ONCE UPON A TIME
IN SAN ANTONIO

Thanks for the
great review!

Steve Fye

ONCE UPON A TIME
IN SAN ANTONIO

Steve Frye

iUniverse, Inc.

New York Lincoln Shanghai

Once Upon a Time in San Antonio

iUniverse books may be ordered through booksellers or by contacting:

iUniverse
2021 Pine Lake Road, Suite 100
Lincoln, NE 68512
www.iuniverse.com
1-800-Authors (1-800-288-4677)

ISBN-13: 978-0-595-34188-7 (pbk)
ISBN-13: 978-0-595-78960-3 (ebk)
ISBN-10: 0-595-34188-8 (pbk)
ISBN-10: 0-595-78960-9 (ebk)

Printed in the United States of America

CONTENTS

▼

MONDAY

Our waiter put a torn slip of paper on the table between us. Bobby and I looked at each other. As I turned the paper around to read the numbers on it, Bobby shoveled up the last forkful of tamales. Two hundred twenty was scrawled on the paper. It wasn't much money for all the food we had eaten.

"You're buying, right, Dave?" Bobby asked between chews.

"Yeah, I'm buying. It's my operation, so it's my check," I confirmed, calculating the exchange rate in my head.

I dug into my pocket and pulled out three one-hundred-peso notes from the roll lurking in the bottom. I slid the bills under my plate. Bobby finished chewing, swallowed and chased the spicy fare down with a mouthful of margarita. I picked up my Tecate and drained the bottle, setting the empty back down on the table with a clunk. My stomach churned a bit. I belched.

"Nice smell," Bobby said, fanning the air. "I'm glad I had a margarita. Much easier to puke up later."

"I think I ate too much."

"I don't think the problem is with the quantity you ate," Bobby observed. "So it might be a good idea to keep a crapper in sight."

"Thanks, I'll try to remember that." I glanced at my watch. It was a couple of minutes after seven in the evening. "Are you ready for this?" I asked, meaning the next steps in our little Mexican adventure.

"As I'll ever be."

"Then let's mosey on over to the hoosegow," I said, exaggerating my Texas drawl, my thumb pointing the way.

We slid our chairs back and stood up. I caught the waiter's eye and pointed to the corners of the bills sticking out from under my plate. When he nodded his understanding, I followed Bobby out onto the sidewalk in front of the dingy café. We stood at the edge of the curb for a moment looking at the town square across the street from us. It was early April and even though the air still had a slight chill to it, a bead of sweat rolled down the center of my back. When it reached my belt line I stepped off the curb. With Bobby following my lead, we rounded the rear end of a slow moving taxi and made our way across the street.

We turned right on the other side, walking down the dirty sidewalk to the corner of the square and then crossed the car-lined street keeping the square on our left. I had thrust my hands into my trouser pockets, the fingers on my right hand brushing against the keys to my Caddy and the fingers on the left jammed against the big roll of pesos. I was consciously willing the next ten minutes to go right. We were two blocks from the Piedras Negras jail.

"Nervous, Bobby?" I asked when we had only one block to go.

"You better believe it."

"Me, too. But we can't back out now. We're too close to being done."

"It's okay. I'm just nervous with anticipation. I'll be glad when it's over."

"Yeah, me too."

We turned right, going around the last corner. The street was dark and deserted. The jail was on the left. A small sign above its door had 'Policia' written on it. There was a tan 1963 Cadillac parked backwards at the curb in front of the door, its big hood facing down the street toward the Rio Grande and Texas. I pulled the keys from my pocket as we approached the big car's butt. I opened the trunk. The interior was dark. I had disabled the fancy trunk light last night and left the spare at our motel on the Texas side of the border. The trunk was nearly filled up with piñatas. At the back of the trunk was a large shopping bag that I pulled out and handed to Bobby along with the wad of pesos from my left pocket. I pushed the piñatas over to the left side of the trunk, making a space about two feet wide on the right. Next I pulled the cardboard liner away from the right front of the trunk. Then, I pulled the key out of the lock, slammed the lid closed and stuffed the key ring back into my pocket. With Bobby holding the shopping bag, I reached into it and removed a black piece of rubber about ten inches long. I put it into my right hip pocket, weighted end first. I left the roll of duct tape, the rags and the snub-nosed .38 in the sack. Then I stood there thinking about details, watching Bobby.

"Looks like we're ready. Let's go," I said, nodding my head.

We walked over to the door under the Policia sign, opened it and went in. There were three desks in the room, two to our right behind a railing and one in front of us. The one in front had a man in a green uniform sitting behind it. He was the only other person in the room. Shift change had taken place at seven and he would be alone until ten. He looked up as we came in the door.

"Buenos tardes, Senor Johnson. How are you tonight?" he asked, standing up to greet us.

"Fine, Miguel. We had a good day shopping. We're full of food and ready to go back to Texas. How's the Cadillac been?" I asked as I moved forward and shook his hand.

"Bueno, Senor. We've kept a keen eye on him all day."

The Caddy was actually a girl. I know because I had looked at its private parts. But I didn't correct him.

"Good, Miguel. Bobby has a gift for you," I said, pointing to my friend.

Bobby was holding the large sheaf of bills and was peeling off several 1,000-peso notes. Miguel turned to get his gift, eyes going wide when he saw the money. As he turned, I reached behind me, pulled the blackjack from my pocket and hit him on the back of the head. He never saw it coming. The sap caught him just behind the right ear and he slumped toward the floor like a rag doll. Bobby dropped the money and grabbed for Miguel. We eased him down, and then pulled him over behind his desk.

"You didn't kill him, did you?" Bobby asked.

"No, he's still breathing. Get the money."

Bobby went back around the desk and began picking up the scattered pesos. Miguel's breathing was a little ragged, so I checked his pulse. I didn't want to kill him, just knock him out. Good, I thought, his pulse was strong. I took the ring of keys he had on his belt and went through the gate in the middle of the railing. To my left was a door, the one to the jail. I found the right key after two tries and opened the door. There was no light on in the jail. In the dimness, I could make out four cells, two on the left and two on the right. The front two were empty. There was someone lying on the cot on the far right one. The far-left one was occupied with stuff, a couple of filing cabinets, some chairs and other junk. It must be the chief's private closet.

"Randy Wilson," I called softly as I approached the reclining figure.

No answer.

"Hey, are you Randy Wilson?" I said louder, with more authority.

"Yeah, I'm Wilson. What of it?" he said at last, sitting up on the cot.

"Well, get your ass up. Your ride's here," I said, fumbling with the cell lock.

"No, shit. That's great. Reed said someone would be coming. I just didn't know when. Good thing, too. Tomorrow they were moving me to Monterey," he said, getting to his feet.

As he got closer I could smell him. Wow! Damn glad he'll be riding in the trunk. I just hoped no one would get a whiff of his mangy tail before we got him back to Texas. The lock came open and the barred door swung inward. Wilson stepped out of the cell. He was six-four, about one-sixty. He'd lost a little weight since he'd been jailed. His daddy had reported his weight at about one-eighty. There would be plenty of room for him in the trunk with the piñatas.

He followed me back to the office. I took the trouble to lock the jail door. It might stall them just a bit to think Wilson was still in there. Miguel was still sleeping. Bobby had just finished applying duct tape to Miguel's ankles, wrists and mouth and was stuffing the big roll of money into his shirt pocket. No sense in leaving the guy with just a headache and an ass chewing.

"Everything okay?" I asked, helping Bobby fold Miguel's legs up and giving him a final shove into the kneehole of the desk. Bobby stood up and grabbed the shopping bag.

"Yeah. He's out, but fine." Then, "Man, did anyone ever tell you that you smell bad?" Bobby asked, nose wrinkling at Wilson standing at the end of the desk.

"This isn't the Holiday Inn, y'know. I'll try to stay down wind from you until I can wash up."

"Enough talk. Let's roll it," I said, walking toward the front door. "I think we've worn out our welcome here in Mexico."

I opened the front door and looked out. The street was still deserted.

"Wait here until I get the trunk open," I told them, as I stepped to the back of the car and fitted the ornate Cadillac key into the trunk lock. The lid popped open. I motioned them forward, handing the keys to Bobby.

"Randy, get into the trunk head first and crawl around to your left behind the liner," I instructed him. "Then fold your legs up and get as small as you can. Once you're in there, don't move and don't make a sound until I tell you. Got it?"

"Yeah, I've got it," he assured me, as he began crawling into the trunk.

When he had gotten behind the liner, I pushed it back in place. In San Antonio I had removed some of the springs from the back seat to make more room. He wouldn't be comfortable, but it would do for a few miles. Then I moved the piñatas around making the contents look even, surveyed my work and closed the lid. As I came around to the driver's side, Bobby reached over and started the car.

I opened the driver's door and got in. Placing the car into drive, I pulled away from the curb and drove down the street toward the Rio Grande. I was sweating and my hands were shaking. I was concentrating really hard on resisting the urge to floor the big car.

"Bobby, got a cigarette?" I asked.

"No, you know I don't smoke. And I thought you quit."

"I did, but I sure could use one now." I said as I took a couple of deep breaths to help settle me down. "How come you look so cool?"

"I'm not. I just don't sweat quite as much as you do. Must be the margaritas."

We had reached the end of the block and I turned right, toward the bridge over the river. I willed my heart to slow down, wiped the beads of sweat from my forehead and then dried my hands on the cloth seat.

"There's freedom," I said, nodding toward the bridge. "Not much farther to go."

"Thank God."

I slowed the Caddy at the last corner before the bridge. No alarm had been raised yet and I didn't expect one. I kept my fingers crossed, anyway. I turned the big nose of the Cadillac toward Texas and eased past the deserted checkpoint on the Mexican side. Clickety-clack over the bridge, then under the lights of the Texas checkpoint. I pulled up to the kiosk and killed the main lights. The customs man peered out at me.

"Well, I see you've made another haul of souvenirs," he said, indicating the piñatas and pottery in the back seat. I recognized the guy from yesterday. We'd been shopping like this for several days, establishing ourselves.

"Yeah, we're just about done shopping for a couple of weeks. We've got the trunk full too. Want to see?" I tempted him.

"Not unless you've got it full of illegals."

"No, none on this trip. If we decide to pick up any, we'll let you know."

"Do you have anything else to declare?" he asked, returning to business.

"Yes, two bottles of tequila" I said, picking up the bottles on the seat beside me and holding them by their necks like trophies.

"That's okay. You're allowed a gallon each. So, you're free to go. Good night," he said in dismissal.

"Thanks. Good night," I said as I turned the headlights back on, placed the car in drive and eased away from the customs booth. I heard Bobby sigh in relief. I did too.

"Nice trick, asking him if he wanted to look in the trunk. I almost crapped when you said it."

"I was just hoping he wouldn't take me up on my offer."

"Yeah, me, too. So, what were you going to do if he'd looked back there in the trunk and found Wilson hiding among the party supplies?"

"Well, we were on the American side, so it probably would have been okay. The U.S guys don't care as much about Wilson as the Mexicans do. Besides," I said in a near whisper as I reached into my left shirt pocket, "I would have just shown them this." I handed Bobby a passport I had gotten from Wilson's father.

"This passport is his!" Bobby said in amazement, mimicking my whisper and pointing to the back seat. "He could have come through sitting up here in the front."

"That's true, but we couldn't risk him being seen in the front on the Mexican side. Besides, what about that smell?"

"Oh, yeah, right."

We were at a traffic light in the middle of Eagle Pass. I made a right turn onto highway 277 toward San Antonio. A half-mile later we turned into the driveway of the Texas Star Motel, a little local inn that we had made our headquarters for the last few days. This was our last stop before going back to the big city. Wilson needed a bath, we needed to pack up the car and I needed a drink. I backed up to the door of number eleven. While Bobby opened the door to the room, I retrieved Mr. Stinky from the trunk and pointed the way to the shower. He was happy to oblige. While he showered, Bobby and I got our gear together and after removing a few piñatas, stowed it and the Caddy's spare in the trunk. We added the souvenirs from the back seat to the piles of stuff we had purchased during our reconnaissance. The plan was to leave it for the maid. We'd brought some of Wilson's clothes with us and I put them on the floor by the bathroom door.

"Your clothes are outside the door," I hollered to him.

"Thanks," he returned, then reached out the door and retrieved his shirt, jeans, socks, shoes and underwear. While he was dressing, Bobby and I opened a couple of beers from our ice chest and toasted our so-far success.

"Here's to the U.S.A. Damn glad to be back in it," I said, raising my Shiner's.

"Here's to the money. Be damned glad to get it," countered Bobby, clinking my bottle.

"And here's to freedom, whatever it cost," said Wilson from the bathroom door. "Now, what do you say we put some distance between us and Mexico?"

"Sounds good to me. We're ready. And this time you can ride up front," I said.

"Good," said Wilson. "I guess that means I can have my passport back now, huh?"

"Yes, it does," I answered with a sheepish grin as I gave him his property. "So you heard us, then?"

"Yeah, I did. That seat fabric isn't very sound proof. But I'll tell you what. I would've wrapped myself around the engine if it would have meant escaping that jail. Oh, and by the way, thank you a whole bunch for busting me out. I don't know what Dad promised you, but I guess I owe you one, too."

"You're welcome for the bust out. Your father paid me, us, plenty. If I need anything else from you, I'll let you know. Oh, damn, I almost forgot. Bobby, get Wilson a beer and finish up in here while I fix up the Caddy."

I went out to the car, opened the driver's door and pulled the Cadillac's real license plates from one of my bags in the trunk. With a screwdriver from the trunk I switched the plates. I'd dump them somewhere on the trip back to town. While I was making us legal, Bobby and Wilson loaded the last of our stuff into the backseat and trunk. They were ready to go when I put the screwdriver away.

"I'll be right back. I need to check us out," I told them as they got into the car. Then I went to the office and settled the bill. I told the clerk that we had left a few things in the room because our eyes were bigger than our vehicle. I went back to the car, got in, fired her up and pulled onto the highway. Bobby and Wilson had finished their first beer and were working on their second.

"No more drinking for the driver," Bobby advised, "but the passengers can settle back and get loaded."

"That's fine, you guys. I'll continue my buzz when we get back to S.A. and get Mr. Wilson on the plane for Dallas."

It had been just over ninety minutes from our entry into the jail until we turned onto U.S. 57 heading east. If everything went as planned, we'd have a little over three hours before the fireworks began. That was just enough time to make the outskirts of San Antonio. The speed limit was 55, but I was cheating a bit. The speedometer needle was just getting to 60.

"Well, I think that's enough beer for me," said Bobby, shoving the empty under the seat. "I'll try for some sleep in case you need relief behind the wheel."

"Thanks, I'll let you know if I get tired."

"Y'know, I'm getting sleepy myself, since the adrenaline's wearing off," Wilson said from the reclining position he was taking in the back seat. "I can drive a car, if you need me to."

"Yeah, I know, but I'm okay for now."

Five minutes later they were both sawing logs.

We passed through La Pryor and Batesville without a hitch. Somewhere east of Batesville, if you look really close among the mesquite trees, you'll see a Texas license plate. It'll be the match of the one you found with diligent work which had been buried in the dumpster behind the Dairy Queen in La Pryor where we stopped for a quick bathroom break. An hour and a half later and we were turning onto Interstate 35 heading north to SA. There was a lot more traffic on that stretch of road from Laredo, which might just give us better cover going north. The trade-off was the increased highway patrolling done on the Interstate. I had to really watch my speed.

"Where are we?" asked a groggy Bobby, waking up as we turned onto the interstate ramp.

"Just getting onto I-35," I replied.

"Are you doing okay? You're not tired are you?"

"No, I'm still okay. We don't have much farther to go. I'll be glad to get back to SA and put this tank into storage for awhile."

"I know what you mean. I'll be glad to get back, too. I could use a shower and a decent meal."

Then, from the back seat, "How are we doing? Are we there yet?"

"Not yet," I said. "We've got about 45 miles to go. So far, so good."

Then I saw flashing red lights in the rearview mirror, a cop car coming up fast. We weren't the only ones on the road so I hoped my 5-miles-over hadn't drawn the wrong kind of attention.

"Folks, we have a highway patrol car behind us," I said as the flashing lights approached, easing the big Caddy over onto the shoulder and applying the brake.

"Shit," said both of my passengers at once.

He must have been doing eighty when he shot past us. I exhaled with a burst of air.

"Damn. Must be for somebody else. He didn't even slow down when he went by."

"Shit, Dave, I wish you wouldn't do that. You about scared the crap out of me that time," Bobby exclaimed.

"Sorry about that. He had me sweating, too. Guess you guys won't be sleeping for the rest of the trip, huh?"

"No, not me," said Wilson. "I'm wide awake now."

"Yeah, me too," said Bobby.

We were beginning to see the glow of the city on the horizon. I don't know which way the cop went. We didn't see him on either side after our close encounter. As we chewed up each mile, I became more confident that we had pulled off our caper. It was ten-thirty when we got off at Military Drive. I drove east on Military to Pleasanton Road toward Bobby's house. Wilson was spending the night with me tonight. His flight was due out at seven-thirty in the morning. Bobby lived on Vestal Street. I turned off Pleasanton onto Vestal and eased up in front of Bobby's house. We divied up our gear and the stuff in the trunk. It took two loads each to get it into the house. When we were done, Wilson got back into the car on the shotgun side while Bobby and I stood on the sidewalk saying goodbye.

"Well," Bobby said just before planting a big kiss on my lips, "you always did know how to show a girl a good time."

"My pleasure," I said, when our lips parted after several seconds. "You are a hell of an operative. Damn glad to have had you along. See you tomorrow at the office."

"Bye, Dave. See you tomorrow," she said after one final squeeze. Then to Wilson, "Good-bye Mr. Wilson, nice to have met you. Have an uneventful flight."

"Thanks, Bobby, for everything. Good-bye."

I walked around the car and got behind the wheel. I started up the big V-8 and waved as we pulled away from the curb.

"Hell of a woman you've got there, Dave," said Wilson as we rounded the corner.

"Yeah, she's great. But she's not my woman. She's her own woman. We used to have a thing going on, but we sort of drifted away from any notion of permanence. We date each other every once in a while, but it's nothing really serious. Mostly, we work together sometimes. I guess you could say we're best friends now."

"So, she's a private eye, too?" he asked.

"No, she's a travel agent. Owns her own business in South Park Mall, back where we turned off I-35. My office is next to hers in the mall. We help each other out, business-wise," I said as I made a left into the southbound lanes of Pleasanton. We were passing a Super's hamburger joint. "Are you hungry now? I only have a few things at home and there isn't much in the way of fine dining out there by my house."

"No, I'm okay for now. I'd just like a long sleep without cockroaches running around in my hair. How far away do you live?"

"About a mile from Bobby's, just off Commercial Avenue on a little street called Escalon. We're about half way there. Unfortunately, we're only going to get about four hours sleep. Your flight leaves at seven-thirty, so we need to be at the airport at six-thirty. Since it takes an hour to get there, we need to leave the house at five-thirty so we can get you checked-in okay. That means we need to get up at four-thirty. Swell, huh?"

"Yeah, swell. How long's the flight?"

"A couple of hours, gate to gate," I answered, making a right on Petaluma and heading west toward Commercial Avenue. "The flight is into Love Field, not DFW, so you'll be a little closer to home."

"Who's supposed to meet me?"

"I believe your father is," I said.

"It's funny," Wilson said, a little sadly. "I'll be glad to see him but at the same time I won't be glad. I was pretty stupid down in Mexico, buying drugs from an undercover cop. I can hardly wait to see the look on his face. Got any armor plate you'd loan me?"

"Sorry, fresh out," I told him. "Just face the music like a man and be glad your family had the resources for getting you out. Most captives in Mexican jails don't last too long."

We obeyed the stop sign when we got to Commercial and I waited for a car to go by before continuing straight across. We stopped again where Petaluma made a tee with Escalon and turned left on Escalon. A minute later I steered the big car onto the gravel track running along the left side of my house, past the '56 TR-3 and a '70 Chevy van parked on the paved driveway.

"Here we are, home again," I said, easing the Caddy around to the back of the house.

"Where are we going?" Wilson wondered.

"To the back. See that big barn-looking shed back there behind the gate?"

"Yeah."

"Well, it's mine, too. We're going to unload our things, then stash the Caddy in the shed for a few days, just in case someone's looking for it. We'll take the van to the airport in the morning."

"Okay with me. Just tell me what you want me to do."

I stopped the car in front of the gate, grabbing the keys as I got out.

"Get some of the gear and I'll let you in," I told Wilson as I got out of the car and headed toward the back door steps.

"Which door is yours?" Randy wondered, pointing to the two doors facing us from the back of the house.

"They both are. The house used to be a duplex, split down the middle, but I converted it," I explained, pulling open the screen door and fitting my key into the deadbolt of the wooden back door.

He followed me up the steps as I opened the door, stepped into the kitchen and turned on the kitchen light. I also turned on the outside porch light so I could see what I was doing out by the gate.

"This is weird," he pointed out while looking over the one large kitchen where two had once been.

"Yeah, I know. There was just one bedroom and one bathroom on each side before I remodeled. I took out most of the wall running down the middle, leaving the part between the bedrooms and bathrooms. I wanted a little privacy in case my mom was visiting when I had a girlfriend over or something."

"It just seems strange, with two kitchen sinks and cabinets on both ends of the room."

"Actually it's kind of convenient. Gives me more storage and more places for dirty dishes. Just put that stuff down anywhere. You're on the right," I said, pointing down the right side of the middle divider. "The bathroom is the first door, then the bedroom. Make yourself comfortable while I park the Caddy."

"Hey, you've got two front doors, too," he observed as he walked down the hall to the front of the house.

"Yeah, cool, huh. Had the mailman confused at first, until I put a box out by the street. You should see the looks on the door-to-door salesmen who come by. I greet them at one door, then at the other. Kind of freaks them out."

"Yeah, I can see where it would."

"I'll be back in a few minutes. I'm going to hide the Caddy."

"Okay."

Before opening the gate, I unloaded the last of my stuff onto the back porch. Then I unlocked the padlock securing the chain around the gate halves and swung both sides wide to accommodate the big tugboat. I got back in, cranked up the V-8, and pulled the Cadillac down along the shed and into the last of six wide stalls. After locking it up, I covered it with a large, gray drop cloth. The left-over piñatas could wait for another day. I walked back the way I had come along the open side of the shed, looking at the lumber stored in the other bays, thinking that some day I would have to clear out all that old stuff the previous owner had left behind. There was enough wood in there to start a lumberyard. When I got to the gate, I locked it and headed for the back porch. Opening the back door and stepping into the kitchen, I could hear Randy in the bathroom on his side. While he was busy I plucked the receiver off the wall phone by the back door and made a call to Dallas. It rang three times before a sleepy voice picked up.

"Hello."

"Hello, this is Dave Harris," I said quietly. "Is this the Wilson residence."

"Yes, it is, Mr. Harris. This is Robert Fitch, his butler. What can I do for you?"

"Well, either I need to speak with Mr. Wilson or you can take a message for him."

"Mr. Harris, Mr. Wilson is unavailable right now. I'll take a message for him."

"Okay, please tell Mr. Wilson that his son is with me in San Antonio and we'll meet him as planned in the morning."

"That's good news, Mr. Harris. Did everything go okay."

"Yes. We'll be there in the morning."

"I'll be sure to tell Mr. Wilson, sir. Thank you for calling."

"You're welcome, Mr. Fitch. Goodbye."

"Goodbye."

I hung up, picked up my two bags of clothes and things from the kitchen floor and walked down the hallway on my side, past the bathroom and into my bedroom. I dropped the stuff on the floor by the bed and retreated to the living room. Without turning on the light, I went over to the window facing the house next door, carefully avoiding cracking my shins on my easy chair and the coffee table. I stepped around the pile of magazines on the floor and looked out the window at my neighbor's house. There was still a light on in the living room. I'd better tell them I was home and pick up my mail and newspapers.

"Hey, Wilson," I called out.

"Yeah?"

"I'm gonna go next door and get my mail. They're still up over there."

"Okay, I'll be here."

I opened the front door nearest my neighbor and went out past the screen door and down the steps. When I reached his house, I opened the screen and tapped lightly on the door. No movement. I tapped again and heard footsteps coming my way.

"It's late. Who is it?" came my neighbor's voice from behind the door.

"It's me, Jose, Dave from next door. I got home a little while ago."

The door swung open and Jose Perez filled the gap. He was about five nine, around one-sixty and in his middle or late forties. He and his wife Rosa had several kids, the oldest one about twenty.

"Hey, gringo, you're up late. You just get back?" he asked in a low voice, holding out his hand. "How was your trip?"

"Bueno, Jose. It was a good trip," I answered, shaking his hand. "Everything here okay?"

"Yeah, sure, Dave. Everybody's asleep but me. I was watching some late TV and having a beer before I go to bed."

"Everything okay at the house?" I asked again thumbing toward my place.

"Yeah, Dave. Same old San Antonio. Same old neighborhood. Nothing happening around here."

"You've got my mail?"

"Sure do, right here," he said moving over to a table with a bunch of letters and magazines piled up on it and picking up the stack. "You sure get a lot of mail, buddy."

"I know. Comes from being stationed in Turkey. Ever since then I've hated an empty mailbox. Even if it's just magazines, it makes me think there's someone out there who likes me enough to send me something."

"Hey, it's your mailbox," he said, handing over the pile. "I also picked up your newspapers, but we read them and tossed them out afterwards, okay?"

"That's no problem, amigo. It was old news anyway. Say, as a thank-you I brought you something from Mexico. It's in the Caddy. I'll bring it to you tomorrow or the next day. I've got to go on another short trip in the morning, but I'll be back tomorrow late. Would you pick up my stuff again tomorrow?"

"Sure, but it'll cost you."

"Oh, yeah?"

"Yeah," he confirmed. Then in a whisper, "You and me gonna go out and have a few. You're my excuse to get out of the house."

"I didn't think you needed an excuse."

"It just makes it easier, you know?" he said, moving his thumb over his shoulder toward the back of the house.

"Sure, Jose. Maybe this weekend."

"Okay."

"Jose, who is it?" Rosa called from the back bedroom.

"It's just the crazy gringo from next door picking up his mail, Rosa. I didn't mean to wake you," I called softly to Rosa.

"It's okay, David."

"Thanks, Rosa. Jose, I've got to go. I'll see you tomorrow or Thursday, okay."

"Yeah, okay. Buenos tardes, Dave."

"Good night, Jose." Then a little louder, "Good night, Rosa."

"Good night, David."

I took my mail and retraced my way home. Before I had gone to Mexico, I had made up the spare bedroom's double bed for Wilson as an act of optimism on my part. He was already asleep when I got back from Jose's. I quietly sorted through the stack of stuff I had gotten from Jose, making sure not to miss any bills or checks. I tossed the culls onto the coffee table. Then I secured the house, brushed my teeth, stripped to the buff and went to bed. I was relieved to be home in one piece.

TUESDAY

I slept like the dead until the alarm went off at four-thirty. Having two hot water heaters is sometimes the best part of my place's makeover, since it was apparent that Wilson liked a long shower. After cleaning up, I put on my usual uniform of slacks, shirt and sports coat, making sure my socks and shoes matched my outfit. I added a red tie with a simple pattern just because I was going to meet a client. Wilson wore what he had on the night before.

"You look pretty fancy today," Randy observed as we reunited in the living room.

"Well, I've got other business today, so I figured I'd dress the part. You ready to go."

"Yeah, but I'm hungry. Got anything to eat here?"

"Yes, but not much," I stalled, trying to remember where the nearest McDonald's was. "We'll get something on the way to the airport, okay."

"Yeah, okay. First place though, right?"

"Right, first place."

We left through the front door on Wilson's side. It was another nice day in the city with light, fluffy clouds dotting the otherwise blue sky. Might be getting some weather in a day or so, I thought. We put his meager bag of things in the Chevy van and headed north to the airport. At Military Drive and Commercial we pulled into a twenty-four hour Jack in the Box. Randy ordered two burritos, a hamburger and a large Coke. I got two tacos and a small Root Beer. We sat in the parking lot until I was through eating, then went west on Military toward I-35. I hated to eat and drive at the same time. It was always too messy and too hazardous.

When we started up the I-35 on-ramp, Wilson started up the small talk.

"How long have you lived in San Antonio?" he asked.

"Since the tail end of 1972, after I got out of the Air Force."

"How long were you in?"

I looked sideways at him.

"Look, I can see where this is going," I told him after a long minute. "You're a likable enough guy, but I consider myself kind of a private person. Also, I'm a loner who doesn't make friends very easily. So, don't pry too much and maybe we'll have a nice conversation on the way to the airport."

He sat there a little stunned by my blunt reaction to his questions. We were deep into the early morning traffic and approaching the I-35 and Highway 90 mix-master on the southwest corner of downtown when he tried again.

"If you won't tell me about you, tell me about San Antonio. You got out of the service in 1972. Why did you stay here? You're not from here, are you?"

I had to give him points for trying. I smiled thinly, beginning to soften my attitude a little in the face of his tenacity.

"No, I'm from Fort Worth, originally. My family lives in the Metroplex. San Antonio is close enough and far enough away, if you get my meaning."

"Sure, that's why I like going to school in Denton. Dad wanted me to go to SMU, but then I'd be living at home under his thumb."

"And you think you're not under his thumb right now, anyway?"

"Yeah, I guess I am, but at least Denton is thirty miles away from home," he conceded. "And I like it. It's a party school and a party town."

"You'd have made better contacts going to SMU," I pointed out.

"Yeah, I know. I just couldn't stand living like a beggar at my folks' place."

"So you're a drug trafficker, instead."

"I wasn't going to sell the stuff. Just be the guy who had the stuff. The chicks are all into it, you know."

"So I've heard. But it's still illegal."

"Yeah, it is. I guess you'd lose your license if you ever got busted with dope, huh?"

"Sure would. Not that I've never tried it. But I have to think beyond today, you know. If I go to jail for dope, I lose everything. And I really like the private eye business."

"How did you think of that as a job?"

"I left the Air Force because of an injury I received on the job. The job was as a security policeman who worked with the OSI. Investigating is one of the only things I know how to do well enough to make money at. Since I was in San Antonio when I was discharged, I stayed. But there are other benefits in being here."

"Like what?"

"Like the cost of living is cheaper. The weather is mild, except for summer. And I'm stuck on the military."

"What do you mean?"

"I mean this is a military town. There are five Air Force bases and three Army posts here."

"There are?"

"Yes, there are. Medina Base is on the west side of town, outside the loop. The officer training school is on Medina along with some training ranges for security police. It also has a couple of huge bomb dumps. Next, going east, is Lackland, the basic training center for nearly the whole Air Force. Next to it is Kelly, which is a retrofit base for nuke weapons. Southeast of downtown is Brooks Field. It used to be a pilot training base during World War II, but isn't used for much now except by the medical command. Then there's Randolph, which is east of town. It's the command center for Air Training Command. Army posts include Fort Sam Houston, Brook Army Medical and Camp Bullis, north of town about ten miles."

"So how many service people are here?"

"I don't know. Probably about half the population, I'd guess. But that's not the best part."

"What's the best part?"

"The best part is what that population is made up of."

"And what's that?"

"It's made up of people mostly under forty years old. And there are a lot of women here. Single military women and women whose spouses are overseas, particularly in Southeast Asia."

"Viet Nam?"

"Not just Viet Nam. All over Southeast Asia."

"So you're saying that there are a lot of young, horny people in this town."

"Exactly. Mix that in with the Latin influence, salsa and sombreros, and this place makes Denton look like a monastery."

"The University of Texas has a campus here, right?"

"Yeah, by Hemisfair Park. And there's a new one out this road," I said, pointing toward the left front of the van. "Where it crosses the outer loop. They've been building on it for a couple of years. Why? Were you thinking of transferring down here?"

"From the way you describe it, maybe I should."

"I think you should stick to business right where you are. You might want to get that one down pat before you start jumping around."

"You sound a little like my dad."

I gave him another sideways look.

"Sometimes it might be a good idea to listen to guys who sound like your dad. It's why God gave us two ears and only one mouth."

He mulled that over a few minutes as we wound around the interchange northwest of downtown that sent us toward the airport. We had to take I-10 north for a few miles until we intersected with loop 410. I had just merged us into the northbound traffic when Wilson cleared his throat and continued his interrogation.

"You ever been married?" he asked at last.

"Now that is a personal question," I pointed out.

"I know. I was really wondering if you'd always been single."

"No, I was married once, for five years," I admitted after considering for a moment if I would answer him at all. "We split up in Turkey. I had a roving eye and I drank too much."

"Your wife didn't like that, huh?"

"Nope," I said without elaboration. Then added, "I still have a roving eye and drink too much, but I'm single now."

"Got a girl friend, besides Bobby?" he wondered.

"Bobby and I are friends, like I told you last night."

"Yeah, I remember. It's just that you two sort of fit together."

"Except we're both very independent types. I have my life and she has hers."

"Is that why you used her as a partner yesterday?"

"Not totally. She's also very reliable. I know I can trust her guarding my back."

"She looks like she can handle herself in a fight, too."

"She's had some karate, I think. I taught her how to shoot a pistol."

"You did?"

"Sure. Can't have a partner who can't handle a gun."

"I suppose not."

The traffic was lighter now as we approached the north loop. Everyone was headed into town, not away from it. I guided the van around the access ramp to the east. We had beaten the morning airport traffic by just a little, so we made good time from there.

A few minutes later, we pulled into the short term parking area. I locked up the Chevy as Wilson retrieved his bag and then walked with him to the check-in counter across the street. I surprised Wilson by checking in with him.

"Are you going, too?" He asked, his eyebrows up a couple of notches.

"Yes, I have business with your father," I explained.

"Why didn't you tell me you were going?"

"No reason. Just a little surprise to see how you'd react."

"You like catching people off guard, don't you?" he accused.

"Sometimes, if I know they can take it. I knew you could, so I did," I said with a grin.

Wilson just shook his head, matching my grin. We were told that our plane wasn't ready to board. We took a seat along a row facing the apron and taxiway. I gazed out the window. Our plane wasn't even at the dock yet.

"How'd you get the job of coming after me?" Wilson started.

"Couple of weeks ago I was called by a detective agency in Dallas that your father has used a couple of times. I'd worked with them on a fraud case involving one of the stores in the mall where my office is. They asked me if I'd be interested in retrieving something lost in Mexico. I said maybe and they gave me your father's number."

"'Something lost' in Mexico? That's one way of putting it. What did you say when you found out it wasn't a something but a someone?"

"I said okay, but it'd probably cost more."

"Like how much more?" he wondered.

"Enough to make my being caught worth the trouble," I answered, not being precise. "Your father was also my insurance policy in case something happened."

"Insurance policy?"

"Yeah, in case I needed bailing out myself. By the way, he's gone to a lot of trouble for you. So have I, but I get paid for it. In his case, I think he cares about you a lot more than you think. My advice for you is to stop with the greasy kid stuff and start paying more attention to him. He didn't get where he is by being stupid. You might learn something from him if you tried."

"Yeah, I know. He's just so wrapped up in business that it's easy for me to forget I have a father."

"So, where's your mother?"

"She does her own thing. Country club stuff."

"And you're supposed to be a good college boy, right?"

"Yeah, North Texas isn't that bad. Like I said, Denton is a party town and it's close enough to home. Then we had the big idea of scoring some cheap weed down in Mexico."

"Who's we?" I wondered.

"A couple of friends at school. But they managed to get away and leave me holding the bag, literally."

"After all the hassle, it would've been a lot cheaper if you had just bought the stuff in Denton or Dallas, huh?"

"Sure would."

"What about the two guys you were with? Where are they?"

"Right now, I don't know. I met them at school. We hatched a plan to get a couple of bales of grass. Thought it'd be a great adventure. It was a great adventure all right," he said ruefully.

"Some adventure, being put under a Mexican jail."

I watched as the plane arrived at the gate. Not much longer, now.

"I thought Dad was going to get me out, but not with a jail break."

"You mean bribe you out?"

"Yeah, whatever it took."

"So, what are you taking in school?" I asked, changing the subject.

"Business. I'm a sophomore."

"How old are you?"

"I'm nineteen. I'll be twenty in July."

"That's what your dad said, but you seem older. I'm only eight years older that you, for Christ's sake."

"Twenty-seven. Wow, you act older than that."

"Thanks. It's not an act. Sometimes I feel older."

A voice on the overhead speaker called the flight. Wilson started to get up. I put a hand out and stopped him.

"We'll wait. I don't want to sit in one of those crowded seats any longer than I have to. We have plenty of time."

"Okay, you're the boss," he said, settling back in his chair.

"So what are you going to do when you get back home?"

"I made myself a promise in that Mexican hell hole that if I ever got out I'd go back to school, get good grades and keep my big mouth shut."

"Sounds good. Nothing like a little third-world-country prison time to drive a lesson home."

"You've got that right. I don't want to ever do that again."

We watched the end of the line of passengers file through the door, waiting until they announced the last call for the flight. It came none too soon for Wilson.

"Okay, now we go," I said, getting to my feet.

"About time. I was getting a little nervous."

We boarded the plane. After settling into our seats and bouncing into the air, we both napped through the flight. A little after nine o'clock we touched down in Dallas. His father was standing at the gate when we walked into the terminal. Wilson walked up to his father, his right hand stuck out for a handshake. His father looked at his son and the out-stretched hand for a few seconds and then shook it. Next, the older man pulled his son in for a one-armed hug. I could have sworn I saw tears in the old man's eyes and I know I heard the word "knucklehead" used at least once. Daddy then looked up and saw me standing about six feet from them. He mouthed a thank-you at me and I nodded. They ended the embrace and I stepped closer.

"Let's go someplace where we can talk," Daddy said. "I have some things for you, Mr. Harris, before you board your flight back to San Antonio."

"Lead the way," I said, as Daddy Wilson turned toward the terminal's innards.

"There's a bar that's open over this way," he said, tilting his head to the right. As we left the arrival area, I noticed a fellow in a nice suit with a brief case falling into step along side us.

"Mr. Harris, this is Mr. Reed. He works for me. He has your papers," Wilson explained.

I nodded toward Mr. Reed. He was my size, about six feet even, and sported my average build, but I suspected he had a few special talents hidden under the nice threads. He nodded back without any facial changes.

When we were seated, the bartender came over and took our order.

"What'll you have, Mr. Harris?" Daddy Wilson asked.

"You serving alcohol now?" I asked the bartender.

"Yes sir, we opened at nine."

"Good. It's early, but we're celebrating. I'll have Glenlivet and water," I told her.

Wilson was buying, so what the hell.

"Coffee with Bailey's, please," said the senior Wilson. "Son, what will you have?"

"Plain coffee for me, please, with cream and sugar," Randy said.

It was apparent that Reed wasn't included in the party when the young lady glanced at him and he shook his head slightly. She retreated with our requests. Mr. Reed set the brief case down on the floor by Daddy and moved over to sit at the bar. He kept an eye on us while also watching the surrounding pedestrian traffic.

"Mr. Harris, this brief case is yours," said Wilson, sliding it over to me. And then to his son, "Randy, would you excuse us a minute. I'd like to talk with Mr. Harris alone."

"Sure, Dad. I need a bathroom break, anyway," Randy said, sliding his chair back and getting to his feet. "I'll be back in a few minutes."

As soon as Randy was out of earshot, Wilson continued, "I want to thank you for returning Randy to the U.S and to me. You did a good job. You'll find the second half of your payment in the brief case along with a bonus for a job well done. It's ironic that I'm paying you much more for the job than what bribing the police chief was going to cost. But he got greedy. He thought twenty thousand was not enough. I could see that his greed might have had no end."

"Frankly, Mr. Wilson, I'm glad he was greedy. And I appreciate you understanding the kind of work and risk involved in freeing your son. It was fortunate that everything went smoothly."

"Not quite, Mr. Harris. Just before you called last night, I received a phone call from a certain irate police chief. It seems that several Anglos broke into his jail, beat up a guard, and escaped with several prisoners. He mentioned that he would probably make an official protest unless a certain sum of money came his way. I told him I knew nothing of the incident and that what happened was probably not even connected with my son or me. I suggested he look closer to home, that it was probably someone else's family who caused the breakout. He wasn't amused. You, Mr. Harris, were never mentioned by name, but I'd be on my guard back in San Antonio. Some of the ranking folks in Mexico have rather long arms over the border."

"Well, thanks for the update and for keeping me out of it so far. I'm afraid all we did was knock out one lone jailer. And there were only two of us desperados. Besides, we left a wad of cash in the jailer's pocket," I said in my defense.

"There was..." Wilson trailed off as our drinks arrived and the conversation stopped. We waited until the barmaid retreated to her station.

"There was no mention of any money," he continued. "My guess is that the chief took it from your jailer."

"Probably. And Miguel probably got himself beaten up for not resisting more."

"Not to mention the anger invoked by having the chief's retirement fund robbed of its human nest-egg."

"Oh, you're right. I hadn't thought of that. I should have stuffed some dough down the poor slob's boot."

"No matter now. You still did a good job from my standpoint. That's why I included a bonus. You might need a good lawyer. I have already alerted mine, in case the chief tries to recoup some of his recent loses."

"Thanks for the advice. I'll be on my guard."

"You're welcome. Now, there is one other thing in the briefcase—an envelope. Inside the envelope, you'll find a note from a woman who is employed by my wife. It's about a bit of work she needs done for her in San Antonio."

"What kind of work," I interjected.

"Missing person. Her fiancé who lives there hasn't called her in a couple of days and she's worried about him. Her telephone number and address are in the note, so you can contact her for details. I included some extra cash in the briefcase to help cover your expenses. I know this may be a pain, but I'd like you to take the case as a favor to me. The woman's name is Maria Garza. She's been with us for a long time. Please do what you can."

"Okay, I'll check it out when I get back. Anything else I can do for you?"

"No, but I may take the liberty of referring other clients your way from time to time, if that's all right with you."

"Sure, I can always use the business. But I would rather work in south Texas than up here in the Metroplex," I stipulated. "Connections, you know."

"Of course. I have some local people I use when I have need for that kind of operation here in Dallas."

Randy was coming back down the concourse. His father saw him as soon as I did and gave him a look that said it was okay to return, that our business was done. Randy sat down and doctored his coffee.

"Here's to freedom," Randy toasted, picking up his cup and holding it out over the table. Wilson and I looked at each other, then hoisted our drinks and lightly clinked Randy's cup.

"To freedom," we chimed in together with less enthusiasm than Randy had voiced.

"Son, your freedom cost a lot. I hope you understand that. Now you'll have to start paying for it, beginning today," Daddy said, sipping his Irish Crème tainted coffee.

"Yes, sir, I understand. I already decided that. I promised myself that I'd knuckle down. Right now I'm making that promise to you, too."

"We'll see how well you do. When is your next class?"

"Tomorrow."

"Good. You'll be there for it won't you?"

"Yes, sir."

"Good. Now let's finish up and go. I'm sure Mr. Harris is anxious to return to San Antonio."

I nodded. They finished their coffees and Daddy stood up, holding out his hand to me. I gulped down my scotch, stood up and shook the elder Wilson's hand.

"Thanks, again, Mr. Harris. I'll be in touch if I need you," Wilson said in dismissal.

"Yes sir, you have my number." Then to Randy, as I took his hand, "Take care of yourself, Randy. Listen to your father. He's smarter than you think."

"Yeah, I know, Dave. I'll be careful. Thanks for everything. I'm glad to be back," he said, pumping my arm.

We said goodbye and separated. I wandered down to my return gate, checked that the departure was on time, and since I had over an hour to kill before the first boarding, went back to the bar and ordered a another Glen, this time on me. I sat back down at the table we had just vacated, opened the briefcase after the drink arrived and surreptitiously inspected the contents. There were several packets of hundred dollar bills under a Wall Street Journal spread out to cover the cash and an envelope on top of the newspaper. I picked up the envelope and opened it. Just as Wilson had said, Maria Garza's name and number were on a sheet of paper. Below her information was the name Robert Garcia with an address and phone number in San Antonio. Also in the envelope were ten one hundred dollar bills. This was turning out to be quite a payday, I thought to myself. Fifty thousand from Wilson and a couple of bonuses. Nice. I wondered if Garza was at the number on the paper. I motioned to the bartender.

"Do you have a phone I could use for a local call?" I asked.

"Yes, but you'll have to come up to the bar to use it."

"Okay," I said, picking up the briefcase and my drink and moving up to a stool at the bar. She reached under the counter and handed over the phone.

"Here you go. Not too long, though, okay? It's supposed to be for business only," she informed me.

"Thanks. It'll probably be less than five minutes," I said as I picked up the receiver and dialed the number from the paper. It rang twice before someone picked up.

"Wilson's residence," said a pleasant female voice. "May I help you?"

"Yes, my name is David Harris. May I speak with Maria Garza, please? I was told I could contact her at this number."

"Please wait while I get her for you," and the line went quiet. I didn't hear the phone being set down. Must be a hold button on that phone. Fancy. Then the line came alive again.

"This is Maria speaking, Mr. Harris. I'm surprised you called so quickly. I thought you'd still be with Mr. Wilson."

"He just left. What can I do for you, Ms. Garza?" I asked, trying to speed things along as I saw the waitress glance at her watch.

"It's my fiancé, Mr. Harris. He usually calls me every day, but I haven't heard from him for three days and I'm worried that something may have happened to him."

"What makes you think that? Have you tried calling him?" I asked.

"Yes, several times every day, but no answer. The phone just rings and rings. I even tried his work number, but they wouldn't give me any information about him. What really worries me is that the last time we talked he said he'd be making a bunch of money on a special project he was working on, but he really didn't give me any details."

"You haven't talked with him for three days. When did you see him last?"

"Three weeks ago, here. His family lives here and he comes up once or twice a month to see them. And me. He seemed okay the last time he was here."

"Has his family said anything about him not calling."

"Not really. I called his sister to ask about him, but she said it wasn't strange that he hasn't called. She said he only calls about once a week. I think she thinks I'm being a little paranoid. Maybe I am, but he usually answers his phone. I'm just worried about him."

"Where does he work?" I asked, keeping things on track.

"At Kelly Air Force Base, in a place he calls swami or sama or something like that. He says it's classified and he can't tell me any more." She apparently didn't know it but SAAMA meant San Antonio Air Material Area, with the classified portion being tied to the Kelly nuke farm.

"Maria, what does he do at SAAMA?" I prompted.

"He writes books, like textbooks, for the Air Force," she answered.

"Okay. Are the address and phone number I have here the correct ones?" I asked, reading them off to her.

"Yes, that's right."

"Good. Now give me his work number, too. I'll try out there myself," I said.

"Just a minute, I'll have to look it up," she said before setting the phone down.

I was getting that look from the waitress as I stood with the receiver to my ear. I held up my empty glass and made pouring signs. The waitress nodded and ordered me a refill from the bartender. I fished a pen from my shirt pocket as I heard the receiver on the other end make bumping sounds.

"Are you still there?" Maria asked.

"Yes."

"Okay, here's the number."

I wrote it on the paper with Garcia's other numbers, then repeated it back to her. My drink came.

"Maria, what does Robert look like?" I asked, taking a sip.

"Oh, he's thirty five years old, a few inches taller than me, so about five eight or nine and he weighs about, I don't know, maybe one seventy? And he's Mexican. Well he isn't, his father is. Robert is an American, but his hair is dark and so are his eyes. He looks Mexican."

"Does he have any scars or marks on him?"

"He has a moustache," she said.

Great, I thought, so do half the people in San Antonio, including me.

"Anything else?" I asked. I could tell by the silence that she was thinking about it.

"He doesn't have any scars that I know of, but he has moles."

"Moles?"

"Yes, moles. He has a big one below his left ear and some on his head covered up by his hair."

I smiled. I really didn't want to know how she'd discovered the ones on his head. Or anywhere else for that matter.

"Anything else that you can think of?" I asked, my pen poised over the paper.

"No, nothing right now. But I could call you if I think of anything else."

"Okay, here's my office number. Are you ready?"

"Just a second," she said, fumbling around. "Okay, what is it?"

I gave her the number.

"Well, that's about all I need right now. I'll give you a call as soon as I find out anything, maybe tomorrow or Thursday; Friday at the latest. Okay if I call you at this number?"

"Yes, anytime. If I'm not here someone will take a message," she said.

"All right then. I'll get to work on it. Good-bye for now," I said.

"Good-bye, Mr. Harris, and thank you very much."

"Your welcome, good-bye." And we clicked off.

I looked at my watch, just under five minutes.

"You barely made it," said the waitress, coming over to collect the phone.

"Less than five minutes," I said, tapping my watch.

"Uh-huh. Are you going to want another drink?" she asked.

"Yeah, one more, please. You can ring me out, too," I told her, pulling two twenties from my front trouser pocket and putting them on the bar by my drink. I waved off the change as thanks for the phone use. Nothing like a big payday to put me in a generous mood.

I mulled over what Maria had told me about her beau, trying to keep an open mind about his current location. There were several possibilities with an unannounced break-up being the front-runner. Three hundred miles is a lot of distance for proper love affair maintenance. There are quite a few curvy distractions in San Antonio. Some other possibilities involved work, drugs and mayhem.

I finished my drink. I noticed that I had a little buzz on as I walked down the concourse to my gate. Good thing I had eaten breakfast. I'd get something else to eat on the plane. It would be nearly three o'clock by the time I got to the office on the south side. There would be just enough of the day left to make a couple of phone calls to try locating Robert Garcia.

I walked out of the terminal in San Antonio at two thirty-two, retrieved the van and headed south. Twenty-five minutes later I was halfway between downtown and the mall, taking the exit off I-35 onto the westbound lanes of Highway 90. I accelerated to sixty but stayed in the right lane because the next exit right led to the main entrance of Kelly Air Force Base. I had two purposes for stopping at Kelly. I had some cash I needed to unload and a phone call to make. I had kept my bank account at the Kelly Air Force Base Credit Union after I left the Air Force in 1971 on a medical discharge. The cause of my medical release was a small caliber bullet wound to my right buttock received during a drug bust while serving as a security policeman. My partner had accidentally shot me with a .22 caliber pistol he had taken from one of the bustees. My discharge was not without some benefits, like medical, BX, commissary, and banking privileges. The credit union also housed my safety deposit box where I planned stashing all but one hundred of the Ben Franklins that Wilson had given me. The rest were destined for my office safe.

At three twenty I had the money stowed safely and returned to the credit union's service desk where I used their phone to call Garcia's office. The woman I talked with told me he hadn't been to work the last few days, but that it was no big deal since she was pretty sure he was taking some vacation time. I called his house. No answer. I got into the van and retraced my tracks back to Highway 90 then drove south on I-35 to the mall. On the way to my office I mulled over the afternoon's information, or rather, lack of it.

Traffic was light and I pulled into the parking lot of South Park Mall just after four o'clock. On the northwest side of the mall, next to the Penney's store there was a mall entrance into a hallway where Bobby's travel agency and my office were located. I parked as close to the door as the busy lot would allow, locked up the van and headed toward the building. The door I went to was one of those fire doors that only opened from the inside with a push-bar. My security key opened the outside lock and I used it as a handle when it released the lock. I stepped into the hallway and the door closed after me. Just down the hall on the left was the office entrance I shared with Bobby. Bobby and I also shared a secretary, Ruth Myers. She had been Bobby's front person for years. Ruth was older than Bobby by ten or twelve years, probably somewhere in her middle forties. She had graying brown hair usually done up on her head in a braided twist affair. She wore glasses and a telephone headset that gave her an 'operator' look. She greeted me cheerfully as I walked through the door that advertised Bobby Nelms's Travel Agency on top and David Harris, Investigations as second billing.

"Hello, Dave. Glad to see you made it. Bobby said you were out tying up some loose ends from one of your wild capers. She wasn't sure if you'd be back today or not, so I told your one caller that you'd phone him in the morning."

"Thanks, Ruth. Who was it?"

"The Penney's manager, Roger Stone. You know him, right?"

"Yes, I do. Did he leave his number?"

"It's right here", she said, holding out a slip of memo paper to me. "Said you could call him at the office tomorrow anytime. I asked him if it was a security thing and he said no, that it was personal."

"Personal, huh? Did he say it was an emergency?" I asked, taking the paper with Roger's number on it. I also managed the security stuff in the mall and the anchor stores, so occasionally one of the mall managers would call me in for something. I did it for a cut in my monthly rent.

"No, he didn't say it was an emergency but he did sound a little stressed on the phone."

"It's early yet. I think I'll call him now", I said stepping over to my office door. "Thanks again, Ruth, you do good work."

"Thanks and you're welcome. So when do I get a pay raise?"

"I'll think about it," I said retreating into my office and closing the door.

"Sure, Dave, sure" I heard as the door clicked shut.

My office is a twenty by thirty rectangle. I think it used to be a small jewelry store or a tax office before I moved in. I had carpet laid over the linoleum floor to muffle any weird noises that I might make. In the front part of the room I had arranged a leather couch and two easy chairs around a square coffee table just for intimate interviews with clients. I had also placed two interview chairs facing my big flattop desk further back in the room. Behind my desk were two filing cabinets and a big floor safe, a Mossberg that I had received from a client who couldn't meet my wage demands with money. Bobby and I had installed a bathroom complete with shower that connected our two offices behind the wall behind Ruth's desk. While the workmen were installing the plumbing, I had them put in a wet bar in the space between my office door and the toilet door. There was just enough room left to put in a small refrigerator for cooling beverages and the odd leftover. Over the wet bar were cabinets which stored a few eats and some coffee stuff for use in the Mr. Coffee sitting on the counter next to the toaster oven. I was all set up for long hauls in the office or entertaining whoever might need some entertaining.

I walked past the conversation pit and the interview chairs and plopped my gift briefcase on my desk. I opened the case, pulled out what was left of the cash and divided it into two stacks. The small stack I folded and put it into my right pants pocket. I took the larger stack and went over to the Mossberg. After dialing in the combination and opening the right hand door, I put nine thousand dollars into a drawer at waist height. The safe had been one of my better acquisitions, holding evidence, photos, a couple of hand guns, my cameras, some important papers and any cash I wanted to keep safely at hand. I closed the big door, twirled the combination and went over to my filing cabinet. I extracted an empty folder, closed the drawer, went over to my desk and put all the information I had about Garcia in the folder. I withdrew a pen from the desk drawer as I sat down and wrote his name at the top of the folder. I set the folder aside. Then I dialed Roger's number.

"Roger Stone's office. How may I direct your call?" his secretary asked.

"Hi, Andie, this is Dave Harris. Roger asked me to call him. Is he in?"

"Oh, hi, Dave. He is. Just a minute while I transfer your call."

I heard elevator music, then Roger's voice. "Hello, Dave. Glad you called back. I need your advice on something and was wondering if you could come by my office in the morning?"

"Sure, Roger. I could even come up now if you'd like."

"No, tomorrow's fine. About nine-thirty, it that's convenient?"

"Yeah, nine-thirty's okay", I agreed after I'd looked at my schedule book sitting on the corner of the desk. The only iron in the fire was Garcia and he wasn't even in my book yet. I could continue the search in the morning after my meeting with Stone.

"That's great, Dave. Thanks. I'll see you then. Have a good evening."

"Okay, 'til tomorrow. Good-bye."

"Good-bye."

Hmmm, I thought. Now what? Ah, nothing like another little mystery to perk up one's life.

I fished through the briefcase for Garcia's number for one more try. Ten rings and no answer. I leaned back in my chair and propped my feet up on the corner of the desk. Mr. Garcia, what are you up to? Let's see. The easy plan had been to call him up and find out why he had been incommunicado. Now, unless he answered later on tonight or in the morning, I was going to have to make a trip out to the west side and check out his abode. Hopefully with him in it. Better plan for the worst; in this case it was probably mayhem.

Since the Caddy was literally under wraps for a few days, I'd need to use my other sedan, a 1972 Olds Eighty-Eight, same tan color as the Caddy, but with a lot more guts under the hood. I kept the Eighty-Eight parked at the mall just in case I needed another car for surveillance purposes. Tomorrow I would again be a real estate agent, complete with magnetic car door signs, for-sale yard signs, a multipurpose clipboard and my handy-dandy 100-foot tape measure. I also had some surveyor's tape, wooden stakes and a few other tools for the realtor on the go. I'd double-check my inventory of gear before I left for home.

As I pondered tomorrow's action, the lack of sleep over the last few days was beginning to make my eyelids heavy. I dozed off.

Suddenly, I was surrounded by Federales, all with their pistolas drawn and aimed at me. As I heard a shot, I woke up. The sound was my office door slamming. Bobby was standing inside the door grinning at me.

"Dave, you going to stay here all night?" she asked.

I looked at my watch—nine thirty. No wonder my neck and legs were stiff and there was a latrine-like taste on my tongue. Hell, the mall was closing in thirty minutes.

"No," I managed to get my mouth to say as I swung my feet off my desk. "I guess I was just tired from all the fun we had. By the way, I have some money for you."

"Good. I was hoping the five grand you promised wasn't just a Dave-dream."

"Ha-ha. No it's real. I'll get it for you as soon as my legs wake up," I said while trying to rub the circulation back into my lower extremities. Bobby waited patiently while I returned the blood flow to my toes. After a couple of minutes, I stood up, walked stiffly over to the safe, played with the combination until the last tumbler clicked into place and opened the door. I took five thousand dollars from the drawer and closed the safe. Bobby was sitting on the couch when I turned around with the cash.

"You know you probably shouldn't just dump this into your bank account," I prompted as I walked over and handed her the wad of bills.

"Yes, I know it's semi-hot. I'll keep your good name from the IRS. Now that we're both sort of rich, who's going to buy dinner, you or me?"

"I will," I said. "You name the place."

"Okay, how about the Café Americana?"

"Okay."

"Tonight?"

"Okay. How late do they stay open?"

"Midnight, I think, maybe later. I'll call while you freshen up," she hinted, nodding her head toward the bathroom.

She made the call while I splashed water on my face, combed my hair and brushed my teeth. She was right as usual. They closed at midnight. I felt a bit more human after the mini-spit-bath. I cleared off my desk and secured Garcia's file in the cabinet. We locked up our offices and took the Eighty-Eight to the restaurant after I quickly checked the realtor inventory in the Old's trunk. We ate a filling Tex-Mex meal at the Americana and closed up the place over sopapias and coffee. I dropped her off back at her car at the mall and drove home for some well-deserved sleep.

Wednesday

Eight o'clock came too early. I was still groggy from the long hours we'd put in for Wilson. I showered and dressed in slacks and jacket, with an open collar shirt. I dropped a package of lock picks and a small flashlight in my jacket pockets. I fished two thin rubber gloves from the box under the bathroom sink and stuffed them into my left inside pocket. Then I retrieved my Beretta 380 from its resting-place inside the hidden compartment on the side of my dresser and slipped it into the holster at the small of my back. I eyed myself in the mirror to check that nothing was too obvious. Everything looked okay.

I left the house at nine and headed for Penney's to meet with Stone. When I arrived at his office, Andie wasn't at her desk. I knocked on Stone's partially opened door and announced myself.

"Roger, it's me, Dave," I said easing the door fully open.

He was on the phone. He waved me over to one of the overstuffed chairs facing his desk. I took a seat and waited for him to finish his call. I ignored his conversation with the caller. After about three minutes he said good-bye and hung up. Then he stood up and stuck out his hand for a shake. I stood and we shook. Then he sat back down and kind of sunk into his chair. I sat, too, watching him carefully. At the moment he didn't look like a successful late thirties-ish department store manager. He looked a little beaten. His bushy eyebrows came together in a frown as he began speaking.

"Thanks for coming, Dave. I need advice and maybe your services as a P.I."

"What's up Roger? You sound pretty serious."

"Well, it's a personal thing. I, uh, I think Marcie's having an affair but I'm not sure," he blurted out. "She's acting kind of odd and I don't know if it's something or nothing."

"What's she doing that's odd?"

"Once or twice over the last three weeks she's had phone conversations that get really quiet when I walk into the room. And she's had a couple of evenings out with her friends, so she says. She never used to do that. I just need to know. I care about her enough that if she wants a fling, I might be able to overlook it. I want to know is all."

"Look, Roger, knowing isn't necessarily a good thing. It could lead to a divorce if you don't trust her and if she thinks she can't trust you. How long has it been going on?"

"About six weeks all together. I'm so upset with thinking what it might be that I don't sleep well at night. And it's starting to affect my work. I can't seem to concentrate very well. That's why I need your help."

"What do you want me to do?" I asked.

"Could you, very discretely, find out where she's going and what's going on?"

"You mean, tail her?"

"Yeah, tail her."

"I'll tell you what, Roger. I'll check it out, but you've got to trust me, too. If I find out there's nothing to it, I'll tell you, and then you've got to believe me and ask her yourself or drop it. One time good deal, okay? And I'll only charge you my expenses, okay?"

He thought about it a minute and then said, "Okay. We'll do it your way. Please be careful. She's seen you before and might connect you with me. It would ruin everything if she made a connection before I know the truth."

"I'll be careful, Roger. I know what she looks like." Boy, did I. Marcie was a striking blonde with a girlie-magazine figure. She was just the kind of woman that you'd want to take home to momma and not take home to momma, if you know what I mean.

"Give me a couple of days to check it out and I'll get back with you about it. I've got another case cooking, but I should have it settled pretty quickly," I told him.

He stood up and again offered his hand.

As I gripped his hand, I looked him in the eye and said, "Meanwhile, you relax. You won't gain anything by worrying. Let me do my work. I'll let you know as soon as I get it nailed down. Could be something, could be nothing. Right now your best action is to plan for it either way. What I'll need from you now is your address and phone number. If she goes out and you know about it, call me at the office or at home and I'll saddle up."

I gave him my business card with my numbers on it. On the back of a second card he wrote his information and handed it to me. A thought suddenly occurred to me.

"Would you mind if I bug your phone? That may be the quickest way to solve this mystery," I added.

"Well, I guess it'd be okay. Do you have that kind of equipment?" he wondered.

"Yeah, I have some. I keep it in the trunk of the Olds. For special cases."

"How are you going to do it with her there?"

"I'm not. Is she home all day?"

"Today she isn't. She usually plays bridge at the Women's Club from two to four-thirty on Wednesdays."

"Good. Can you meet me at your house at about two-thirty?" I planned on being there just a little bit earlier than that.

"Yes. I can get away then. How long will it take?"

"Thirty minutes or so without problems. How many phones do you have?" I asked, deciding if I'd need enough equipment to bug each one or just the main junction box.

He thought a minute and said, "Five, if you count the one in the garage."

Junction box it was.

"Okay then, probably closer to an hour. We should be done in plenty of time before she gets home."

"Thanks, Dave. I knew I could count on you. This means a lot to me," he said walking me to the door.

"I know. I'll see you at your place at two-thirty," I assured him as we parted.

On the way out of the mall, I stopped by my office. I needed another cup of coffee before I drove to the west side. I also wanted to call Garcia's house one more time. Ruth was at her desk engrossed in whatever she was typing for Bobby so I just said hi as I headed for my door. She nodded without looking up from her work. I retrieved my cup from its shelf by the sink, loaded it with creamer and a dab of sugar and stole a mugfull from Ruth's half-full pot without disturbing her. Back inside my office, I sat down and dialed Garcia's number. It rang eleven times before I gave up. No such thing as the easy way with this one. I sipped at the hot liquid until it was gone. Time to earn my money. But first, one more phone call.

I pulled the card Roger had given me from my pocket and dialed his home phone. It rang twice, then Marcie's voice came on the line.

"Stone residence," she said.

"Marcie, this is Dave. Roger's onto us. To throw him off I offered to tap your phones. He wants to do it today, after you leave for bridge. So watch your phone calls after you get back."

"Dave, do you think tapping the phones is a wise thing to do. What if I slip?"

"You won't. Just be careful. I'll come by to see you tomorrow or the next day."

"Okay. But now you're making me nervous with all this spy stuff," she said with an edge in her voice.

"Try to settle down. We'll get this to work out. Everything will be okay. We just won't use the phones until things blow over. Trust me."

"Famous last words, Dave."

"Yeah, I know, but it'll be okay, Marcie. Have some faith."

"Okay, I'll try."

"Good. See you tomorrow. I've got to go now. I've got another case I'm working on. Bye, Marcie."

"Goodbye, Dave."

I slowly hung up the receiver. This thing with Marcie was complicated, but it would be over soon, thank God. I took my empty cup over to the wet bar, washed it out in the sink and upturned it on a towel to dry. Now, I said to myself, it's time to earn your dough.

I walked out the mall side door and toward the Eighty-Eight. There was some people traffic in the parking lot so I made my next actions deliberately casual. I opened the trunk and pulled out two magnetic signs that announced I was from Branson's Realty, with the real number for Branson's at the bottom. I placed one of the big magnets on each front door. I retrieved my clipboard from the trunk and placed it on the front seat. There was a metal "For Sale" sign in the trunk, ready to be implanted in Garcia's lawn if need be. Under the sign was a 100-foot tape measure. I was setting up for worst case and hoping for best case. I closed the trunk and slid behind the wheel. The big engine sprung to life and I drove over to the southbound entrance to I-35. As I accelerated up the on-ramp I glanced at the clock on the dash. It still worked, amazing but true, and the time was ten eighteen.

I drove south on the freeway to the I-410 loop, then headed west. Near Medina Base, where the Air Force trains its new officers, are some housing developments by Ron Ellis. Ellis built tract homes with GI wallets in mind. Garcia's house was one of them. The neighborhood I needed was just west of the freeway with Medina Base as the other boundary. It took me twenty minutes from the mall to the turnoff. I looped under the freeway and headed back along the east-bound access road. I was driving a bit too fast and had to brake hard to make a right onto Lake Valley. I paused at the intersection of Lake Valley and Sun Valley, getting my bearings, then drove straight paralleling Garcia's street and checked the addresses. Garcia's house was on the next block to my right. At the corner, I turned right and right again onto Garcia's street. I judged his house to be about midway up the block on the right side. There were medium sized cotton-wood trees lining the street, with enough overhang to provide some shade and bird droppings for those lucky enough to park on the street.

I eased the car up to the curb in front of a frame house with half brown brick and half tan siding—a Ron Ellis special. I switched off the engine after placing the big car in park. The street was quiet. Moms were no doubt resting after seeing their kids off to school. I grabbed my clipboard and stepped out into the street. As I closed the car door I could hear the traffic on the freeway. I also heard a blue jay from his perch in a tree down the street loudly announcing my arrival. I rounded the Eighty-Eight's big nose and walked up the front walk to the house. I stood at the door a moment before I pushed the bell. I heard it ring inside. No answer. I rang again. Still no answer. For prying eyes, I looked at the paper on my clipboard, made a couple of fake notes and walked back to the car. My original plan was to meet Mr. Garcia as a real estate agent and once I gained the interior of his house, confess my real mission. The backup plan was to gain entrance to his house and nose around. To do that with a semblance of normalcy, I got my gear out of my trunk.

I carried the sign, the tape measure and my clipboard to the middle of the yard. I stuck the sign in the ground facing the street. I turned around and faced the house. The bedrooms appeared to be left of the front door. There was also a wood fence that started to the left of the house. I didn't see a gate. The driveway on the right of the house led back to a doublewide carport. The gate to the back was probably there. If I were going in, I'd do it from the side or the back. I walked over to the left corner of the house. Hooking the metal end of the tape on the brick, I started measuring the house, carefully noting my findings on the clip-board. Working my way past the bedroom windows, I tried to get a glimpse inside, but drawn blinds thwarted my intruding eyes. I sketched the front porch, keeping up my charade. I then measured the living room and ended up on the driveway.

As I strung the tape along the carport side of the house, I saw a door about a third of the way down the wall. As I passed it, I tried the handle. Locked. There was a wooden gate between the house and the wooden storage area that spanned the end of the carport. I finished my notes at the gate. I gave it a rattle, hoping that there was no dog protecting the back yard and if there was one, hoping that the rattle would alert the dog and warn me of its temperament. No barking; no growling. I took a breath and flipped the latch. The gate swung open with a slight moan of rusty hinges. Then I was in the backyard. The yard was surrounded with the wooden fence, six feet tall for privacy. How convenient for me. Along the back wall of the house was a slab patio with some cheap lawn furniture, a barbecue and a bench near the back door.

I continued my act to the back door, pulling at the screen door. It opened. Standing between the screen door and the solid wooden door, I tugged on my evidence gloves and gave the knob a twist. It turned and the door opened. I stepped into the kitchen and quietly closed the doors. I didn't smell any rotting corpses and I heard no movement in the house but as I glanced around the kitchen, I could tell it had been burglarized. Either that or Garcia was one messy housekeeper. The cupboards were all open and there was kitchen stuff all over the counters. Some of the cabinet drawers were standing open. There were a few bowls and utensils on the floor. The trashcan had been knocked over. I propped the clipboard against the back door and leaned the tape against it, so their falling would tip me off if anyone should try to sneak up on or away from me. I slid the Beretta from its holster and held it at the ready. It didn't feel like anyone was in the house but me, but I didn't want to chance it. I crossed the kitchen floor, avoiding the debris and entered the living room. It was in the same condition: sofa cushions strewn about, chairs upturned, books out of place. The bedrooms and bathroom were down the hall to my right. I inspected each one. The searchers had been pretty thorough, the tank lid on the toilet had been set aside on the sink. Only the bedroom in the back left corner of the house hadn't been touched. Either the culprits had found what they were looking for before they trashed that bedroom or they had to leave before they were done.

After returning the Beretta to its hiding place on my belt, I gave the room a quick once-over to see if I could find something out of place. I looked in the usual places, which for me included the backs of the drawers in the dresser and nightstand and the inside walls of the closet. I saw nothing obvious. The internal clock in my head was flashing its alarm that I'd overstayed my time and I headed toward my entrance point. Back in the kitchen I looked at the refrigerator, its humming compressor keeping the contents fresh and tasty. I wondered if they'd checked out the oldest hiding place since the icebox had been invented. Probably, but what the hell. I opened the refrigerator door. The sparse contents inside included half a carton of milk, some plastic containers of unidentifiable and probably inedible foods, some condiments in the door, and the usual vegetable keeper with some-not-so-fresh lettuce, an onion and half a soggy tomato. The meat drawer was hiding a package of sliced bologna and a partial half-moon of Longhorn cheese. I closed the refrigerator door and opened the freezer door. There were Tupperware containers with frozen stuff inside and three half filled ice trays within the frosty lining. It didn't appear that any of it had been moved lately. I shuffled the stuff around. Under the frozen leftovers was a plastic bag with a flat newspaper-wrapped object in it.

Well, what have we here? I guess it doesn't hurt to check out the obvious after all. I freed the bag from its resting-place among the frost particles and shook off the frozen pieces. The bag was a zip lock about twelve inches square. The contents felt like a thick magazine. Funny place to keep his Newsweek. I slid the package from the plastic wrapper and added the bag to the trash on the floor. The newspaper wrapper covering the inner package was held together with clear tape. I debated tearing it apart in the kitchen or waiting until I had more time to peruse the contents back at my office. My curiosity could wait. Besides, I was running low on trespassing time. I lifted the tail of my jacket and wedged the package in the small of my back between my shirt and the Beretta. It was cold and I wiggled a bit to get my jacket to drape more naturally. Satisfied that the bulge wasn't too obvious, I closed the freezer, went over to the back door, retrieved my clipboard and tape measure and turned the back door knob.

I opened the back door, snapped off both gloves, stuffed them back in my pocket, and exited the house. No change in the outside noise or activity level. I kept my step casual as I left the backyard through the gate and walked down the driveway to the Olds. Opening the driver's door, I tossed the clipboard and tape onto the front seat. I left the For Sale sign on guard in the front yard in order to sustain my cover. It would be the only testimony that I had been near Garcia's house. I fished out my keys and cranked up the engine. Easing from the curb, I took one last look at the house.

At the end of the street I stopped at the sign, looked both ways and turned right. One block over I turned back onto Lake Valley and made my way to the entrance ramp to the 410 loop. Gunning the big car up the ramp, I drove south, then east toward I-35. When I reached the I-35 cloverleaf, I aimed the Olds northward toward downtown San Antonio, planning on making my exit at I-35 and Military Drive. It took about ten minutes to cover the distance. I got off at Military and took the turnaround under the overpass to point me back toward the mall. I eased through the parking lot until I neared the mall exit by my office.

I found a parking place close to the door, rolled up the windows nearly all the way, got out and locked the car doors. I took a minute to pull off the magnetic signs and stow them in the trunk before I entered the mall through the fire door. I went down the hallway and pulled open the door to Nelms and Harris. Ruth was at her desk, the telephone headset glued to her head. She nodded to me when I came in. I mouthed a hello and opened my office door. As soon as the door was closed, I pulled the package from my back and rounding the corner of my desk, plopped it onto the desk protector. I took off my jacket and draped it across the back of the chair. I tugged the Beretta's holster from my belt and after sitting down in my chair, dropped the gun rig and then my lock-pick case from my jacket into my right-hand desk drawer. I locked the drawer, then retrieved the letter opener from my pen and pencil jar and slit the newspaper open on one end. I dumped out the contents, hopefully expecting to find a folder full of diamonds or at least some good hash-hish.

What I held in my hands when I pulled the newspaper away was a loose-leaf book bound with screw posts. The cover was blue, about a quarter-inch thick and the size of a Time magazine. One look at the writing on the cover told me that Mr. Garcia had been a very naughty boy. Damn, this book was a hot potato that I needed to find a proper home for. The only person I knew that could handle my find was a guy on Kelly Air Force Base. I made a quick decision. Kelly it was. I grabbed my phone number flip file, slid the indicator to R and hit the button. The file popped open and Ramirez was the fourth one listed. I dialed the number.

"Major Ramirez's office. Sergeant Acres speaking," the female voice said.

"Hi. I'm Dave Harris. May I speak with the major, please?"

"He's in a meeting right now, sir. May I take a message?" she asked, politely.

"Yes, please tell him that Dave Harris called, that I'm on my way over to see him with some important papers."

"I'll tell him but he'll probably be gone to lunch before you get here."

"I'm leaving now and will be there in twenty minutes," I said, stretching the truth a little. "It's important, so please tell him not to leave until I get there, okay?"

"Yes sir, I'll give him your message," she promised.

"Thanks, goodbye."

"Goodbye."

I hung up, then stuffed the book back into its wrapper, stood up, grabbed my coat and headed for the door. On the way out, I returned the book to its place against my back and tugged my jacket on. Ruth was still on the phone. I mouthed "Gotta go" to her and left the office, retreating down the hall the way I had come in. Fishing my car keys out of my pocket with one hand, I hit the bar on the fire door with the other and I was out in the sunshine. I unlocked the driver's door, slid behind the wheel, fired up the big eight cylinder and took off through the parking lot toward the freeway just a bit less carefully than before. Good thing the shopping crowds hadn't hit yet, I thought. I'd hate having to thread the human needle right then. I didn't slow down much when I reached the street and bounced onto Military Drive heading east to the I-35 intersection. Luck was with me. I arrived at the light just before it went to yellow and turned left onto the access road heading to the city center. I roared up the entry ramp onto I-35, tires squealing a bit at my heavy throttle job. Five minutes later and I was braking hard going into the cloverleaf at I-35 and Highway 90.

I'm sure I was exceeding the recommended ramp speed when I took the exit onto Highway 90 west. The tires on the Eighty-Eight complained until we straightened out and zoomed up onto the four-lane. Two minutes later, the entry ramp leading to General Hudnell Avenue was sharp enough to cause me to slow to thirty. I followed General Hudnell around toward Kelly until it dumped me at the base's main gate. I drove up to the guard shack, was waved through and proceeded onto the base. A couple of minutes later I pulled into the parking lot of a two-story office building near the center of the base. The guy I was going to go see was an old friend. After securing the Olds, I entered the building and took the stairs to the second floor.

At eleven forty-three by the big Air Force clock on the wall, I followed the nice behind of Sergeant Joan Acres as she ushered me into the office of Leo Ramirez, the local commander of the Office of Special Investigations for Kelly Air Force Base. Leo and I had been stationed together in Turkey for two years. We'd been reassigned to Kelly nearly simultaneously whereupon he, in the line of duty, had accidentally shot me in the buttocks and landed me in civilian ranks. Since then he had changed jobs and been promoted a couple of times while I plied my trade on the outside. He gave me a big grin and had his hand outstretched as I entered the room.

"Dave, good to see you. How's your ass?" he asked with barely suppressed laughter.

"Fine, Leo. How's yours?" I countered, stepping over to his desk and gripping his big paw. Leo was about six four and weighed in at around two thirty. He had the rounded face of a guy who enjoyed his work and ate too much.

"I'm great, Dave, just great," he said pumping my arm. "It's been a damn long time since I've seen you. It was at that Halloween party last year, wasn't it? You were with, what's her name, the cute brunette from General Whigg's office?"

"Julie Newton."

"Yeah, Julie Newton. How did that go? I never found out."

"It went okay," I said, sitting in the chair he waved to in front of his desk. "We dated a while, then the general moved on up to the Pentagon and Julie was reassigned along with him. Early December it was. I got a Christmas card."

"That's too bad. She was a looker." Then he switched gears. "So, what brings you into my office on this fine April morning?"

"Well, I brought you a little gift," I said.

"A gift, huh? Where is it?"

"Right here," I said, leaning forward. I reached back and extracted the package from the back of my trousers.

"Seeing where you got that from, I'm not sure I want your so-called gift. What's in it, explosives?" he asked with a grin.

"No, but the contents could be explosive. I retrieved it today from the abode of a gentleman who works on your base. At the nuke farm."

I had Leo's undivided attention with that one. His smile had disappeared.

"At SAAMA?" he repeated. "What is it?"

"A book. But before I show it to you, I need your promise that when I give it to you my involvement will be strictly backstage."

"Dave, I can't promise you that and you know it. At least not until I know what I'm dealing with."

"Leo, do you trust me, just a little?"

"Yes. At least enough to put a bullet in your butt."

"Good. Then let me tell my tale and at the end of it you'll have your book and know how to handle it."

"Is this a long story?" he pressed.

"Five, ten minutes tops."

"Then I'll indulge you. Shoot."

"I'm working on a case right now, since yesterday. My client is a young lady who lives in Dallas and whose fiancé lives in San Antonio. Problem is she can't seem to get in touch with him for several days. She claims he mentioned making some big bucks and now he's apparently disappeared from the scene. I figure it's for the usual reasons. But I'm getting paid well, so I take the case."

"You found him yet?"

"Nope. I called his work, at SAAMA, where he's 'on leave'. And since there's no answer at his home on the west side I mosey over there this morning to have a look-see."

"So you go over there, peep through some windows and what did you find?" he injected, trying to speed up my story.

"Not him, that's for sure. But the place had been, uh, inspected by someone other than my man."

"Well, I know you better than to think you just peeped in the windows to determine that a search had taken place. Is that when you found the book?" he asked, eyes dropping to the paper bag.

"Not exactly. I may have interrupted the inspectors. One of the bedrooms was pristine. On a whim, as I was leaving, I took a quick look in the equally untouched freezer and found what I'm about to give you. And when I show it to you, you'll know exactly what my man was hoping would make him rich. Problem is, I'm not sure who was going to cash him in."

"Is that it?"

"Pretty much. Now for your gift," I said extending the newspaper bound package over his desk.

I upended it, plopping the screw-post-bound soft-covered book onto Leo's desk protector. The book landed face down. What was written on the back cover was enough to make Leo's face turn slightly pale. Bold print announced that the book's contents were classified as Secret. And worse, it contained Critical Nuclear Weapon Design Information.

"Holy shit!" was Leo's one exclamation as he flipped it over.

Printed on the front was the same secret warning. In the center of the cover was a block with: "Render Safe and Disposal Procedures for the W-28 Warhead including the B-28 External, B-28 Retarded External, and B-28 Full-Fusing Internal Bombs".

"You found this in some guy's freezer? Who's the guy?" Leo demanded.

"His name is Robert Garcia. He works as a tech writer for SAAMA. You want his work number?" I asked innocently.

"Damn right I do," he said, getting to his feet, leaning on his desk.

I had written down Garcia's numbers on a piece of paper which now resided in my shirt pocket. I gave the paper to Leo.

"Look, I've got a couple of calls to make. Sit tight. Don't go anywhere. I'll have Acres bring you some coffee if you want," he added on his way out of the office with the book in his hand.

"I want," I said to his back. As the door closed I could hear Leo issuing orders to his secretary.

A few minutes later Sergeant Acres came in with a mug of coffee that she placed atop a coaster on the edge of Leo's desk nearest my chair.

"Here's your coffee. Do you use anything in it?" she asked.

Acres was a cute, curvy blonde with her hair up in a military style bun to keep it off her uniform collar. She had a pretty, slightly oval face, wide eyes and clear skin. Her skirt was at the knee and she had nice legs. I had already been eyeing her assets and decided on a flip answer to her question.

"Irish Crème if you've got it," I answered.

"We don't," came her professional tone. "Anything else? For your coffee?" she added before I could render another inappropriate reply.

"Some sugar and creamer would do nicely," I replied, the playfulness gone from my voice.

"Okay, I'll be back in a minute," she said, retreating through the door.

She wasn't gone long. When she returned, she set a plastic spoon and two packets of creamer and one of sugar down near my mug. I tried engaging her again.

"How long have you worked for Leo?" I started in.

"I've been assigned here for eighteen months. I came here from Vandenberg in California," she volunteered. "Now if you'll excuse me, I have some calls to make."

"Sure," I said. Cut off for the second time, I thought. "We can talk later."

"Sure," she said, her tone softening a bit, as she headed back out to her desk. The door closed with a click behind her.

Thirty minutes later and I was still staring at Leo's desk. I'd had my cup of brew and stood up to stretch. I was getting the kinks out as the door opened and Leo stuck his head in.

"Sorry to leave you hanging. Had some people I had to round up. I have a few other calls to make to figure out what's going on. It shouldn't take long."

"Hey, if you want, I could come back later. Or since you've got my story and all the secrets, I could just go," I countered.

"No, I'd rather you stayed until I find out who, why and where. I might need some other info from you, okay."

"Well, okay for now, but I've got an appointment that I can't miss at one-thirty," I lied. "So no matter what, I need to be going by about one o'clock."

"I understand. I'll have things under control by then. Just don't leave quite yet. I haven't had Acres strip search you yet for hidden material," Leo joked.

"Leo, while I wouldn't mind Acres peering at my nether parts, I don't think she likes me much."

"Oh, why do you say that?" he wondered, a sly grin creeping across his face.

"Her attitude seems a bit clipped is why," I answered.

"It should be. First thing I did was warn her about you," he said devilishly. "Told her what a lady-killer you were."

"Great. Thanks for the leg up, Leo. Anything else I can do for you?"

"Nope," he added. "I'm having a good time just giving you the needle. I'll be back in a little bit," he said pulling the door closed behind his retreating head.

A few minutes later Acres came back in, probably at Leo's bidding.

"More coffee?" she asked, picking up my empty cup.

"Yes, please. And I'll get the next one if you'll tell me where the pot is," I offered.

"It's no problem. The coffee's back down the hall, but I think the major would rather I get it for you," she replied.

"Oh, I get it. Secret areas and such, huh?" I guessed.

"Something like that. So, just let me know if you want more."

"Okay, I will. Changing the subject, Sergeant Acres, I understand the major warned you about me."

"Not exactly," she said, eyeing me closely. "He just told me you had a big ego and little penis and a bullet hole in your ass. That's all."

I was laughing by the time she got to the bullet hole part. I made a mental note to kill Leo at the earliest opportunity.

"So he told you I had a little penis, huh," I repeated.

"Yes, he did," she confirmed, smiling.

"The part about the bullet hole is true, but the first two things are really descriptors of your boss," I informed her.

"Is that so? Sounds more like it's true of both of you. But don't tell him I said that. He does write my performance appraisals."

"To keep me quiet, you'll have to have dinner with me sometime."

"Hmm," she pondered my offer. Then, "I'll think about it. Of course, now that I know what you have to offer accepting might be anticlimactical."

"Ha, ha. But at least think about it."

"I will. Now back to coffee. I'll be back in a minute," she said, making her exit.

She returned in a few minutes with my refill.

"Here you go. And here I go. Duty calls," she said closing the door.

"Come back when you can stay longer," I said to myself.

By the time I had finished the coffee, it was after twelve thirty, the second hand on my watch slowly winding its way around the dial, pushing the minute hand ever closer to the twelve. Leo has fifteen minutes, then I'm making my break, I thought. Fifteen minutes.

At ten minutes before one o'clock, Leo reappeared.

"Well, I don't have all the details, but it looks like your boy was going to sell his goods to someone from the Middle East or Africa. That's all I can find out from my contacts so far. Looks like you're out of the loop on this one. Need to know, you know, Mr. Civilian. So, you're out of here," Leo said, extending his hand in farewell.

I stood up and shook his hand.

"Can't say I'm not glad to be out of the loop, Leo. Except for a couple of things. You're going to notify the police, right?"

"Right. If you insist."

"Well, yeah. Even though the evidence belongs to your Air Force, Garcia was a civilian and so is his address. As I remember, breaking and entering is still illegal. And of course there's the missing Mr. Garcia himself. I didn't get a chance to look in the attic for bodies."

"Assuming there is one and Garcia's not just a guy on the lam."

"Yes, assuming that. And speaking of Mr. Garcia, what do you propose I tell the bride-to-be?"

"You'll have to stall her, Dave, until I can find out what's happening and where Garcia is. I have some more checking to do and I'll let you know what I find out about him. He's your only connection, right? I get the low down on him and you're out of the game, right?"

"Yeah, except for the fee I collected in advance. That's why I need to know what's happened to him. So, call me ASAP, okay? The fiancé and I will be waiting," I said, fishing out a business card from my pocket and handing it to Leo.

"Still at South Park Mall, eh?" he asked, looking at the phone number and address on the card.

"Yep, it's cheaper than uptown and I have a little mall security thing going on," I admitted.

"Mall security? You're a little young for that gig aren't you?" he said as we moved toward his office door.

"It helps pay the bills. I'm not with the government anymore, you know. Something about a bullet in the butt. Speaking of which, I owe you a little something extra for your warning to your secretary."

"I guess you do," Leo laughed. "I'd forgotten I'd poisoned that well for you. Didn't want you corrupting my staff so I had to cut you off at the pass," he said, seeing me out.

We'll see who cut off whom, I thought, then said, "Keep in touch, Leo, about Garcia."

"I will," he assured me. "And if you find out anything more about the case, call me."

"I will," I said, turning to shake his hand again. I noticed that Sergeant Joan wasn't at her post. Probably off on some Leo-errand.

"And Dave, watch your ass on this one, okay?" he cautioned.

"After you, Leo, I always do," I answered with a grin, leaving Leo standing in his doorway.

It was five after one when I cranked up the Olds. I mentally reviewed the directions to Roger Stone's house. Depending on the traffic, it would take me about twenty-five minutes to get there. If I goosed it a bit I'd arrive just in time to see Marcie leave for her afternoon out. After leaving the air base, I goosed it.

Roger's street was one of those all-American suburban boulevards situated on the north side of San Antonio, just inside the 410 loop. The trees were young and pruned just so; the lawns were green and well manicured. I half expected to see little gardeners popping up from behind every shrub, clippers in hand. I passed the Stone residence, continued on down the block, made a u-turn at the next intersection and headed back up the street. Two houses before Stone's, I pulled up at the curb and stopped the engine. I made a show of playing with the city map while watching the action at Roger's house. His place was a single story brick affair with five windows facing the street. The driveway went around to the left of the house to the garage in back. The front yard had been freshly mowed and there were evergreen bushes flanking the sidewalk leading to the front door. The only activity on this part of the street was my Oldsmobile, my map and me, just waiting.

I had arrived about ten minutes before Marcie was scheduled to leave for her appointment. Several minutes after I had begun my map act, a dark green Ford station wagon pulled out of the driveway. The woman behind the wheel was Marcie. It was five minutes after two. Roger was due to arrive in about twenty minutes.

She looked at me as she drove past and stopped her car beside mine. She rolled her window down.

"Are you lost, mister?" she asked mockingly.

"No, ma'am. You're just the person I wanted to see. Sorry about the phone thing today, but I figured that would be the only way we could get Roger side-tracked."

"How am I supposed to handle not using the telephone?"

"Marcie, you can still use the phone. You just have to be careful what you say. Our plans aren't changing, are they?"

"No, everything's the same. Say, weren't you supposed to come over tomorrow or the next day?"

"Well, yeah, but I came by early just to reassure you that things will be okay."

"Okay," she said, pausing, then "Well, I have to go now. I'll see you later."

"Right. 'Bye, now."

And with that she gave me a look, rolled up her window and drove away. I could only hope she would be able to keep it together as we had planned. I went back to studying the map.

I was down to reading the individual street names on the map when Roger drove by my car several minutes later. He tapped lightly on the horn and with an index finger, indicated that I should follow him into the driveway. I cranked up the Olds and eased after him around the side of the house. I stopped behind him, switched off the engine and got out. The garage was attached to the house, sharing a common roof. The back door of the house was to the right of the double garage door. Roger was standing at the back door, his keys in hand.

"Roger, are you sure you still want to do this?" I asked as I approached him.

We shook hands and he said, "Yeah, I'm sure. What do you need me to show you?"

"Well, I've thought about it and I think the best plan is to hook up my tap to the telephone's main box, which may be outside or possibly in the attic. Do you know where it is?" I asked, getting down to business.

"It's in the attic, I believe. Come on, I'll show you."

"In a minute. I've got to get the stuff out of the car," I said, walking back toward the Olds. I retrieved a hinged wooden box the size of an overnight case from the trunk while Roger waited for me at the back door. The box held a recorder and other electrical components that I'd used for surveillance in the military. I had accidentally retained possession of the box when I was discharged. It was times like this when my larcenous ways paid off. When I returned to him, he silently unlocked the door and we went into the entryway like two sneak thieves. After the entry we were in the laundry room. The kitchen was through a door on our right and the garage was to our left. He opened the garage door and we went into what has got to be the cleanest garage I've ever been in. Not a grease spot on the floor or thing out of its assigned place. There were garden tools hanging on the walls that looked unused. The workbench to our right had a shadow board with every shadow covered.

"Nice garage, Roger. How do you keep it so neat?" I had to ask.

"I force myself. Otherwise I wouldn't be able to find a damn thing. Besides, my wife reminds me to keep it cleaned up," he said, leading me over to a cord hanging from the ceiling.

The cord belonged to the pull-down stairway leading to the attic above. He pulled on the string and the trap door opened halfway. He pulled the lower stairs down, locked them in place and started up the stairs. Halfway up he stopped, flipped a light switch mounted on the framework of the stairs and the blackness in the attic changed into seventy-five watt light. He continued up the stairs and when he was at the top, I followed. The interior of the attic was only slightly less clean than the garage. The temperature felt about twenty degrees higher. Most of the floor was covered with plywood, which made walking over the joists less hazardous. The place even looked like it had been swept lately, there being only a little dust in the air. I had to ask.

"Roger, do you sweep up here?"

"I use the shop vac up here once every couple of months. I'm a little sensitive to the dust and it's easier to do some cleaning than to put up with a stuffy and runny nose."

"You're a better man than I," I commented. "Where's the phone box?"

"Over here," he said, leading me down the center of the attic to the place where the garage roof met the house.

Just past the tee, Roger stopped, turned and pointed to a gray plastic box mounted to one of the two-by-four uprights supporting the roof. There were several telephone lines coming out of the box, each going off to their respective phones below. There was one larger wire bundle feeding into the box. The main, I guessed. While Roger looked on, I unscrewed the lid to the box, located the main input and after extracting two lead wires with alligator clips from my recorder box, plugged into the phone line. Now I needed power for the recorder. It was activated by the small amount of electricity from the phone line and voices but needed house voltage to power the tape machine.

"Do you have a plug-in up here?" I asked. I suspected he'd have one. Where else would he plug in the vacuum?

"Yes. Right there," he answered, pointing to a box attached to a two-by-four down one from where the telephone was mounted.

I removed a coil of extension cord from the recorder box and plugged in the machine. I turned it on and readied the tape.

"All we need now is a test call. Why don't you go downstairs and call your office so I can see if it works."

"Okay. See you in a minute," Roger said, stepping around me and back to the hole in the floor.

A minute or two passed, then the tape began to turn. I could just hear Roger talking to someone on the phone. A minute later and the tape stopped. I rewound it, pressed play, turned up the volume and heard Roger talking briefly to his secretary. I stopped the tape, rewound it to the ready position, turned the volume back down to minimum and closed the lid to the box. To ensure that I'd be the first one to hear what the tape recorded, I used a key on my key ring and locked the tape box. As I stood up, Roger was just coming up the stairs. I started toward the hole and reached it as he emerged headfirst.

"All set, Roger. Now we wait," I said, reaching the stairs.

"Good," he said, retreating backwards down the stairs. "Turn off the light on your way down, will you."

I hit the switch, plunging the hot attic back into darkness. Roger stood waiting at the bottom of the stairs. After I stepped off the last rung, he picked up the stair half, set it onto the top half and with a flick of his hand engaged the springs that returned the ladder into the ceiling.

We both slapped our hands together to get rid of the excess dust, then exited the garage.

When we were outside, Roger said "Thank you, Dave. I really appreciate this." He shook my hand.

"Roger, I locked my recorder box," I confessed. "I want to listen to the tape first, then we'll listen to it together. If it turns out to be something, I want to pursue it a little first. If it's nothing, you'll be the second to know. Okay?"

"Okay. But don't hide anything from me," He warned, trying to have a little control in the operation.

"I won't," I assured him. "Just remember, we're doing this my way. And, Roger, trust me."

"I do, Dave," he said, letting go of my hand.

"I'll check the tape in a couple of days, when she's gone. You set up the time and I'll come over."

"I'll give you a call when the coast is clear."

"Okay. I'll be waiting. Try not to let our spying show," I said, walking over to the Olds and opening the driver's door.

"I won't spill the beans," he promised.

"See you back at the mall, Roger."

"Yeah, see you, Dave."

I got behind the wheel, closed the door and fired up the big engine. Roger returned my wave and I backed out of his driveway.

Back out on the street, driving away from Roger's, my stomach growled, reminding me that I'd missed lunch. It was only two forty-five, really too early to quit for the day, but I needed some time to think. What was Garcia up to, I wondered. And what the hell was I going to tell his fiancé? I talked myself into going over to the west side of town where the Black Fox was, just off Military Drive. The Fox was a small local bar with jukebox music, pool tables and several cute barmaids and waitresses. It had a postage stamp dance floor surrounded by six or eight intimate tables. The place was dimly lit and it usually took several minutes for pupillar adjustment if one entered the establishment during the daytime. The bar was a sunken square in the middle of the place with comfortable swivel chairs around the perimeter. Patrons sat at eyelevel with the bartender. Off the main floor where the bar and dance floor were, there were three pool tables in a step-down room, like a sunken living room. There were several high wooden-backed stools and elevated round tables around the walls for those waiting their turn to shoot. The lights over each table gave the room just enough illumination to be cozy.

There were probably fifteen other bars in San Antonio that were very similar in layout. Locals called them icehouses. A guy I had been stationed with in Turkey had told me about the Fox and it was now my favorite hangout. In the afternoon, the place was usually empty until quitting time on Lackland and Kelly Air Force bases. It was an after-work watering hole for thirsty troops. I decided to grab a hamburger at one of the fast food places near the Fox, take it to the bar and eat it there, washing down the plastic food with a cold beer.

It took me nearly thirty minutes to drive from Roger's on the north side to Military Drive where it crosses Highway 90 on the west side of town. I pulled onto Military drive and stopped in at the McDonalds by the Fox. I ordered two burgers and a large order of fries. No telling if the day bartender had eaten yet. The Fox was a half block off Military Drive, so I had to drive out of the burger joint, then turn up the street to the Fox's parking lot. It was empty, except for a blue Ford Falcon parked in the far corner of the lot. Unless I was mistaken, it belonged to a brunette named Niki, who was one of the usual day workers at the Fox. I parked up by the front door and killed the engine. I rolled up the Olds windows until there was just a crack at the top of the glass to let the heat out. Then I grabbed my food sack, got out and locked the door. When I went into the Fox, I had to wait a minute for my eyes to adjust or else risk cracking my knees on the bar chairs.

While standing there blinded, Niki said, "Dave, is that a hamburger in your bag or are you glad to see me?"

"Both," I answered into the spots in my eyes. "Just a second and I'll share a burger with you. In the mean time, you could pour me a cold beer, please. My mouth's been watering for one ever since I decided to come over here."

"One beer coming up," she announced.

Niki was maybe twenty-five, about five foot-four, with short brown hair. I think it's called a shag cut. It went well with her oval face, high cheekbones, brown eyes and inviting lips. She had that been-around look to her, a confident walk and she smiled easily. She usually wore a loose shirt and tight jeans. I could only guess what her figure was like under the shirt, but the jeans accentuated her athlete's butt and slender hips. One day she might wear a tighter blouse and I could make better note of the rest of her figure. It might even be today, but I'd have to wait until my eyes adjusted to the dim light to tell.

It took a couple of minutes before I could finally see. Loose shirt, I noted. I walked to the right around the bar toward the sunken poolroom. There were seven low-backed swivel chairs lining the side of the bar facing the tables. I went down the two steps into the pool pit, around the end chairs and plopped the sack of food down on the bar in front of the middle chair. I pulled my jacket off, draped it across the back of the chair, unbuttoned my shirtsleeves and rolled them up twice. No sense getting mustard on my cuffs. I sat down with my back to the pool tables, opened the sack and spread the contents on the bar in front of me. Niki tossed down a coaster and put a twelve-ounce glass of beer onto it.

"Here's to cold beer, nice looking bartenders and burgers and fries," I toasted, holding the beer up and offering a sandwich to Niki.

"I agree, thanks, and thanks, respectively," she said. "So, what brings you in so early? Besides me?" she added, unwrapping her burger.

"Well, I wanted to see you, of course," I said, peeling the wrapper off my sandwich and spreading out the paper on a counter.

She offered a salt shaker from the bar and I sprinkled white crystals onto the patty.

"Then there was the growling stomach problem I was having. Also, my alcohol-low-level light was on. And last but not least, I'm working on a case that has a couple of wrinkles that I'm trying to iron out and figured I might come here to do some thinking."

"Anything you'd like to share with a friendly barmaid, besides the burger?" she asked, taking a bite of burger and leaning on her edge of the bar, batting her eyelids at me in mock seduction.

"Sure, Niki," I answered between bites, leering back at her. "There are a couple of things I'd like to share with you, besides the burger. Most of them involve being in a lot less clothing and something to do with baby oil and plastic sheets."

"Sounds pretty kinky. But you'll just have to wait until I get off work at eleven, Romeo. By then you'll probably be too tipsy to find the oil. So I guess we'll just have to wait for a better time for our steamy rendezvous."

"Well, how about now?" I offered. "There's no one here but you and me. We could make hot love on one of the pool tables."

She studied me for the count of five or six. She looked like she was deciding something.

"I'll tell you what," she said with a serious tone in her voice, waving the remnants of her hamburger at me. "If you aren't too trashed and some young cutie hasn't taken you away from here by the time I get off work, I'll let you take me to breakfast at Shorty's."

"Breakfast?"

"Breakfast. Then we'll see what happens after that."

It was my turn to contemplate her. I ate a few more bites, savoring the moment, watching her chew.

"Okay, it's a deal," I answered, wiping my hand on a napkin and extending my arm over the counter to seal it with a shake. She popped the last bite into her mouth, wiped her fingers, then took my hand and shook it. Our grasp lingered just a bit as our skin pressed together.

"So, as a consolation prize, how about a game of pool, before it gets too busy?" she asked, releasing our handhold.

"Sure, I guess that's one way to get you onto one of the tables," I joked.

"It's the only way, right now," she laughed. "But finish your burger before I beat your socks off."

"Beat my socks off? Now who's being kinky?"

She laughed again, then came up two steps out of the bar tender's pit. I stood up, wadded up the wrapper and plopped it into the trash behind the bar, banking the shot off a beer cooler. I followed her over to the middle table.

"Give me a quarter and I'll rack," she said, squatting down by the coin slot at the side of the table.

I fished into my trouser pocket and withdrew several coins. I sorted them, returning all the non-quarters to my pocket.

"Here's four," I offered, holding them out to her. "That's assuming we'll have a chance to use them before the four-thirty crowd hits."

"We should have enough time for at least one game before then," she said, sticking one into the machine. "I'll put these others right here on the rail for later use, either by you or by us."

With that she pushed the plunger and the balls were out of the chute with a loud bang. Niki went around to the end of the table, retrieved the rack from its hiding place, and began filling it with balls. As she arranged them for eight ball, I selected a cue stick from the wall rack and rolled it across the table.

"I'm a fair shot, but worse with a crooked stick," I said, frowning at the decided wobble of the last ten inches of the stick.

"I'll bet you are," she remarked, getting the last ball in place and positioning the rack over the end spot.

I chose another cue and repeated my test.

"That's better," I said, chalking up the end. I found the cue ball in its hole at my end of the table and put it on the table just to the left of center behind my breaking line. As I lined up on the lead ball, the yellow number one, Niki deftly lifted the rack away and gave it a spin as she returned it to its home in the slot at the end of the table.

"Something tells me you've done this before," I said, stroking the cue through the bridge I'd made with my left index finger and thumb.

"Once or twice," she said, grinning at me as she moved over to retrieve a cue stick. "And then only for money."

I laughed, then smacked the cue ball into the triangle at the other end of the table. Balls went racing around the table, bouncing off the cushions and each other and finally came to rest spread out over the green surface. I hadn't made a one.

"Your shot," I invited.

Niki approached the table, screwing the chalk onto her cue tip, surveying the layout.

"Well, it looks like you've given me no choice but to beat you with the stripes," she said, taking aim at the thirteen ball and smacking it into the side pocket.

"One down and seven to go," she predicted, lining up the nine.

With confidence she fired the cue into the nine which rolled to the corner and obediently dropped into the pocket. The white ball meanwhile had bounced off the seven and come to rest with good shape behind the eleven. She chalked up again.

"I guess you have done this once or twice," I said stricken slightly with awe.

"Only for money," she repeated, looking up from her shot, flashing that big grin again. She shot the cue and another ball fell and another shot was lined up perfectly.

"I'm impressed. If I ever get a shot, I guess I'd better not miss."

"Not if you plan on winning. I've been shooting pool since I was ten. Just over fifteen years. My dad taught me on a pool table in our garage. So don't be surprised if I'm hard to beat."

"Why is it I've never seen you shoot in here before?"

"When I'm here I'm usually working. I live over by Brackinridge Park and hang out at the Bombay Bicycle Club. That's where all the wannabes shoot pool. The pool money's better there, but working's better here."

"Might have known I'd make a pass at a pool shark. And then ask her for a game of pool."

"That's sharp, as in clever. But don't worry. I won't be too hard on you. I like you, even though you've only flirted with me before and never acted serious about it."

The fourteen ball found its way in the side pocket.

"Well, I'll let you in on a little secret. For the couple of months that you've been working here I've been wanting to talk with you more or do more than talk with you, but there's always someone else around, customers and such."

"Are you telling me you're shy around women?"

"Maybe a little. I like talking with women, flirting, using a lot of sexual innuendo. But the truth is I am a little tentative when it comes to taking the next step. Especially with someone as attractive to me as you are," I added hesitantly, not knowing how she'd take it.

"Thanks for the compliment. But flattery won't help you with this pool game," she added, sinking the last of the stripes.

"I see that," I said, watching her line up on the eight ball.

A finesse tap and the eight ball fell into the corner pocket, joining the others.

"Rack 'em, please," she ordered politely.

"Okay," I obeyed, squatting down by the coin intake and feeding the machine another quarter. "So tell me what's the easiest way to get past the flirting stage," I asked as I pulled the balls from their hiding place and added them to their mates on the table.

"Well, you've already done that."

"I have?"

"Sure, you're taking me out for dinner. Remember?"

"That was breakfast, at Shorty's, right?"

"Yeah, breakfast. But anyway, you took the next step without even knowing it. Besides, you've already broken the biggest secret about women, anyway, even though you may not realize it."

"I have? What secret?"

"Look," she said, coming over to me and looking me in the eyes. "Men generally make their first mistake with women by just going after their bodies. If men would engage a woman's mind first, her body will follow." Then she added in a lower tone, her mouth curling up at the corners, "You seem to already know that."

"I do?" I asked, swallowing hard. She was just inches away from me, our faces nearly touching. I could smell her perfume. Her eyes were light brown, teasing me. I could already taste her lips on mine.

"Yes, you do," she said softly. "You brought me something to eat and made a crude pass at me, but the whole time you were looking at my face and my eyes, not my boobs or my ass like most guys do. That was a big plus, just not doing what most guys do."

"I did look at your boobs and ass," I confessed. "But I tried not to be obvious about it. I consider it rude to gawk."

"Gawk?" she grinned, her eyes widening, and the spell was broken, sort of. "Where did you learn that?"

"Gawk is a real word."

"I know. It just surprised me to hear it just then. Just as I was about to reward you with a kiss."

"You were? It's not too late, you know," I said in a low voice, leaning toward her.

She reached up and put her hand on the back of my neck, pulling me the last few millimeters toward her. I pulled her hips toward me. Our bodies touched. Our lips touched.

"Hey, anybody here?" came a booming voice from the doorway.

We both jumped like we'd been shot.

"Jesus, you scared us," Niki shouted toward the door. "I'll be with you in a minute."

"Damn, so close."

"There'll be another chance, but you'd better hide that while I wait on this guy," she said, glancing down at my crotch. "So, you are glad to see me, after all."

"Yes, ma'am, I am," I said, looking down at the bulge in front of my trousers that was giving away my true feelings for her.

She retreated to the bar as I walked around to the head of the table and did as she asked. To cover my recovery, I began placing the pool balls into the rack, plopping the eight in the middle and alternating stripes and solids around the outside. Shoving the rack onto the spot and making sure the balls were tight, I attempted to spin the rack off the balls as Niki had done. The rack slipped out of my grasp and landed in the middle of the balls, spreading them out over my end of the table.

"I can see that you haven't done that before," Niki joked, coming back over to the table.

"Never for money," I said, regrouping the mess I'd made into a colorful triangle.

"Yeah, I'll bet."

I applied the rack again and took it off gently, not trying any tricks.

"Better," she said, stroking her cue stick.

I had barely time to step aside when the cue ball smacked into the lead ball with a crack. Her break was wilder than mine, with three balls finding the pockets, two stripes and a solid. I went over and sat down. I picked up my beer and took a long drag from the glass. Times like these made me want to start smoking again.

Niki's customer had ordered a draft and sat down with it a couple of chairs away from me.

"Sorry to bust in on you two like that. I'll call ahead next time."

I looked at him. He was older than me by several years, wearing a blue Air Force uniform, and sporting close-cropped brown hair, a wide smile and six stripes on his sleeve.

"It's no problem, Sarge. There'll be another time."

"Looks like it's stripes again," Niki prophesied.

And it was. We watched as Niki worked the table methodically, quickly eliminating all the striped balls.

"She's a damn good pool stick," said the Sarge.

"Yeah, she is," I concurred. "So, eight balls later and it's game time again," I said to Niki as she lined up the eight ball. "Well, ten if you count the two solids you knocked in by accident."

"Do you think I knocked in the five and one by accident?" she asked, looking up from her shot.

"You did that on purpose?"

"Sure," she said, taking aim on the eight and sinking it in the side pocket. Then she added, "Well, not really, but it made a good story. Tell you what, since it's your money and I'm spending it, I'll rack, you break. That way if you sink anything, you get to shoot again. We'll see how long you can last."

"I've heard that line before," I joked.

She laughed. The Sarge laughed.

"Okay, sounds like a deal to me. But first I've gotta use the head," I said, getting to my feet and walking around the back of the bar to the short hallway where the storeroom, office and toilets were. "Be back in a minute."

"Take your time. I'll be here," she said, putting another quarter into the ball release and pulling the lever.

When I came back, the balls were racked nicely, but now there were a few more customers in the place. It was after quitting time on the base, so the partiers would be out in force. Niki was in the bar pit fixing drinks for her new customers. When I got back to my chair, she came over.

"Well, my son, looks like you're on your own now. Good luck," she said, extending her hand.

When I took it, she pulled me toward her and gave me a quick kiss on the lips. "That's for luck and for later."

"Thanks, I'll take both," I told her, our hands lingering together for an extra moment before she turned back to her customers.

The Sarge had been watching.

"Well, I won't give you a kiss," he said, "but since you lost your pool partner, I'd be willing to take you on for a game of eight ball. I think you'll stand a better chance beating me than her."

"Depends," I replied, taking a last look at Niki before turning to the Sarge. "But, anyway, you're on," I told him, picking up my stick and chalking up for the break. "Loser buys."

"Okay with me."

We shot pool. He was good but I was luckier. I won. He bought. We played again. I lost the next one and by that time there had been challenge quarters put onto the table edge. The place was filling up with people. I sat out a couple of games before my turn came up again. Niki made an occasional pass by my chair, flirting a bit each time. I flirted back. Each time she came by, I noticed something else about her that I liked: long, slender fingers with closely trimmed nails, no polish; simple pierced earring studs in her earlobes; the way she handled herself around customers; her walk.

My turn came up to shoot some more pool, so I did. Three games later and I was sitting on the sidelines again, keeping an eye on my next turn and watching Niki whenever I could. Just before eight o'clock, she brought me a beer that I hadn't asked for and set it on a coaster in front of me.

"This is from the lady over there in the slinky black dress. Says she knows you," Niki said, her tone a little icy. She turned her head to indicate a dark haired woman sitting opposite the bar pit from me. "Do you know her?"

I looked more closely and recognized her. She was Julie Newton.

"Yes, I know her. She's an ex-girlfriend," I said, getting to my feet. "She lives in Washington, D.C. Must be in town for something."

"More likely, someone."

I looked Niki in the face and said, "Look, Niki, I said ex-girlfriend. We split up in December when she moved to D.C. We've written a few times, but that's all. Besides, you and I are just at the getting-to-know-each-other stage and already I'm detecting some jealousy here"

"You'd be some detective if you didn't," she said flatly. "Besides, I was really looking forward to eleven o'clock."

"Me, too. I still am. But I've gotta go over and at least say hi. Okay?"

"Yeah, okay. Sorry to be such a bitch. I just wanted more than one interrupted kiss."

"Oh, you'll get more, I promise. But with Julie, you've got to trust me. This will be your first test of trust."

"First?"

"You know what I mean."

"Yeah, I do. No go on, before she snares someone else and I change my mind."

I rolled down and buttoned my sleeves and pulled my jacket off the back of the chair. I picked up the beer glass she had sent over and walked around the bar to the far side where Julie was sitting, putting on my jacket as I went. There weren't any open chairs next to her, so I placed the beer on the bar and kneeled on one knee beside her chair.

"Well, long time no see. What brings you to this neck of the woods?" I started lamely, trying to keep my hurt feelings at losing her and my excitement at seeing her again out of my voice.

"Dave, it's good to see you, too. And I like you on your knees. I'm in town with the general on some Air Force business. Say, am I interrupting your move on the cute bartender?"

"Yes, you are."

"Don't worry about it," She said, resting her hand on my arm. "I'll square it with her. I'll only be in town a few days and I wanted a familiar face to look at on my time off."

"Judging from your dress, I'd say you shouldn't have any problem making friends."

"Thanks, Dave, I'll take that as a compliment. But you're the friend I wanted to see tonight. I guessed you'd be here and wore my little black dress to entice you."

"You are certainly enticing," I said looking her over. "Black hair shining in the bar light, dark brown eyes wide with anticipation, makeup perfect, smooth, flawless skin, lipstick dark red, pearly white teeth smiling seductively, a tempting bit of cleavage showing above a clingy, black dress with spaghetti straps, a great set of dancer's legs showing below a hem that's just a bit too short, and three inch heels to accentuate the whole look. Did I miss anything?"

"Yes, you did. I'm not wearing a bra or panty hose, my panties are black and very small, my whole body is athletic and tanned, and my hands are pretty with short nails, just like you like them. Also, these are pumps," she added, wiggling her footwear, "easy to slip on and off."

"You sure know how to get to a guy. Especially the part about the underwear."

"That was the idea. So, how about it? I borrow you for a few days and return you to your friend when I leave," she offered. "And I'll square it with her so you won't be getting the icy looks she keeps throwing our way."

"Well…"

"Trust me. That's what you told her before you came over here, wasn't it? Trust me?"

"How did you know that?"

"Since I saw you last I learned to lip read. Comes in handy every now and then."   •

"I'll bet. Remind me to cover my mouth," I said. "So, if I agree, what's the plan?"

"First, you take me dancing."

"Dancing? Where?"

"The Back Way Inn. They have a band every night, remember?"

"Yeah, I remember. You gonna teach me how to dance?"

"You know enough steps, as I recall. Just let your body move with the music. I'll do the rest."

"I'll bet you will."

"Now, you go to the men's room and I'll talk with your lady friend. Take your time."

I stood up, eyeing her suspiciously. I had been in love with the woman, but her career had come first. Now that she was back in my life, I could sense things getting more complicated. I looked at Niki. Her back was to us. I had begun to like her and now I was going to hurt her. I must be drunk.

"Go on. Trust me," Julie said as I turned toward the toilets.

Nope, I decided, I'm not drunk, just crazy.

I peed, washed my hands, splashed water on my face and took my time drying off. Here I was, stuck between two good-looking women. I had fleetingly entertained the idea of being the meat in a two-woman sandwich, but now I felt more like I was being sandwiched between two women. Best case I could end up with both, worst case I could end up with both or neither. Too bad there wasn't a back way out of the Fox. At this point I was just cowardly enough to take it. I stood up from leaning on the sink, checked my look and decided it was time to face the music or pay the piper or something.

When I returned to the bar, Niki and Julie were talking and looked up at me together. It was a good thing that I had evacuated my bladder a few minutes before. Their faces weren't mad looking, just determined, like two lionesses sizing up a wounded gazelle on the Serengeti. I mentally took two mighty bounds toward the door and sprinted for cover among the trees. Physically, I paused a second on my way around the bar toward Julie. They must have noticed, because they both smiled at my misstep.

"You two look too cozy there together," I tried, when I finally got back to Julie's chair.

"We've decided that I get you while I'm in town these next few days and that Niki gets you after I leave," declared Julie matter-of-factly.

Niki nodded her head.

"Do I get a say in this?" I wondered aloud, while inwardly sighing in relief that things might work out after all.

They looked at each other and then back at me.

"No," they said nearly simultaneously.

"There are two of us and one of you and that's the way the vote went," said Niki. "Take it or leave it."

"I'll take it," I agreed. Damn, what a punishment. "What do we do now?"

"Well, you and I go dancing at the Back Way and Niki goes back to work."

I looked at Julie, then at Niki. Niki nodded.

"That's what I agreed to," Niki confirmed. "My father once told me that all we really have in this life is our word. And I stick by my word. You two have a good time tonight. Now get out of here."

"Thanks, Niki," Julie said, holding out her hand. "I'm really glad to have met you. I know he'll be safe in your hands when I have to go back to D.C."

"Same to you, Julie. Don't wear him out too much, okay?"

"I won't. He's young. Good-night, Niki."

"Good-night."

"Thanks, Niki, I owe you one on this one," I said, bending toward her over the bar and squeezing her hand.

"Yes, you do. More than you know. Call me at home when Julie leaves," she added, handing me a napkin with her phone number on it.

"I will," I promised, letting go of her hand. I fished into my pocket and came out with two twenties that I handed to her. "This should cover our bill. Thanks again, Niki. Good-night."

"Good-night," she said, taking the money.

I turned and followed Julie, who had gotten to her feet and headed to the door. We both looked back at Niki. She waved, that determined look on her face again. We waved back. I was liking Niki more and more. I watched the back of Julie walking out the door. I was liking her more and more, too.

Outside, we paused at the nose of the big Oldsmobile.

"This is yours, isn't it?" Julie asked, patting the fender of the big car.

"Yes, it is," I confirmed. "How did you get here?"

"I took a cab from the La Quinta across the freeway. That's where I'm staying. I was counting on you being here to provide transportation."

"You know me too well. That's a little scary," I noted as I walked her around to the passenger side, unlocked and opened her door. She sat on the leather seat, flashing a bit of leg for my benefit, then slid across to unlock my door.

"Thanks," I said, "both for the door and the flash."

"You're welcome, for both."

I closed the door and walked around the back of the car. I opened my side, got behind the wheel and started the engine. She moved over to sit next to me. We backed out and after waiting a minute for a break in the traffic, went north on Military Drive. The Back Way Inn was situated at the back of a strip shopping center about half a mile from the Fox. It was another icehouse that had a few pool tables, a bigger dance floor and a band nearly every night.

"Julie," I started, after turning left onto Military, "what did you say to Niki to get her to agree with your plan?"

"Just what I told you and what you already know," she said, smiling. "That I wanted a familiar face near me for a few days. That yours was the most familiar one I knew in San Antonio, that we had been lovers for a while and that I still care a lot for you. But that you aren't interested in coming to D.C. and I'm pursuing my career with the Air Force, wherever that leads. I told her she and I could be friends and have you at the same time if we were willing to be reasonable. I also told her that I liked her and that while you and I make a good couple, you and she make a good one, too. We eyeballed each other a bit, then shook on it. Then you came back. That's it, okay?"

"That's pretty amazing, since I had considered taking off through the back door of the Fox. I figured I'd blown it with Niki, with your help, of course. I wasn't sure she'd be that agreeable. And to be truthful, I'm not sure of my feelings for you. I'm still a little hurt at your leaving for D.C., even though I understand why. But I also still get a great rush whenever I'm near you."

"Thanks, me too. But you and I agreed about our feelings before I left, remember? I thought we were okay. We are okay, aren't we?"

"Yeah, I suppose we are."

"And about Niki, remember you told her to trust you. Now maybe you should trust her, too."

"Yeah, you're right. I did tell her to trust me, didn't I?"

"Yep, you did," she confirmed, patting me on the right thigh. "And I told you to trust me, too, didn't I?"

"Yes, you did. And I do," I said as we pulled into the strip mall where the Inn was. I noted that her hand hadn't left my thigh. I was getting a certain tingling sensation in my crotch. Buddy, be careful, I thought, that thing down there has a mind of its own.

We rounded the corner of the row of stores where the Inn's door was and the parking around the place was nearly filled. I finally backed into a tight spot with a dumpster flanking the Olds on the passenger side. We were so close to the dumpster that Julie would have to slide out the driver's door. When she did, I got a better flash of her legs than when she'd gotten in the car.

"Goodness," I remarked. "Nice legs, lady."

"Thank you, sir. The better to dance with," she replied, standing up beside the car. "I left my purse in the car, if that's okay with you."

"I guess that means I'm buying?" I said, locking the car doors.

"Yes, you are."

We moved from in between the parked cars and walked to the door of the Inn, side by side, arms around each other.

"Feels like old times," I observed.

"Yeah, it does. It's good to be back with you, even for a short time," she said, giving me a sideways squeeze.

We reached the door. I opened it and Julie went through and past the coat checkroom, pausing at the entrance of the saloon to take in the scene. To the left was a rectangular shaped bar, with swivel chairs around the counter top and a few tables between the bar and the outside wall. There were also some tables scattered around the dance floor in front of us. There was a five-piece group on the bandstand to the right of the dance floor. They were playing some rock-and-roll. Several couples were gyrating to 'Jungle Boogie'. A waitress came up to us.

"C'mon, there's an empty table over at the far side of the dance floor. Follow me," she invited loudly, over the music.

We walked single file around the dance floor, the waitress leading the way. Julie's hips were swinging to the music. The guys we passed eyed Julie. She truly looked good enough to eat. When we reached the empty table, we sat where we could watch the dance floor.

"Hi, I'm Kim," the waitress said after we sat down. She put two square napkins on the table. "What'll you folks have tonight?"

"A sloe comfortable screw for me," said Julie teasingly, a smile curling the corners of her mouth.

I looked from Julie to Kim and back to Julie.

"That was just exactly what I want, too. And to drink I'll have a Glenlivet and water, please," I said, matching Julie's little smile.

They both laughed at my rude joke.

"One screw and one scotch coming up," Kim repeated, the smile still on her face. We nodded and Kim retreated toward the bar.

"Well, big boy, time to face the music" Julie putting her hand on my arm.

The band had finished their hot number and started their rendition of 'Midnight at the Oasis' sung by the female keyboard player. A slow song, my favorite kind.

"Okay, let's see how good my legs are. I already know how good yours are."

Smiling, she took my offered hand and stood up. When we were on the dance floor, I pulled her close to me and tried out a few turns.

"Hey," she said stepping away from me a little and looking up at my face, "you're better than I remember. Did you take a lesson or something?"

"You're not the only one who learned something while we were apart. You once told me that women like guys who are good dancers. You said that it was a promise of how they'd move later. It made sense what you said, so I took a few lessons after you left. Nothing much, a little Foxtrot and some Swing. You'll have to teach me anything more."

"I think you're doing just fine. However, I believe Mr. Shorty should stick to faster dances where we aren't too close," she said, gently thrusting her hips at me to indicate what she meant.

"Don't worry about him, Julie. He's just glad to see you. He has a long memory, you know. Besides, honey, he won't hurt you."

"I'm not worried about that. It's just that this song will be ending soon and your cover will be blown."

"I've got some news for you. Every guy in this place has the same problem I do since you walked in here."

"Oh, yeah?" she asked softly, pushing her pelvis against me again.

"Julie, you're really making it hard for me to concentrate on dancing."

"I think both are true at this point," she agreed, pushing at me again. "Dancing and hard."

The song ended and she turned abruptly toward the table, holding my hand and hiding my erection with her skirt. The band was taking a break. It'd give me time to get 'Mr. Shorty' back to normal.

"You are such a tease," I whispered into her ear.

"You ain't seen nothin' yet," she promised, her hand brushing against the front of my trousers as we arrived back at our table. "Oh," she whispered in my ear, "nice cock."

"Thanks," I whispered back. "You're really giving me a hard time, you know."

"Just preparing you for later."

Our drinks had arrived in our absence. I fished out a ten from my pocket and placed it under my napkin for Kim to retrieve at her leisure. I took a gulp of Scotch and set the drink back down. Julie was sipping hers through a straw, looking at me over the rim of the glass. She put her glass down and leaned toward me, her hand again on my thigh.

"I'm glad you still like me, baby, even after I left you for the big city and all."

I put my arm around her and scooted her chair closer.

"Julie, it's hard, er, difficult not to like you, even if I'm not with you. You have a special way of making things all right, you know."

"Thanks. I've missed you, too," she said, giving my leg a squeeze.

"So, tell me what you've been doing since you left," I tried, changing the subject to something less stimulating.

"Postponing the inevitable, I see. Okay," she said softly, not relinquishing her grip on my thigh, "I've been dealing with Belt-way bandits who have been trying to get the general's attention for the last several months. It's been nothing special. Probably not as exciting as you'd expect, certainly not as exciting as your life's probably been. What have you been doing?"

"Not much the early part of the year. I went skiing at Taos a couple of times. Had to take lessons, but I'm getting better. Same old thing at the mall, just pushing shoplifters toward the courts. More recently I sprung a stupid kid from a Mexican jail and gave him back to his father for disposal. And now I'm on a weird case involving a missing fiancé who's also a local government employee stealing secrets. Actually I gave the government part of the case over to Leo Ramirez. Remember him?"

"Yeah, the big Mexican dude who shot your hiney, right?" she recalled, sliding her hand from my thigh around to my right cheek and giving it a squeeze. "Right here, wasn't it?"

"Yes, dear, right there. I'll show it to you again later, if you'd like."

"Oh, I'd like," she said, squeezing my ass again before moving her hand back to my thigh. This time her hand came to rest a bit higher on my leg with her fingers just brushing my right testicle.

"Julie, you seem a bit tense tonight. Have you had sex since you've been gone?"

"Yes, once. And yes I'm horny. Have you screwed anyone since December?"

"Twice, but both times I was thinking of you," I assured her.

"How flattering. Sometimes you say the sweetest things."

"Right now we'd better either leave and take care of Mr. Shorty and your horny problem or dance, since the band's coming back."

"Decisions, decisions. Let's see what they play first."

After a little tune-up the band started in on 'Doctor My Eyes.'

"Dance it is. Let's see what you've got," she said removing her titillating hand from my thigh, standing up and pulling me to my feet.

I did my best to keep up with her, doing a fair job. We stayed on the dance floor when it was over and started up again when the group went right into 'Your Momma Don't Dance'.

"You're doing pretty good. Looks like those lessons paid off," Julie remarked halfway through the song.

"I'm doing okay, but one more like this and it's break time."

"I agree."

The band did a better job than I expected transitioning into 'Nights in White Satin' to slow things down a little. The already dim lights on the dance floor went nearly to black. I pulled Julie into me and we were plastered together, my arms encircling her. I could feel her hard nipples against my chest as she wrapped her arms around my neck.

"Now this is more like it," I said into her hair.

"I'll say," wiggling herself just a bit closer and tilting her face up to me.

We kissed, slowly at first, our tongues touching tentatively. Then we were in a full-blown tonsil check. Her lips were soft and hungry, pulling at my lower lip. One of us moaned. I think it was me, but I couldn't be sure. Our lips finally parted.

"God, you taste good."

"So do you. Did you moan," she giggled slightly.

"Mmm, I think so. We need to go now while it's still dark in here," I said, grinding my erection into her.

"Yes, we do. I want you now, baby. Bad," she said, returning my pelvic pressure.

"Do we have anything over at the table?"

"Just the drinks."

"Forget 'em, let's go before the song ends."

"I'm with you," she agreed, unwinding her arms from my neck and propelling us toward the door.

I used her skirt and my jacket to camouflage my hard-on. With every opportunity, Julie's hand brushed against me, just making matters worse. Out the door, we fairly ran to the car. I pulled out the keys and unlocked my door, swinging it open for her. She slid onto the seat all the way over to the far door.

"Where are you going?"

"Come over here," she invited, patting the middle of the big bench seat.

I slid in, sticking the key in the ignition and pulling the door closed behind me as I scooted over to her. She hopped onto my lap, straddling me with her legs, her knees gripping my hips, our crotches grinding together.

"Now I've got you where I want you," she said before kissing me.

I moved my hands up her back, holding her close, her firm breasts and hard nipples pressing into my chest, our lips and tongues doing an intricate dance of suck, push, taste, nibble. She hurriedly began unbuttoning my shirt, running her hands over my chest when the last button gave way. Since I consider groping a woman impolite unless she first has something stiff to hold onto, I took her left hand and placed it firmly on the bulge in my trousers. She squeezed my erection, then began undoing my belt and trousers. Our kiss broke.

"You sure you want to do this right here?" I panted, glancing outside to be sure we weren't being watched.

"Oh, yeah," she confirmed, smiling that great smile as she finally freed my hard-on. "I want this big cock inside my pussy right now," she said, stroking me.

I moaned, moving my hands down her back and onto her ass, squeezing her cheeks. I eased my hands up her legs, starting at her calves, making slow circles on her hot, smooth skin until I was under her skirt, massaging her inner thighs. I was going to take her panties off, but couldn't find them. In my search, I brushed against her small triangle of pubic hair and slid my right hand down along her wet pussy lips, my middle finger finding its mark and entering her while my other fingers caressed her outer folds. It was her turn to moan.

"Hey, what happened to your slinky black underwear?" I whispered.

"Oh, God, that's good. I, um, I took them off, oh, yeah, back at the Fox when I got into the car," she breathed between moans.

"Pretty sure of yourself, weren't you?" I teased, my probing finger sliding back and forth across the ripply skin in the deepest part of her vagina.

She lifted herself up slightly and yanked my trousers and shorts down to my knees. She had a grip on my cock that I would have to teach my hands about later. With her left hand she pulled my teasing fingers from her slippery crotch and aimed my throbbing penis at her hungry pussy.

"This is what I want," she growled into my ear, pushing the tip of my cock into her molten wetness, "all six inches of it."

She rubbed the head around the opening, then slowly sat down on my cock, easing me fully into her. She moaned the whole time, her back arching and her head thrown back, her breasts pointing at me. The inside of her felt like hot honey, slick and burning, and her vaginal muscles were tight, squeezing the blood into the end of my dick. I almost came right then when she stopped and tilted her head forward, looking at me with a hunger and a softness that I had never seen in her eyes before. I lost myself in her look as I reached up and slid the straps of her dress off her shoulders, pulling the fabric slowly down to her waist, freeing her breasts. She began to slowly push her hips back and forth as I cupped her breasts and rolled her nipples between my thumbs and index fingers, marveling at their half-inch length.

"Baby, I love you. Do you know that?" she whispered, making her strokes just a little longer by lifting up her ass just a bit with each thrust.

"Yeah, honey, I know. I love you, too. But if we keep this up, I won't last very long."

"It's okay," she assured me, making each thrust longer and longer. "I know you're good for more than one round. I want the easy one out of the way before we get down to some serious loving."

I was nearing the end of the easy one, so I pulled gently on her nipples until they were touching my chest, then moved my hands to her back, bringing her closer as we kissed. I was breathing really fast, my hips thrusting into her. Our lips parted.

"Fuck me, baby, fuck me hard," she panted into my ear.

Her vaginal muscles were beginning to contract around my cock. I couldn't hold it any longer and groaned loudly as my sperm shot forth. It felt like my climax was starting at the bottom of my feet. I was racked with spasm after spasm, then Julie began coming with me.

"Oh, yes, yes, yes," she cried out, arching her back again. "Oh, God, yes."

We were so loud that I looked out the windshield to make sure we didn't have an audience. No one in the parking lot but the empty cars and us. I glanced at the clock on the dash. It had only taken us about five minutes for the easy one. It had seemed like a lot longer. Julie was just coming down from her climax and was gently rocking back and forth on my still-hard dick.

"See, there's plenty left for another round," she observed, wriggling her pussy around on my cock.

"You've just got me way turned on, with the way you look and feel. And the way you make love with me."

"Mmm, me, too," she cooed in my ear. "I think we need to go back to the motel right now. There are some other things I want to do with you that are done easier on a bed."

"There are, are there? But this feels so good. Maybe I can drive with you sitting right where you are. It's only a few blocks away."

She laughed.

"I can see this now. 'Officer, we haven't seen each other in a while and now we're stuck together. Could you throw some cold water on us,'" she giggled, still wiggling against me.

"Don't move. Someone's coming out of the Inn," I told her as I saw two people leaving the doorway. They started in our direction then must have realized where they parked their car because they turned abruptly away and went over to a dark colored muscle car. They unlocked it, got in and backed out, driving away from us.

"Okay, now you can move."

"Dave, I never stopped moving," she corrected me, sliding up and down on me a couple of times for emphasis. "But I do think it's time we went to a more private place."

"I agree."

"Do you have anything we can use so we don't make too big a mess? Like Kleenex?"

"Yeah, under the seat," I said, reluctantly giving up my hold on her back to reach under the driver's seat and retrieve the box. I set it on the seat beside me.

She began pulling the straps of her dress up, but not before I gave each breast a thorough going over with my lips and tongue. I had her panting again as I sucked on those fantastically hard nipples.

"I think they like you, Davie. I don't think I've ever seen them as hard."

"I like them too. They're just delicious," I confirmed, giving each a final kiss before covering them up with her dress.

She raised up and I glided out of her. She grabbed some tissues and dropped them in my lap. I began wiping our combined juices off me as she pulled some more out of the box and reaching under her skirt, did the same with her wetness. When her hand reemerged, she took the tissues from my hand, folded the used paper together and dropped the damp package over the back of the seat onto the rear floorboard.

"A souvenir for you," she laughed.

"Thanks, I'll never clean out this car again," I said, recovering my trousers and zipping up my fly over my still stiff boner. "After you, I may have to beat it against a fence post just to get it to go down."

"I've got something better to beat it against," she offered, licking her lips.

"I'll bet you do," I agreed.

I reached for the key and brought the big engine to life. She had moved over to sit very close to me, so I wrapped my right arm around her. She turned her face up to me and we kissed again, savoring the afterglow. She placed her right hand on the lump in my pants and kneaded my erection.

"Drive me home, baby," she said softly when our kiss broke.

"Yes, ma'am, anything for you," I said as I put the car into gear with my left hand and we eased from the parking slot.

We drove quickly to her motel, kissing and rubbing against each other the whole way. It was as if we couldn't get enough of each other's touch. We made more love that night than on any other I could remember. I was exhausted and exhilarated at the same time. We finally fell asleep in each other's arms. I never looked at the clock. I was so happy I didn't care what time of night it was or what century we were in.

THURSDAY

I awoke with a start at six-thirty when the telephone rang.

"Yes, this is Miss Newton," Julie said when she finally picked up the noisy beast. Then, after a slight pause, she said, "No, it's okay. Thanks for waking me."

"It was the front desk. My wake-up call. The general and I are supposed to be at a meeting at nine," she explained after hanging up and resuming her place by my side, her hands exploring my chest and then areas further south.

"Hey, what's this?" she asked, squeezing yet another erection of mine. "I thought you'd be all used up by now."

"Well, it's a gift for you."

"And I thought I'd opened all my presents last night," she said happily. "Tell you what. If you go pee and come back and it's still like that, I'll let you use it on me."

"It's a deal," I said, jumping out of bed and heading to the bathroom, my penis sticking out like a flagpole in front of me.

I grabbed Julie's toothpaste on the way to the commode. I squeezed a dab of paste on my finger and gave my teeth a scrubbing while I emptied my bladder into the toilet. When I finished, I flushed, put the seat down and bounded back to the bedroom. Julie was on the phone again.

"So you'll be alright without me?" Pause. "Okay, yes sir, I'll have a good time." Pause. "Right, right, yes sir. I'll see you on Saturday." Pause. "Thanks, general, you're wonderful." Pause. "Yes, sir. Good-bye and thanks again." And she hung up the phone.

"I had to call the general, to ask for the day off. He said fine, be careful. But the best part is I don't have to be back until Saturday," she said gleefully. "We have today and tomorrow together. Isn't that great? Oh, no, now look what's happening," she said sadly, pointing to my penis.

It had begun drooping a bit.

"Hmm, you can fix that, I bet."

"I can, but let's fix it in the shower."

And we did.

After our sensual cleansing, we decided on breakfast at the Denny's by the motel. I wore my slightly rumpled clothes without the jacket. Julie put on a form-fitting blouse and jeans with white socks and tennis shoes. After doing-up her hair and make-up we left the room and walked around the building to the restaurant arm in arm, happy as two clams.

"So what do you want to do today? River Walk? Lay in bed and have sex? Take a long drive? Have sex?" she teased.

"Have sex, then lay in bed, then River Walk, then long drive, then sex. But not neooooarily in that order."

"Okay, we can fit all that in after breakfast."

"Yes, we can. Something else I have to do is make a couple of phone calls to check on the progress of my little cases that are still cooking."

"Okay, after breakfast and sex," she joked.

Denny's breakfast was spectacularly Denny's. We languished a bit over coffee, playing footsy under the table, making goo-goo eyes at each other. It was nearly nine-thirty when we walked back over to the motel. I noticed that the weather was changing. The partly cloudy skies of the last few days had been replaced with a near overcast. Rain wasn't far behind, I thought, probably later on today or tomorrow. Back in the room I used the phone while Julie tried to distract me.

Ruth answered on the second ring, "Nelms Travel Agency, Harris Investigations. How may I help you?"

"Hey, Ruth, it's Dave. Anything for me?"

"Well yesterday, after you bolted out of here two guys came in looking for you."

"Who were they?" I asked, my suspicions rising.

Julie had stopped nibbling on my ear when she caught my serious tone. She sat next to me on the bed, being very still, listening to my conversation with Ruth.

"I don't know. They came in right after you left. They wanted to know if a man had come in who drove a big, tan Oldsmobile. Said something about the driver scraping off some of their paint in the parking lot."

"What did you tell them?"

"Well, nothing at first, but they described you and your Olds pretty much to a T. So I said there was a guy that might have a car like that, but he wasn't in right now. I asked for their names, but they just wanted to know when you'd be back. I told them either later today or tomorrow. They said they'd come back later to talk with you. They didn't come back yesterday afternoon, so I guess they'll be here today."

"That's funny. If their car got scraped it wasn't by me. I parked on the end and didn't touch another car. What did they look like?"

"Both were dressed nicely, slacks and shirts. They looked sort of Mexican."

"Sort of?"

"Well, their skin color was a little different and their noses were bigger. They could have been Arabs for all I know. There are a lot of them in town going through the schools at Lackland, you know."

"Yeah, I know. Did they have an accent?"

"Yeah, kinda clipped or strained. Oh, wait, they talked to each other in a language that wasn't Spanish, so they weren't Mexican. Probably Arabic, now that I think of it."

"And they said they'd be back? Today?"

"Dave, I don't know. Probably. What should I tell them if they come in again?"

"Just have them sit tight and I'll be in. I'm not home right now, so I'll call you every so often to see if they're there. Otherwise, try calling my house. That's where I'm going in just a little while. Main thing is I want to meet them where I can arrange for backup. I had a little run-in with some Mexican dudes a few days ago and I want to make sure these two guys aren't them, okay."

"Yeah, okay, I get it. Stall them until you call or I call you."

"Right. Thanks, Ruth. I'll probably see you in a bit. Good-bye."

"Wait, Dave. There's one other thing."

"Oh, yeah. What's that?"

"Leo Ramirez called yesterday afternoon after your two visitors left. Said you needed to call him about some book. You want his number?"

"Sure," I said, opening the drawer on the nightstand. There was a pen right next to Gideon's Good Book. I picked it up and used the pad by the telephone to record the number Ruth recited. I read it back to her.

"That's the number. See you later, Dave."

"Okay, Ruth. I'll be in later on this morning."

"Good-bye."

"Good-bye," I said, looking at the number for Leo and wondering what he wanted.

"What was that all about, Dave?" Julie asked, rubbing my arm.

"A couple of guys came into the office yesterday looking for the guy driving a tan Oldsmobile matching the description of my car. Said I scraped it or something in the mall parking lot. Well, there's not a scratch on the Olds, so I don't know what they were talking about. Might even be someone else's car they saw."

"Maybe so. So what's the big deal about a little mistaken identity?"

"Maybe its mistaken identity. Ruth said they described me pretty accurately. I told you I had a couple of cases cooking. I told you that one of them involved a guy in a Mexican jail that I helped liberate. By freeing him we pissed off the sheriff who was holding him and trying to extort money from the guy's father. They might have come looking for me."

"Doesn't sound too likely they could find you this fast in a town the size of San Antonio."

"Yeah, that's true. Besides, Ruth said the guys yesterday didn't speak Spanish. Only other thing it could be about is the book I found yesterday at my other case's house. Ruth said the guys came in right after I left to take the book to the base. I wonder if they followed me yesterday from Garcia's house. Damn, I didn't even notice. I must be slipping."

"Either they followed you or you scraped their car in the parking lot and didn't know it." Julie said with some excitement in her voice. "What kind of book was it?"

I looked at her. The excitement was showing on her face, too.

"It was a classified tech manual my missing person had taken from work. I think he planned on selling it to someone. Those guys looking for me might be involved, since I was at the guy's place. I didn't want anything to do with stolen secrets, so I took the book to Leo Ramirez. You remember him, don't you? The O.S.I. dude at the Halloween party?"

"Big Mexican guy, wasn't he?"

"Right. Anyway, I gave him the book yesterday and Ruth said he called back yesterday afternoon. So now I'm wondering what Leo wants. Probably no big deal. I'll call him when we get to my place. So, come on my junior private eye, we aren't gonna solve this mini-mystery sitting here, are we?"

"No, we aren't. Does that mean our sex, sex, drive, river are cancelled?" she wondered.

"No, just rearranged. First we drive over to my house where I get a change of socks, et cetera. Then we have sex. Then we go for a drive to the office where hopefully we meet up with the mystery men. Then we have sex again. Then we drive to the River Walk."

"Then sex again, right?" she cut in.

"Greedy, greedy, greedy. Okay, sex again," I kidded.

"Good, sounds like my kind of day. Let's get started."

And we did.

Some thirty minutes later we pulled up in the driveway of my Escalon place. As we dismounted the Olds, I scoped out the house.

"Everything looks normal here," I observed, closing the car door behind Julie.

"Sure does. You still have the old Triumph, I see. Can we use it today?"

"I'd love to, but I need to work on the engine a bit. It hasn't been running very well lately."

"Oh, well. Maybe next time. Say, when does the yard man come?" Julie wondered. "September?"

"Funny. I'll have you know it's only April. I've already mown twice this year."

"Right. Needs it again, though, don't you think?"

"Yeah, but now you're here, maybe we can do it together tomorrow."

"That's okay with me, but you get to rake."

"Great, my favorite job," I said, opening the screen and unlocking the front door.

I swung it open wide, holding the screen door for Julie.

"Well," she started, stepping across the threshold. "Now I know what happened to the yard man. He ran off with the maid."

"Have a little sex and a little breakfast and you're a real comedian," I observed, jabbing a finger into her passing ribs.

"Ow," she yelped, jumping at the poke, then laughing at my defensiveness.

"I'm a bachelor, lest you forget. So, it's a little messy. That's my style."

"I'll say," she agreed, moving away from me before I could jab her again. "But, David, you need to pick up your stuff just in case a young beauty, such as me, comes over for some entertaining. While we'll baby you, baby, we ain't your mother. Know what I mean?"

"Yes, mother, I do," I said, straightening up the place a little.

It really wasn't too bad. There were some paperback books strewn about on the couch and floor, magazines spread out here and there and a sweatshirt and sweatpants tossed over the back of my easy chair. I hadn't cleaned up much before my Mexico trip and hadn't bothered to clean up the place for Wilson either.

"At least there isn't any dirty underwear lying around. I guess you do have your standards."

"Wait until you see the bedroom."

"I'm not so sure I want to see it. At least not with both eyes."

She peeked around the corner into my bedroom. The bed was unmade and there was a pile of dirty clothes that needed laundering heaped next to the closet. The top of the dresser had a jumble of stuff on it, including a bunch of change, a stack of receipts, some clean clothes that I hadn't put away yet, and other odds and ends.

"I guess it could be worse. Someone could have thrown in a hand grenade."

"True," I agreed, going into the bedroom to retrieve some clothes. "I presume we'll be staying at your place?"

"Either there or here. I don't have a preference as long as we're together. But here might be more convenient. You still have cooking facilities, don't you?"

"Sure, but I don't use them much." I said, opening dresser drawers and picking out fresh underwear and socks.

"I'll see what you've got," she said, walking toward the back of the house.

I changed quickly into tan slacks and a short-sleeved tan shirt that matched. I pulled on a sports jacket so I'd have extra pockets. It was my idea of a purse for men. Then I transferred the money and wallet from my discarded clothes into my pockets. I checked my look in the mirror. It would do. I met her in the kitchen where she was looking through the cabinets.

"Looks like we'll be eating out," she said, eyeing the meager contents of the pantry.

"Now that sounds okay to me, but where will we be getting our food?" I teased.

"Ha, ha. But seriously, Dave, do you ever eat food here?"

"Yeah, sometimes. But I prefer cooking by telephone. You know, 'I'd like a reservation for one, please'," I pantomimed, making a hand telephone with my little finger and thumb extended and holding it to my ear.

"Yeah, I get it. But now you'll have to make it for two."

"Like this?" I asked, holding both hands up to my head as mock telephones. ·

"So see, a little sex and you've become a comedian, too," she said, closing the pantry door and turning toward me. "But, that's one of the things I like about you, you know."

She stepped closer and put her arms around my neck, her fingers fussing lightly with my hair.

"I know. One of the things I like about you is the way you smell," I said softly, pulling her to me, our eyes embracing. Our faces were nearly touching.

There was a loud knocking coming from the vicinity of the front door. I waltzed Julie over to the hallway where I could get a look at our visitor. It was the neighbor. I untangled myself from Julie and moved toward the front of the house.

"Hey, Joe, what's going on?" I asked as I arrived in the living room. Julie was close on my heels.

"Not much, Gringo," he said, opening the front door and letting himself in. He stopped when he saw Julie. "Oh, sorry, I didn't know you had company."

"Joe, this is Julie Newton. You should remember her from about six month ago."

"Oh, yeah, we met last year. Hi, Julie. Good to see you again."

"Hi Joe. It's good to be back in San Antonio," she said, sticking out her hand to shake his.

After their shake, Joe turned back to me.

"Well, I just stopped by to tell you that yesterday afternoon two men came to the house. I was in the yard and asked them what they wanted. They said they needed to talk with you."

"Did they say what they wanted?"

"No, just that they wanted to speak with you."

"What did they look like?"

"Like touristas. They were about five foot ten or so, average builds. Dark skin, but not Mexican because I tried Spanish at first and they didn't understand. Their English was okay. Since they didn't tell me what they wanted, I just told them you'd be back later. Then they left."

"What were they driving?"

"A 1973 or '74 dark green Cadillac four-dour. I didn't get a license number. Didn't know it was important."

"It's probably not. Thanks, Joe. Did they come back last night?"

"Not that I know of. I looked out a couple of times during the night, but didn't see anyone."

"They're probably the two guys I need to meet later at the office. They've got some business for me," I lied.

"Yeah, okay. I just wanted you to know you had visitors," Joe restated, moving toward the door.

"That's fine, Joe. Thanks for keeping a lookout for the place. Never can tell who'll be popping up, huh?"

He was halfway out the door by now. I followed him out onto the porch.

"No problem, Dave. Glad to be of service," he said. Then, shaking his hand for emphasis and rolling his eyes toward the living room, he added in a near whisper, "Nice looking woman, Dave."

"Thanks, Joe. See you later."

"Adios," he said, backing toward his house a few steps before turning and walking the short distance to his front door.

"So my two new friends know where I live. That's not such a good thing," I said to Julie back in the living room.

"We can stay at my place, if you think that's a problem," she offered.

"It may be. I don't know yet."

The phone rang. It rang two more times again before I picked it up on the extension in my bedroom.

"Hello."

"Mr. Collins, this is Ruth with the Nelms Travel Agency. Those two tickets you wanted finally came in. They'll be here for you whenever you want to pick them up."

"I'm guessing that's code for my two guys are sitting there in front of you, right?"

"That's right, Mr. Collins. They're ready for you whenever."

"Ruth, we should be over there in about twenty minutes. I'll be sending in Julie Newton ahead of me. Do you remember her?"

"Yes, Mr. Collins."

"Have her wait in Bobby's office. I'm also going to find a couple of the security guys and have them cover me. One of them should show up just after I take my two gentlemen into the office. Okay?"

"That's fine, Mr. Collins. See you this afternoon."

"One other thing, Ruth. Any funny stuff and you call the police, okay?"

"Yes sir, I will. Thanks, Mr. Collins. Good-bye."

"Good-bye," I told the receiver and hung it back on the hook. Then, "Julie, it's time to go. Those two guys are waiting for me and I need to see what they're up to."

"Not yet. You were going to call Leo, remember?"

"Oh, yeah, I forgot. Thanks for reminding me. I'll do it from the office after I see my mystery men."

"Okay with me. Wow, we sure did get serious all of a sudden," she said with some disappointment in her voice. "Guess this kinda messes up our day, huh?"

"Not too much. We'll go meet these guys and then get back on track," I countered, giving her a light peck on the lips before ushering her out the front door.

"So what's the plan? You told her you'd be sending me in first."

"Yeah, I want you to get a look at the two guys just in case. I trust your intuition about people and I may need that insight later, okay?" I said, closing and locking the deadbolt.

"So I'm your back-up, huh?"

"My mental back-up. Anything more than that and that's why I'll have two of the boys there, in case things get ugly," I explained, opening the driver's door for her.

"You really think things will get ugly?" she asked, sliding across the seat.

"I don't know. What I do know is those two guys probably followed me from a house that had been ransacked and the house's owner is missing. That makes the situation a little unstable," I said, getting in behind her.

I closed the door and fitted the key into the ignition. I turned the key and the big eight-cylinder came to life. We backed out and headed north on Escalon toward the mall.

"I'm a little scared about this," she confessed.

"Don't be. I'll handle it okay. I'm adding security to this because I just don't want to get caught with my pants down."

"That would be okay with me. I like you like that."

We laughed at her joke.

Less than ten minutes later we pulled into the parking lot on the south side of the mall. After locking the car, we walked to the entrance by the K-Mart.

"Just go in, tell Ruth who you are and that you're supposed to see Bobby. She'll take you into Bobby's office. Go into the bathroom between our offices and just eavesdrop. After I get the two guys into my office, one of the two security men will be in the waiting room by Ruth's desk. The other one will be watching the hallway and tailing the guys when they leave. Remember, it's all just for in-cases."

"Yeah, I know. And if things get rough or whatever, we bust in and jump the guys, right?"

We reached the mall doors. I opened it for her and we went into the temperature-controlled air of the mall.

"No, the security guy will bust in," I continued. "You just hang tight. I don't want you in on that action. These guys could be armed. Let security and me handle them. You're our backup. And if you sense things are going badly, call the cops. I already told Ruth to be ready for that possibility."

"How far behind me will you be?"

"A few minutes. I've got to find the two guys I want to back me up. One's working this end of the mall and the other one should be around Penney's. It'll take me a couple of minutes to find them and give them a briefing. You go on now. I'll be behind you shortly."

"Okay. Here I go. Hey, how about a kiss for luck?"

"Sure. Anything for you."

We kissed a little too long for just luck.

"Whew," she breathed when our lips parted. "If that was a kiss for luck I should leave now and go play the ponies."

"Yeah, me too. Nice kiss. Now off you go. See you soon."

"See you," she said, waving and going off down the mall corridor toward my office.

I found Richard Sanchez wandering through the K-Mart keeping an eye on any larcenous customers. He was carrying a shopping bag for cover. I came up behind him and stuck a finger into his ribs. He jumped just a little.

"Rick, this is a stick-up."

"Some stick-up. What are you up to?"

"I need your help for a few minutes. There are a couple of guys waiting for me over at Bobby's. They followed me from a job yesterday and I need some back up in case they get rowdy. Care to help?"

"Sure, I'm just making some rounds. What do you want me to do?"

"C'mon, I'll explain while we walk down the mall and find Jack Deets," I said, ushering him toward the mall door. "There are two guys at Bobby's in the waiting room. I'm going to take them into my office for a discussion. After I get them into my office, you come into Bobby's and have a seat in the waiting room with Ruth. I want Jack to wait in the mall near the hallway where he can keep an eye on Bobby's door. When those two come out, you and Jack tail them, discretely.

If you hear any funny stuff while we're in my office, come on in. If you don't and I buzz Ruth, come in. I mainly want you there to prevent their exiting if they get fresh with me or something. Got it?"

"Right, sounds easy enough. I needed to take a load off anyway."

"That's fine. Just stay alert."

"Okay."

"Jack was supposed to be at Penney's, right?"

"Yeah, but he was covering the hobby store, too."

"If we don't find him in the hobby store, you locate him in Penney's and come on over to Bobby's. I should be set up by then. Oh, I also told Ruth to call the cops if it starts looking bad."

"Sounds okay with me."

We found Jack Deets in the main part of the mall between Penney's and the hobby store. I briefed him and left the two of them standing near the Impressions T-shirt stand in the middle of the concourse. They were to follow me in five minutes. I took a deep breath and rounded the corner to our office door. When I opened the door there was no sign of Julie. Ruth looked up when I came in. So did the two men seated in our little waiting room.

"Dave, these two gentlemen are here to see you," Ruth said, with a wave toward the men.

They came to their feet. They were both about five-ten, around one-eighty and were dark skinned—not Mexican, I reckoned, more likely Saudi, but I wasn't sure. There were a lot of trainees from the Middle East at Lackland. These two could be some of them. They had serious looks on their faces.

"Mr. Harris, my name is Mustafa Gengis," the obvious leader said, sticking out his hand for a polite handshake. I took it. His palm was dry and his grip was not too firm. "This is Mohammet Achbar," he said, indicating his sidekick.

The two men were dressed in slacks and short-sleeved shirts like Ruth had described them as wearing yesterday. They looked to be in about their mid-thirties. Both men were clean-shaven except for carefully trimmed moustaches. Mustafa's hair was more closely cropped than the other man, probably to disguise his receding hairline. He was the nicer looking of the two, with clearer skin and a smaller nose than his partner's. Mohammet had a little darker skin, some small pox scars on his cheeks and his eyebrows were nearly touching in the middle. His dark brown eyes appraised me with some indifference, rather like a shopper deciding which box of cereal to buy. They appeared calm and confident but not surly.

"David Harris," I said shaking Mohammet's outstretched hand. Same limp grip. Turning back to Mustafa, I added, "What can I do for you?"

"It's a private matter," said Mustafa with a glance toward Ruth. "Can we go into your office to discuss it?"

"Sure, this way," I said, thumbing toward my office door. I opened it for them. "Go on in and have a seat. I'm going to get a cup of coffee. Either of you want some?"

After a brief discussion, Mustafa said, "No, not now, thank you."

I opened the door and ushered them into my office, indicating with an open palm that they should sit on the couch or the chairs by the coffee table. They sat, Mustafa on the couch and Mohammet in the chair opposite him. I noticed that they both perched on the edge of the furniture with their feet under them rather than relaxing back into the soft brown leather. I turned back to Ruth's desk.

"Mind if I have some?" I asked her, indicating the half-filled carafe in the maker on the counter behind her desk.

"'Course not, help yourself," she offered. "It's not that old."

I flipped over one of the half-dozen cups resting on a folded hand towel by the pot and poured the cup about three quarters full. I added two spoonfuls of creamer and a sugar lump from the bowl beside the creamer cup. I stirred the mixture until my additives dissolved. The coffee and I returned to my office. I closed the door, went over to my two interview chairs and turned one of them around to face my two guests. I didn't want to sit too close in case I had to take defensive action.

"Now what is this about?" I asked after I sat down.

I took a sip of coffee. Hot. I put the cup on the corner of my desk blotter.

"Mr. Harris, we believe you have something that we've paid for and is rightfully ours," began the one called Mustafa, leaning toward me.

His expression was that of a slightly dissatisfied customer at one of the stores in the mall. There were no frown marks between his bushy eyebrows. His partner had the same bland expression.

"What might that be?" I asked.

"A book," he said matter-of-factly.

"What book?" I asked, forcing innocence into my voice.

"One that we saw you take from a man's house yesterday."

"You saw me take a book from a man's house yesterday?" I threw the question back at him, raising my eyebrows to emphasize my innocence. He didn't buy it.

"Yes. We saw you enter our business partner's back door, search his house and leave with a book that belongs to us."

I must be slipping, I thought. I had figured the wood fence between the houses had protected anyone from seeing my breaking and entering.

"I believe you are mistaken."

"No, we're not," he insisted, his tone rising just a little.

He was restraining himself pretty well, I thought.

"After you left his house, we followed you here and waited for you."

"So, who is your business partner?" I asked, changing subjects.

"You must know him. You were at his house. His name is Robert Garcia."

"Do you know where Mr. Garcia is?"

"No. We paid him for the book. He said he had it. Then he disappeared before he delivered it to us."

"He disappeared," I repeated flatly. "That's the reason I'm interested in him. I have a client who wants him found. But I don't know anything about a book."

"Don't play with us, Mr. Harris. We saw you leaving his house yesterday after going inside through his back door. We know you have the book he promised us."

"Are you two with the police?" I asked, knowing they weren't.

"No, we are not. Now would you please give us our property?"

"You said you paid for it. Why didn't you get it when you paid?"

"We gave Mr. Garcia a down payment with the balance due on delivery. He never delivered."

"A down payment. So, you didn't really pay for it. Sounds like you have a problem you'll have to take up with Mr. Garcia when you find him."

"Not if you have the book."

"What makes you think I have it?"

"Mr. Harris, we'll give you what we were going to give Garcia for the book if you turn it over to us," he said, side-stepping my question, exasperation coming through in his tone of voice.

"What were you going to pay him?"

"Seventy-five thousand. We already paid him twenty-five."

"Do you know what was in the book?"

"Certainly."

"Then, assuming I have it, I'd say it's worth a lot more than that."

"So is your life," he said without much emotion in his voice.

"Is that a threat?"

"Mr. Harris, we are businessmen. We are willing to pay for the book. What is your price?"

Think fast, Dave.

"Assuming I have the book, it'll cost you a quarter million dollars."

He looked a bit shocked, but not much. Maybe I should have gone higher.

"That's a lot, assuming you have the book."

"If you want it, that's the price, assuming I have it."

Mustafa turned to his pal and they spoke to each other in what I took to be Arabic. At least it wasn't Turkish or a European language that I'd ever heard before. After a lengthy discussion, they appeared to reach an understanding. They turned back to me.

"Agreed," said Mustafa. "We'll bring the money tomorrow. You bring the book, if it isn't already here," he added, looking around me at the big Mossberg safe.

"Assuming I have the book, I'll meet you here tomorrow at eleven am."

"Nine would be better."

"The mall opens at nine-thirty, the stores open at ten. I get here at ten. So, let's compromise and make it ten-thirty."

They looked at each other. Mustafa spoke to his crony. They both nodded slightly.

"Alright, ten-thirty," Mustafa said, getting to his feet. Mohammet and I rose with him. "But, please, Mr. Harris, no tricks," he added with just a hint of menace in his voice. "We're running out of time and patience."

"Not to worry. You just show up with the cash," I assured him.

Mustafa stuck out his hand to shake on the deal. I shook his hand, then Mohammet's. I'd been getting the feeling that Mohammet didn't speak much English.

"Until ten-thirty tomorrow, then," I underscored the time, showing them to the door. When I opened it, I saw Rick sitting in one of Ruth's chairs. He looked up at us, then back at his magazine. My two gentlemen left through Ruth's door, turning left toward the mall where Jack was waiting. A few seconds after they left, Rick followed them at a moderate pace.

I stepped back into my office, easing the door closed. Just as I did, Julie opened the bathroom door and stuck her head around it.

"Is the coast clear?" she asked, coming into the room when she saw I was its only occupant.

"It is. But if it hadn't been, what would you have done then?" I wondered, smiling at her entrance.

"Oh, right. Guess I'd have blown it, huh?" she sounded a little embarrassed.

"Probably. But no matter. What did you think? You were eavesdropping, weren't you?" I accused, guiding her over past the chairs to the couch.

We sat facing each other.

"Of course. You told me to," she reminded me. Then, "Did you say a quarter million?"

"Yes."

"Dollars, right?"

"Yep, dollars."

"And they agreed to that, right?"

"Yes, they did. But it isn't over until it's over. They could still pull a switche-roo or hijack me or give me counterfeit money or something. Besides, I don't have the book, remember? I gave it to Leo Ramirez yesterday. Now, to get the money I have to deliver the book. That means I have to get it back from Leo, somehow."

"Wait, aren't you forgetting something?" she asked, reaching out and touching my knee.

"Like what?"

"Like that you'd be selling secrets to some foreigners, probably terrorists. I think you can go to jail for that, right?" she admonished.

"Do you really think I'd actually go through with it?" I asked, trying not to sound hurt at her tone.

"Sorry, but for a minute there you sounded like you might."

"I'm still very much an American, you know." I said, keeping my voice light. "And I still have a scruple or two left. My plan is to pull a switch on them and keep at least part of the money for my trouble. The problem will be getting Leo to go along with it and giving the book back to me. That means I have to go back to Leo's."

"I can go too, can't I?"

"Sure. Now it's time to call Leo, find out what he wanted and tell him we're coming over," I said, standing up and walking over to my desk. On the way I picked up the coffee cup and tested its contents. Just right. I gulped a couple of mouthfuls before I plopped into my chair. I set the cup down, noticing that the flip-file phone number keeper was still set on R. I pushed it and up popped Leo. I dialed the number while Julie looked on in silence. Acres answered.

"Major Ramirez's office, Sergeant Acres speaking. How may I help you?"

"Hi, Sergeant Acres. This is Dave Harris. I need to speak with Leo, please, if he's in."

"He's in, but on another line. I'll put you on hold and tell him you're on the line. Okay?"

"Yeah, that's fine, as long as you tell him it's about that book I gave him yesterday and that I'm returning his call" I added, hoping to speed up the connection.

"Sure, I'll tell him. Hold, please."

The line went silent for about a minute. I held on patiently, glancing over at Julie. She was sitting very still, watching me.

"Are you on hold or ignore?" she finally said.

"Hold, I hope. I'm beginning to wonder."

And then Leo was on the line.

"So, buddy, I'm glad you finally called. That book you gave me was fishy."

"Fishy how?"

"Fishy in that it's only half here. It looks like Garcia was being cute. Or maybe you were."

"Only half there, huh. Well it wasn't me, pal. Must have been Garcia. Not only that, but I just had a visit by two, I think they were Arabic, characters who wanted that book. Said they had a deal with Garcia and already gave him some money up front. They apparently tailed me from Garcia's house and figure me for taking the merchandise. They want me to finish the deal he started."

"Did you see them tail you?"

"No, but they came into the outer office not long after I got here yesterday, so they must have. I, um, wasn't paying that much attention when I left Garcia's."

"Kind of sloppy, don't you think?

"Yeah, I guess so," I admitted. "But anyway, the guys want the book. They're coming back tomorrow with the cash."

"How much cash?"

"The rest of what they agreed to pay Garcia."

"So, how much?"

"Fifty thousand," I lied, watching Julie's expression. She smiled and shook her head. "They claim to have already given him twenty-five."

"Fifty isn't much for that book. You could have gotten more but that's not bad for the half we have."

I wonder where the other half is, I thought to myself. Maybe I'd have to have another go at Garcia's.

"Which half is missing?" I wondered.

"My guys say the back half, the best part."

"Maybe Garcia was just being careful so he wouldn't get ripped off."

"Yeah, maybe. But we've got to have the other half if we're going to make the deal work."

"Wait a minute, does that mean you're going to go along with it?" I wondered.

"Maybe, if we can get the whole book. Anyway, you need to come to my office before we talk about this any more. Hell, for all you know, your phone could be tapped."

"We'll be over in a little while," I said, bypassing his sarcasm.

"We?"

"Yes, we. I have a general's secretary with me and I don't want to release her yet."

"General's secretary? Julie Newton, I bet."

"Yes, you're right. She arrived last night and we were going to do some sight-seeing until this thing with the two foreign gents came up."

"Fine," he said, "Bring her along. The more the merrier."

"Okay, see you in a bit."

"Yep, see you," he said.

The phone went dead. I hung up the receiver. While I was talking with Leo, Julie had stood up and come over to my desk, standing by my chair with her hand on my shoulder.

"We're going to Leo's office, right?"

"Yes, we are, but first we've got something else to do. And we'd better get going. The bad guys are getting away."

I stood up and pulled her toward my office door. It opened and Deets was standing there with his hand on the knob.

"Which way did they go?" I asked.

"Down the mall toward K-Mart. Sanchez is following them."

"Good. I need you and Sanchez here at ten o'clock in the morning," I directed. "Now, any idea where they parked?"

"No, probably on the north side," he pointed past me.

"Maybe we can catch up," I told Julie. "See you later, Jack. Thanks."

"Need any help?" he wondered.

"No, we've got it," I called over my shoulder as I launched us down the short hallway to my private entrance.

We stopped just outside the door, watching the pedestrian traffic from the mall entrance by the grocery store and K-Mart. We were just in time to see our two culprits emerge from the entrance with Sanchez following discreetly behind. Julie and I used the parked cars as cover as we stalked them and made our way over to my white Chevy van two rows over. I fished the keys from my pocket and

Thursday   87

we entered the van through the back doors so the bad guys couldn't see us. I guided Julie around the footlocker and other gear I kept in the van. We waited in the dark interior, watching our culprits out the front window until they had reached their car, then we took our seats up front.

They got into a dark green Cadillac four-door and started out of the lot, heading toward Military Drive. I started the Chevy and we followed at a distance. They reached the sidewalk at the edge of the street where the driver put on his left blinker. I could see they would be stuck for a while waiting for the traffic to break, so I wound through the parking lot toward the traffic light at Zarzamora, hoping to catch them at the intersection. We had better luck than they did and made a left onto Military Drive while they were stopped at the light. We drove slowly in the right lane until they could catch up and pass us. We maintained our position in the right lane, changing to their lane only when ours ran out at Laredo Street. We kept four or five cars between us. The height of the van made us easy to spot but it also made it easier to keep their car in sight without getting too close.

"Pretty quick thinking," Julie observed.

"What? Following these guys?"

"Yeah, that. And what was that back in your office about half a book?"

"Leo says I brought him only half a book yesterday. The back half of it's missing."

"What does that mean?" she wondered.

"It means that Garcia was probably holding out on those guys in case they pulled a fast one on him. Or he was going to pull something himself. Get more money, maybe, by selling the book in pieces. Either way, for me, or us, it means going back to Garcia's. The other half of that book has got to be there."

"What if the bad guys already have the missing half?"

"They didn't act like they had any of it, yet, but it's possible I guess."

"So we're following them to their lair?"

"Yeah. They followed me yesterday. It's my turn to find out some stuff about them, don't you think?"

"That's fine with me. Got any idea where they're headed?"

"Well, you know there are a bunch of foreign students at the Defense Language Institute on Lackland. My guess is these two birds are skipping their English class."

"You're probably right."

We were just passing through the southern tip of Kelly. We maintained our interval, shifting lanes once or twice and avoiding too much sameness in their rear view mirror. Our pigeons drove through Lackland and made a left on Luke, the last entrance to the base. We followed discretely. My guess had been right. We passed the language school and proceeded down Ent toward the row of barracks that housed foreign students. The Caddie pulled up in front of one of the two-story buildings and the passenger door opened. We eased on past the parked car and I saw Mohammet get out of the car and go up the walk to the barracks. We drove around the block. When we arrived back to watch the car, it was gone.

"Damn, now where did he go?" I asked with irritation.

"There! I just saw him on the next block, going south on Hughes," said Julie, excitedly, pointing out the Cadillac.

"Yeah, I see him."

We twisted around a couple of streets and ended up at Truemper. Our driver had turned right on Truemper and was heading off the base toward Medina. We turned right and broke the base speed limit a little as we closed the gap. Truemper turned into Valley Hi after it left Lackland and then crossed the freeway. Valley Hi loses its name again as it enters Medina Base. On the other side of the freeway, the Caddie turned left onto the southbound access road. Now the traffic was light, so I stayed well back of him. He took the same route I had taken when I went to Garcia's yesterday. But instead of going around the block as I had, the Caddie stopped at a house approximately over the back fence from Garcia's. We were back far enough to allow Mustafa to exit the car and walk up to the house before we drove past. There was a brown Ford van parked in the driveway.

"Looks like we found their lair," I observed as we reached the end of the block.

"Looks like. Now what? They're watching Garcia's, aren't they?"

"Maybe. But since they think I have the book, their guard may be dropping a little. It might be just enough for us to go snooping in Garcia's."

We continued down Roy Ellis drive to the intersection it made with Medina Base Road. At the intersection, I made a right into the parking lot of the 7-Eleven, parking away from the store's door a bit.

"Time for me to change into different clothes," I said, switching off the engine and going into the dark interior of the van. "Gotta put on some coveralls so I'll look the part of a plumber. With what you're wearing, you already look like a plumber's helper."

"Thanks for the compliment, I think."

I opened the footlocker in the back of the van, pulled off my jacket and hung it on a hook behind Julie's seat. I pulled some navy blue coveralls from the footlocker and wiggled into them. I set a tool belt near the back doors and turned to model my attire.

"What do you think?" I asked, showing her the 'Joe's Plumbing' emblazoned on the back of the one-piece.

"Looks good. Glad that it's coveralls you're wearing."

"Why is that?" I wondered.

"No butt crack to show."

I laughed out loud.

"Trust you to make light of a serious situation," I pointed out, still chuckling.

"What are we planning to do, anyway?"

"Go boldly back into Garcia's cleverly disguised as plumber types," I answered, digging into the footlocker for a couple of baseball caps with "Joe's" on the front.

"Here's your hat," I said, tossing her one of the caps and donning my own.

"Great, now I'll have a hat head."

"It'll be okay. Later we'll trade it for bed head."

It was her turn to laugh. While she was recovering from my bad joke, I opened the side door of the van, retrieved two magnetic signs from inside the footlocker and exiting the van, quickly affixed them to the sides of the van. We were officially Joe's Plumbing. Back in the driver's seat, I started up the van and rolled out of the lot the way we had come.

Five minutes later we pulled up in front of Garcia's. I backed the Chevy up the driveway into the carport. My accomplice and I got out and walked to the back of the van. I opened the van's doors to block the neighbor's view, pulled out my tool belt and cinched it in place. We confidently approached the back door. I knocked a couple of times. With no answer after a couple of minutes, I tried the handle. Locked, like yesterday. I pushed sharply on the door, heard wood tearing and we were in. Cheap locks, gotta love 'em, I thought.

"So, officer, we're going to add breaking and entering to the charges of treason," Julie said in a barely audible tone.

"Too, late," I said, stepping across the entryway. "I did all that yesterday."

"I'm sure you did," she said as she closed the door behind her and followed me into the house. "Where do we start?"

"Well, yesterday, I looked the place over pretty good, even though someone else had beaten me to it. Today we need to look in the unusual places, like under the kitchen appliances, under all the drawers and in everything. But be careful on the side of the house facing the back. We don't want the peepers over the back fence to get wise to us."

"Where do you want me to start?" she asked.

"Take the front side of the house. I'll start in the kitchen."

"Good hunting," she encouraged as she bent over to walk past the kitchen doorway.

"You, too," I told her as I did a duck walk into the kitchen to avoid the window over the sink.

We had been looking for nearly an hour when Julie found me in the laundry room.

"I haven't found anything, so far, except something weird," she offered.

"Weird? What do you mean?"

"Well, weird. Out of place weird," she explained.

"What did you find?"

"A ladder in one of the front bedroom closets."

"Show me," I said, following her down the hall.

Sure enough, there was an eight-foot stepladder inside the closet of the bedroom at the end of the hall. It was leaning against the wall behind the clothes bar in the closet. I pulled it out of its hiding place and set it against the wall in the bedroom. There was a tuft of some fuzzy stuff stuck in between the hinge on the right side. I plucked it out and looked closely at it. It was rock wool, the stuff used in attics.

"Where's the attic access?" I wondered.

"In the hall?" Julie guessed.

We retreated to the hall and looked at the ceiling. By the hall light was a square of sheet rock set into a wooden frame.

"I'll get the ladder," I said, returning to the bedroom and folding the ladder so it would fit through the door.

I set the thing up under the door and climbed up, pushing the sheet rock square up as I went. When it cleared the insulation I set it aside. The attic was dusty and dark except for a faint glow of light from the ventilation louvers at the ends. I probed around the itchy insulation nearest the hole, then stepping up another riser, fanned out in a greater arc. I found what I was looking for quite by accident. The book was lying flat against the ceiling and I would have missed it had I not been using a scooping motion to move the insulation. When I pulled it out of its hiding place I received a big nose full of dust. I sneezed, dropping my find onto the ladder where it tumbled down toward the floor. Julie stopped its fall by trapping it against the ladder.

"Gesundheit, Sneezy," she teased. "You sure are making a mess down here."

"Sorry," I said, sniffling. "Dust got me."

"Is this it? Doesn't look like much."

"It's only about twenty or thirty pages. Probably the important part," I pointed out as I fitted the door in place and descended the ladder.

"It's wrapped in newspaper."

"Yeah, just like its better half," I joked, folding the ladder and taking it back to its hiding place.

When I returned to the hall, Julie had torn open the package and was looking through the pages. I came around her side and looked, too.

"There are pictures in the back," she noted, thumbing through the material.

The last ten pages or so had several pictures of a large silver bomb surrounded by navy-looking guys. The pictures had been taken on a ship and were in what appeared to be chronological order. The sailors had partially taken the thing apart and were working on the front of it. A green colored bucket covered the exposed end. An access panel on the side of the bucket had been removed and the men had attached a screw to one of the components in the bomb and were twisting a rope with a stick through it to tighten the rope. It looked like they were trying to pull out the red box that was attached to the rope. The last picture showed them holding up the red box like a trophy.

"Interesting," Julie said at last.

"Yeah, plumber's friend. Let's get out of here and go to Leo's."

"Okay with me," she agreed, stuffing the book back into its newspaper wrapper and following me out through the living room.

We backtracked the way we had come in, not bothering to clean up our mess. I doubted anyone would ever notice out efforts. The street was clear when we buttoned up the van and drove away. Julie had set the package on the floor of the van between us and I eased us out of the driveway.

"Glad that's over," she said as we turned up the street.

"Why is that?" I wondered.

"You couldn't tell I was shaking with excitement and a little fear?"

"Maybe a little. But for a raw recruit, you did pretty good through the whole thing."

"I did, huh," she said, not turning it into a question.

I turned to look at her. She had a small self-satisfied smile on her face.

"Yes, you did. Ever done anything like that before?"

"No. Every time before when you had a case, you'd shoo me off when it came to stuff like breaking and entering. Remember?"

"Yeah, I guess I did. Trying to protect you, no doubt."

"I suppose. What made you change?" she wondered.

"I don't know. Probably because we were in hot pursuit and I didn't have time to think about it."

"That's good," she said. "I'll be your partner anytime."

"Glad to hear it."

At Sun Valley, we turned left. No sense in giving the bad guys another look at the van. We took 410 north and made our way onto the loop a few minutes later. At the Highway 90 exchange, we went east and got off the freeway at Kelly. We had made good time and arrived outside Leo's office after a twenty-minute drive.

"Just over twenty minutes," Julie echoed my thoughts as we eased into the parking lot by Leo's office.

"Yeah, not bad. We're fashionably late. Keeps the suspense going," I said squeezing the van into a parking place between a blue Air Force pickup truck and another Yank-tank nearly the size of the Chevy.

"We'd better go out the back. Wouldn't want to get any blue paint on my van," I said, leading the way past the engine to the back of the van. I shucked my jumpsuit, folded it into the footlocker and smoothed my shirt and trousers. I pulled on my jacket and helped Julie back past the engine box. We dropped our caps in the footlocker and picked up the package before I opened up the back doors. She surveyed my parking job as I secured the van.

"Tight fit," Julie noted.

I looked at her.

"Nice try," I said, pointedly ignoring the opening she'd given me. "But I'll play it polite at this point. No sense in starting something that would delay us further."

"Ha, ha, coward," she accused, laughing at my joke.

And then I remembered I'd made a sort-of pass at Acres yesterday.

"Of course, you know that showing up here with you is going to blow my chances with the cute sergeant Leo has working for him," I warned as we walked to the main entrance of the building.

"You're telling me that so I won't be surprised at the daggers in her eyes, aren't you?" she observed correctly. "Look, I've already done one favor for you last night at the Fox. And as a woman who loves you, I want you to know it wounds me a little to have you ogling every cute girl you see. I know you're a horn-dog, but you have to give it a rest. Later on, I'll bite you in a very tender spot if we go into his office and you treat me like just a casual friend, cute sergeant or not. Okay?"

"Okay, you're right. Sorry, I didn't mean to hurt your feelings," I said, wrapping my arm around her as we entered the building.

"Besides, goofy guy, when a woman sees that you can commit to another woman, it gives her just a little hope that not all men are assholes," she advised.

"You're right again. But, I think Acres may already believe that after yesterday when Leo told her I was a womanizer with a little dick."

Now Julie was laughing out loud, her mood changed by my idiocy and Leo's reported comment.

"He said that to your cute sergeant?"

"Yep. He also told her I had a bullet hole in my ass."

Another round of laugher, this time just outside Leo's office. I opened the door and ushered Julie into the outer office. Sgt. Acres looked up as we came in.

"Hello, Mister Harris, Leo's waiting for you in his office," she said, waving us in.

"Sgt. Acres, this is my dear lady-friend, Julie Newton. Julie, Sgt. Acres," I opened, figuring that attack was better than avoidance at this point.

Julie stepped forward to shake Acres' hand as Acres came from around behind her desk and reached out her right hand.

"Nice to meet you," Acres said.

"Nice to meet you, too. I've heard a lot about you," Julie said without a glance in my direction.

"You have?" Acres wondered, their hands still clasped.

"Yes, I have. From Dave," Julie added, finally dropping the handshake. "And I must tell you that he does have a bullet hole in his ass. Leo gave it to him. But his dick isn't small. Trust me, I know."

I started laughing at Julie's blunt remarks and the two women joined in.

"What are you three laughing about?" Leo was eyeing us suspiciously from his doorway, having opened his door at the noise in the outer office.

"Oh, nothing," I assured him. "I had just introduced Julie to Sgt. Acres and told them a crude joke about two horses, a pig, a sheep and two midget wrestlers. You remember Julie Newton, don't you Leo?"

"Yes, we've met once or twice. The last time at the Halloween party," Leo confirmed.

"Good to see you again, major. How have you been?"

They shook hands.

"Good, Miss Newton. What brings you to town?" Leo wondered.

"You can call me Julie. I'm in town with General Whigg for a couple of meetings. I found Dave at the Black Fox last night and thought I'd keep a close eye on him while I'm here," she nodded in my direction, shot a look at Acres and glanced down at the package I was holding. "Wouldn't want him to get in trouble down here in San Antonio all on his own."

"Yeah, he needs watching all right," Leo confirmed. "So, Dave, come on into my office and we'll talk about half a book. Sergeant, keep Julie company while we talk."

Leo headed back into his office. I followed him, giving Julie a shrug and raised eyebrows, hoping she'd understand it wasn't my decision to exclude her.

"See you in a bit," I offered in consolation. Then, softly, "Sorry."

After closing the door behind me, I took a seat in one of Leo's chairs.

"So those jokers want half of our secrets, huh?" Leo started.

"More than half, Leo. I paid Garcia's another visit and look what I found in the attic," I said, tossing the package onto Leo's orderly desktop.

"Well, well. The missing half. Looks like it's been opened," Leo accused.

"It was. I wanted be sure I had the damn thing this time."

Leo picked it up and ruffled the pages.

"I'll give it to one of my guys to check out. Now that we've got the whole book, I guess we're ready to sell some secrets."

"Looks to be. Do you have any idea what they're up to? Or where Mr. Garcia is?"

"From the intel I have, those two Libyans are trying to buy a classified tech manual to impress their boss."

"Libyans, huh? How'd you find that out?'

"I have my methods."

"Guess you can't tell me, huh?"

"Nope. The source is classified."

"Can you tell me who their boss is?"

"No. It would be a guess anyway because I'm not sure myself. And I couldn't tell you even if I knew for certain."

"What about Garcia?"

"We haven't found him yet, but we're still looking. That's where you come in."

"What do you mean?" I asked, a guarded tone in my voice.

"Well, after you came in yesterday, I up-channeled the info you gave me. Then my boss in Washington told me to have you make the deal with those two characters. Right after you do, we'll pick them up and, um, talk with them."

"I see."

Talk meant interrogate, I thought. Maybe even torture.

"Are you going to pick up the Libyans before or after the exchange?"

"After, so we'll have them in possession of classified material."

"What about the money?"

"Well, against my advice and better judgement, my boss said you can have it."

"That's nice, but won't you guys need it as evidence?"

"No, because we're treating these two guys as spies and they probably won't be tried in this country."

"Do you mean…"

"I can't go into any details, but as spies, they get special treatment courtesy of the United States government. And you don't need to know about it."

"Okay, so where do we go from here?"

"Now that we have both halves, the guys over at the Nuke Farm will be trading the halves for a better version. It should be ready this afternoon."

"Better version? What are they going to do, bug it?"

"Not quite. What they're getting together is a special version of the book. You didn't think I'd give you the real deal, did you? The one you're going to exchange is a fake, but real looking enough to fool nearly anyone."

"So, I expected a trick from them. I hope yours is good enough to fool the bad guys."

"It will be, trust me," Leo guaranteed.

Where had I heard that before?

"You said this afternoon. When?"

"Have you and your girlfriend had lunch?"

"No," I answered, ignoring the 'girlfriend' reference and waiting for him to answer my question.

"Good. Go have lunch and be back here sometime after fifteen-thirty. They should be done with your merchandise by then."

"Okay," I agreed, getting to my feet. Leo stood, too, and walked me toward the door.

"By the way, how much of this does Newton know?" Leo asked quietly with his hand on the doorknob.

"Enough, but she's not in on the details" I lied.

"Good. Let's keep it that way, okay? Less loose ends to tie up."

"Okay with me."

When Leo opened the door, Julie and Acres were sitting at Acres' desk. Julie had pulled up a chair to the side of the desk and the two women were talking over cups of coffee. They looked up as we came into the room. Then they both stood up. Julie walked over to me.

"Through with him, Leo? It doesn't look like you roughed him up much," she said, inspecting me for wear and tear.

"He didn't put up much of a fight. Told me everything without me laying a hand on him. Take him to lunch, will you? He's looking weak."

"Oh, he's not that weak," she disagreed squeezing my right biceps and tossing a wink to Acres which was out of Leo's line of sight. Then, "You two want to come to lunch with us. We're going to Mamacita's."

"No, thanks," Leo declined. "We have some work to do before you get back."

"We're coming back?" Julie asked.

"Yes. Leo wants us to come back after three-thirty today to pick up a package. So we might as well go eat," I informed her, taking her arm and guiding her toward the hallway door.

"That's fine with me," Julie agreed.

"We're done for now, right, Leo?" I asked, passing by him as he held the open door for us.

"Right. See you after three. Have a good lunch."

"Bye, Miss Newton. It was nice to have met you," chimed in Sgt. Acres.

"You, too, Joan. See you later," Julie said turning back to face her as we left.

We weren't even down the steps when Julie's curiosity overcame her.

"So, how did it go?" she whispered conspiratorially.

"Fine," I answered, matching her whisper. "We're on for tomorrow." Then in normal volume, startling her, "And he's going to let me keep the money."

"How nice for you," she said, matching my loudness. "I was trying not to be too obvious, Mr. Spy. In case someone was listening."

"They probably know what's going on anyway, so there's no reason to be too sneaky," I observed as we left the building in our wake.

"Whatever you say, sir."

"C'mon, let's go eat."

"Since it's on the way, we're going back to the mall and trade the van for the 88."

"Good, because sitting all the way over on the other side of the van doesn't give me nearly enough opportunities to molest you."

"That goes for me too," I said, giving her a sideways squeeze as we came up on the van's tail end. "Last time to enter this way, I hope."

We climbed up inside the van, ladies first. I gave her butt a light slap as she hopped up.

"Hey, buddy, watch it," she yelped.

"Sorry, plumber's helper, I couldn't help myself. All the snooping around and I forgot to fondle you," I apologized, scrambling in after her.

"Don't squeeze the help. It'll give 'em ideas."

"I'll bet."

A few minutes later we left the base via General Hudnell. We drove at a normal speed on Highway 90 eastbound, changed directions at I-35 and five minutes later I put on the right blinker for Military Drive. After exiting the interstate, we made a right and then entered into the mall parking lot. We swapped transportation and then we traveled east on Military, proceeding the six blocks to a small building on the right side of the street. Hand painted on the outside cinder block wall was a southwestern-looking mural, complete with cacti, burros, and a pueblo with a cantina. Written in bright yellow through the cloudy blue sky above the scene was 'Mamacita's Café'. There were four other cars in the parking lot in front of the building. We joined their ranks.

"I hope this is as good as I remember," Julie said I as locked up the car.

"It is, my dear," I confirmed. "For me there's nothing like good Mexican food, sharing it with a good-looking woman and then washing it down with cold beer."

We were greeted just inside the door by the Mamacita, herself.

"Hello, David Harris. How are you today?" asked the short, heavy-set proprietor.

"Fine, Louisa. And I've brought an old friend, a lady-friend, with me. Do you remember Julie Newton?"

"Of course. Miss Newton, how have you been?"

"Good, Louisa. It's good to see you again. I've been dreaming about your food for months."

"That's good, pretty lady. It'll be especially good today. Juan is cooking and he's just a little tipsy. He makes better food that way, I think," she confessed, grabbing two menus from the rack by the cash register and ushering us to a booth by one of the few windows in the place.

"Here are your menus. What would you like to drink?"

"For me, water and what kind of beer do you have?" asked Julie.

"American beers and Corona, Dos Equies, and Tecate."

"I'll have a Corona."

"Make that two waters and two Coronas, please, Louisa," I added.

"Bueno. I'll bring you some chips and my special salsa."

"Sounds good, thanks."

Louisa left us alone to ponder the menus.

"So, what do you want?" I prompted.

"Mmm, it all sounds so good," Julie answered, not looking up from her reading. "What are you having?"

"The Mamacita special plate. It has a bit of everything, beans, rice, taco, tamale, quesadia, enchilada, and a couple of other things that always taste good but I'm not sure what they're called."

"Is it hot?"

"Not as hot as you, but it will burn your tongue," I offered.

"You're a flatterer, you know," she said, looking up at me. "But you're still not quite out of the dog house, yet."

"Oh?"

"Uh-huh. I had a little talk with Joan about you. She said you were cute, but a butterfly. I told her that's why we get along well. I am, too."

"Which, cute or a butterfly."

"Both. We fit together, you and I."

"I'll say, which brings up another topic. Didn't we agree that lunch would be in between the sheets or something."

"Well, your tryst with Leo kind of put that particular lunch special on hold."

"You're right about that. Because after we get the book from Leo, we need to go back to the mall and lock it up in my office safe."

"I suppose you're right," she said wistfully. "Oh, well, it'll just delay our afternoon of loving a bit. It'll do us good to agonize over our ecstasy."

"Ooh, some pun," I groaned as Louisa returned to the table with our drinks and chips.

"What will you have, señor and señorita?" she asked when she had finished arranging the water glasses and beer bottles to her liking.

"It looks like we'll both have one of your special plates, the Mamacita, Louisa," Julie answered for us.

"Good choice. I'll tell Juan to make it up extra special for you. Not too hot and not too mild, okay?"

"That sounds good to us," I said, both of us nodding approval to Louisa.

"Bueno. Enjoy your cervezas. The food will be out in a few moments," she informed us as she turned back toward the kitchen.

"Here's to Mexican food and Mexican beer that you can't get in D.C.," toasted Julie, holding up her beer bottle for me to clink with mine.

"Cheers," I saluted, touching longnecks with her. "It won't be long until this beer makes it all the way to Maine, even if the makers do pee in the vats."

"Oh, yuck. That's just a rumor, right?" she asked around her sip of beer, nearly afraid to swallow it.

"Who knows. If they do, I say it just improves the taste over Lone Star. That stuff gives me a headache after just half a can."

"It does me the same way. This is much better, with or without the additives."

And then our food arrived. Service was much faster if you have the specials.

"Watch the plates. They are very hot," Louisa warned. "Everything look okay?"

"It looks wonderful," Julie complimented, picking up her fork and diving in. "Mmm," she added with her first mouthful. "Delicious."

"Thanks, Louisa. The food's great," I agreed.

"You're welcome, David, enjoy," she beamed and left us to stuff our faces.

It didn't take us long to put a dent in the platefuls of food and fill our stomachs. We were almost done in just twenty minutes with hardly a word spoken while we ate. Once during the meal, Louisa came back over to check on our progress.

"Everything still okay?" she asked.

My mouth full, I just nodded.

"It's great. Best I've had since I left town last year," Julie said between bites.

When we finally pushed our plates back, Louisa returned.

"So, sopapillas for dessert, yes?" she insisted.

"Okay, you talked us into it. And coffee, too, please," I added.

"I'll be back with them in just a few minutes," she promised, clearing away some of the used dishes and heading off toward the kitchen.

I waited to make my move until Louisa was out of earshot.

"Julie, it's only a quarter to two," I observed, leering over the table toward her. "If we hurry, you can be my sopapilla in time for us to meet with Leo."

"Baby, although being covered with honey and having you lick it off me is an interesting idea, we'd never make it back in time to pick up the fake. Besides, after eating all that food, if you were to bounce on me, I'd probably barf."

"Good point," I agreed, a little disappointed. "Wouldn't want indigestion to interfere with romance."

"Or just plain old sex, horn dog. We'll have plenty of time to play oinky-boinky after we park the package."

"I think your vocabulary has changed since you moved away," I remarked at her surprisingly novel description of the sex act.

"Maybe. I haven't shown you everything I learned since I saw you last. There is a lot of opportunity for instruction inside the Beltway, you know."

"For students and for teachers, I suppose," I said, giving her the benefit of the doubt.

"Yes, for both. Ah, here comes the best part of the meal," Julie observed as Louisa arrived with a tray full of coffee and sweets.

"Two for you and two for you," she said, placing a saucer with a pair of sopapillas in front of each of us. She put the honey container between so we could fight over it and set a mug of steaming coffee down next to each saucer. Last off her tray was a small bowl with creamers and a sugar pourer.

"Anything else?" she wondered.

"That looks like everything, Louisa. Muchas gracias," I thanked her with just about the only Spanish I knew.

"De nada," she answered, and left us to get sticky with honey.

We had a couple more cups of coffee and it was nearly two-thirty when I asked for the bill. By the time we each took a potty break and made it out to the Olds, it was almost three o'clock.

"Well, if we mosey slowly, we won't be too early," I observed.

"That sounds fine," Julie said, again finding the cuddling spot next to me. "Take me the long way."

"Anything for you, my sweet."

We went the semi-long way.

After heading west on Military Drive and hitting all the red lights possible, I turned right onto Quintana and drove toward the southeast gate of Kelly. It was just after three p.m. when we passed through the Quintana gate. Five minutes later we parked outside Leo's building.

"Okay, Buttercup, ready to go in and get a book," I said, unwinding from Julie.

"If we must. I was really comfortable being your second skin, you know."

"I know, Mrs. Horndog. But Mr. Horndog says it's time to rock and roll. So let's rock," I encouraged, stepping out of the car and pulling Julie after me.

We walked arm-in-arm up to the building. I opened the door and followed her up the stairs.

"Seriously fine ass," I said under my breath, watching her mount the stairs.

"I heard that, fella," she warned, stopping on a step. "You'd better come up here beside me so you won't get into trouble."

"Okay, but you're spoiling my fun."

"I'll show you fun," she promised as we continued to climb side by side.

"I'll bet you will," I agreed, patting her derriere.

"Hey, fresh person, do I know you?" she complained with false indignity. "I can't even trust you when you're beside me."

"Sorry, Hon, but I've been looking at your assets all day and I'm in agony over the ecstasy I'm being deprived of."

"Ouch. Your pun was worse than mine," she observed as we reached the second floor and turned right to Leo's domain.

"I'm just trying to match you tit…"

"Don't say it. It's just too obvious," she pointed out, turning the knob to Leo's outer office door and swinging it inward.

Acres looked up.

"So how was lunch?" she wondered.

"Fine," Julie said walking into the room with me in tow. "Except my lunch partner has been playing grab-ass all the way back."

"I have?"

"Well nearly."

"Don't give me any details, please, about the grab-ass or the food. I haven't eaten since breakfast and I'm starved. The Major is going to let me go a little early. Where did you say you ate?"

"Mamacita's. It's on Military Drive, east of where I-35 and Military Drive intersect. The easiest way to get there is Billy Mitchell to General Hudnell to Highway 90; south on I-35 to Military Drive, then left or east on Military Drive. It's down on the right about five or six blocks. It has a mural painted on the outside of the building. You really can't miss it," I explained as she watched my hands making lefts and rights in the air. "Got it?"

"Yeah, I think so. It's east of South Park Mall, right?" she asked and I nodded. "I'll go there as soon I get off work." And then into the intercom, "Major, Mr. Harris and Miss Newton are back."

"Thanks," came the metallic voice. "I'll be right out."

Leo emerged from his office a couple of minutes later.

"Okay, Sergeant, you're out of here," he told Acres, his thumb jabbing toward the door.

"Thanks, Major," Acres said, gathering her purse and hat. "See you tomorrow. And I'll see you two later, probably. Thanks for the tip on a good eating spot."

"How was lunch, folks?" Leo asked, killing time while waiting for Acres to leave.

"Lunch was fine. I ate too fast, I think. But it was a really good meal," said Julie.

"Just about the best in San Antonio, as far as I'm concerned," I added, closing the door behind Acres.

"Okay," said Leo, his tone lower. "Here's the deal. Tomorrow, when those two clowns come back, you play it straight. No heroics. I'll have the place surrounded. The idea is to do the deal and then do nothing. Stay put in your office. We're after the bosses, not the peons, so our pigeons must fly away home with no suspicions. Okay?"

"Okay. That's fine with me. Where's the merchandise?"

"Right here," he said, producing a brown paper wrapped package he'd kept under the side of his jacket. "This will fool anyone but a trained mechanic. Put it somewhere safe tonight, okay? I don't want any foul-ups."

"All right, Leo," I said, taking the package from him and tucking it inside the back of my trousers, just like when I had brought in the first half to him. "We're going back to my office and lock it in the safe. It'll be fine until morning."

"Sounds good," he encouraged, pulling open the hall door. "Might not let anyone see you go into the mall tonight. Wouldn't want you to get hijacked."

"Good idea, Leo. I'll go in the back way just to be sure. But I think my customers believe the item is already in my safe."

"Possible. Just be careful," he cautioned, letting us out into the hallway.

"We will be," I said shaking his hand in farewell.

"See you, Major," Julie said as good-bye.

"Good luck," he said to our retreating backs.

"Does he suddenly trust me or something?" Julie wondered aloud on the way back to the car.

"Maybe. At our first meeting today, when you and Acres were getting chummy, he asked me how much you knew. I told him enough, but not all the details."

"You lied to him."

"Well, yeah. I didn't want him to think you were in on the whole thing. That would complicate you getting clear of it when the good guys move in. That way you can also just walk away if the shit hits the fan. Besides, he didn't have the need to know what you know."

"Makes sense, I guess. Of course, if he figures we're sleeping together, then I might just know everything."

"Maybe. He never asked, although I expected him to. He's in the nosey business, you know, just like me."

"Honey, I like your nose," she teasingly cooed, touching my nose with her index finger. "Especially next to mine."

We were at the Olds and I unlocked it for her. She slid over to her now-familiar spot just to the right of driver and I got behind the wheel.

"How are we going to sneak into the mall?" she wondered, as I kicked the engine to life and pulled out of the parking lot heading east on Billy Mitchell toward the freeway.

"We aren't going to sneak in. We're going in through the Penny's main entrance and right over to my office. If the bad guys are lying in wait, they'll have to pull a hijacking in front of everybody. And I don't think they'd do that. Besides, like I said at Leo's, they were eyeballing my safe today so I think they think it's in the Mossberg."

"Sounds like a plan to me. I'm coming inside with you, right?"

"Sure. Just a couple of lovey-dovey folks out shopping at the mall."

Twenty minutes later and we were locking up the Eighty-Eight in the parking lot outside the west door of Penny's. Arms entwined, we strolled into the store, traversing its width to the mall entrance. Just past the entrance, we turned down the hallway to Bobby's and my offices. The office door wasn't locked. I could see Bobby at Ruth's desk, talking on the phone. I held the door for Julie. Bobby looked up when we came in and waved at us without missing a beat in her conversation. I saluted her and we went into my office.

"What time does Ruth go home?" Julie wondered.

"Six I think. But Bobby comes in later and goes home later so the place is covered until the mall closes. The mall has a rule that stores and kiosks have to open when the mall does and then stay opened until the mall closes at ten. They'll fine you twenty-five dollars if you don't keep mall hours," I explained.

"How do you get away with not being here?"

"Part of my contract is that I don't have to abide by those rules," I said as I pulled the package from its place under my coat and laid it on the desk. "Besides, Ruth or Bobby has the front office staffed, so it looks like someone is here. I also think Bobby has the same contract as I do, one with an exception."

"I didn't realize the mall management fines you if you don't stay open."

"Yeah, it's a way to keep customers interested. If the stores opened and closed whenever they wanted, mall traffic would be intermittent," I said, finally getting the Mossberg open. I swung the left door outward and put the package on the lower shelf, underneath my loaded CZ-75. Tomorrow, I wanted the book in one hand and a pistol in the other. I did not trust those two Libyans any further that I could throw them one-handed.

"What do you want me to do tomorrow?"

"Same thing as today, okay. Just wait in the bathroom. Leo doesn't know it but the two security guys will be here tomorrow, too. They're ex-military and fairly competent, so I trust you and them to cover me. We'll play it Leo's way to not scare off the bad guys, but I won't feel safe unless I have my own backup."

"I agree. I'll feel much better with them here plus the agents in the mall."

I spun the dial on the big safe and tried the handles. Locked tight.

"Well, what shall we do now?" I asked, turning to look at Julie.

"You promised me that you'd take me to the Riverwalk. So let's go. I remember that there's a great place for cheesecake called the Kangaroo Court."

"Honey, you're all the cheesecake I need," I said, stepping over to her and encircling her with my arms, giving her a big squeeze.

"Oof. There's that flattery again. But what will you do when I've gone back to D.C.?" she mock-pouted.

"Oh, I have other cheesecake lined up, thanks to you."

"Yes, you do, thanks to me," she said, jabbing me in the ribs.

"Ow. At the Kangaroo Court," I corrected.

"Okay, let's go get some," she said, freeing herself from my clutches and pulling me toward the office door.

"Do we need to change clothes before we go clubbing?" I wondered.

"Nope, I think we look fine for San Antonio. Besides, we aren't going to be out that late. I have other plans for most of the rest of the evening."

"Other plans?" I asked, eyebrows arched. "Do those other plans include me?"

"Oh, most assuredly, sir."

"How delightful," I said, locking my office door behind us.

Bobby was nowhere in sight.

"Just a second. I want to see if Bobby's still here."

"Okay."

I opened Bobby's door and she was behind her desk arranging some brochures or something.

"Bobby, we're leaving now. Oh, you remember Julie, don't you?"

"Sure. She's your friend that moved to D.C. last year, right?"

"Right. She's in town a couple of days with her boss. They're leaving Saturday. Anyway, we're headed to the River Walk right now. Tomorrow is what I wanted to tell you about. I'm meeting a couple of nefarious characters about ten-thirty and want some backup listening in the bathroom. I've got Sanchez and Deets covering. Is it okay if we use your office as a throughway?"

"Sure. I don't have a client coming over until, just a minute while I look," she said pawing through the papers on her desk until she unearthed her appointment book. "Right, one o'clock. So, no problem. There isn't going to be any shooting is there?"

"Gad, I hope not. I haven't been to the range lately and would hate shooting up the office," I said half-joking. "Seriously, no. I just don't want to take a chance of being mugged without muscle support."

"Yeah, that's fine, Dave. You're going to tell Ruth in the morning, right."

"Uh-huh. I'm coming in early to scope it out and set things up, so I'll make sure she knows what's happening."

"Sounds okay. You two have fun at the River Walk. Eat a cheesecake for me."

"Oh, I will, Bobby," I confirmed, grinning widely. "You can count on it."

"You are something," she responded to my leering look, shaking her head and giving me a shooing wave with both hands. "Good afternoon."

I waved good-bye and eased the door closed. Julie was waiting patiently in one of Ruth's customer chairs.

"Gave her a heads up, huh?" she guessed, getting to her feet.

"Yeah, figured it'd be better if I asked permission this time."

"Smart idea. Buddy, let's go walk off some enchiladas so we can make room for more fattening desserts," she said, taking my hand and leading me out into the hallway.

"Say, just for fun, let's do a figure eight on the way back through Penny's," I suggested before we reached the main concourse of the mall.

"Figure eight? What do you mean?"

"We'll be checking for tails. I figure we weren't followed from Leo's, but we may have picked up a tail when we came into the mall. I just want to be sure. Here's what we do: you and I split up when we go into Penny's. I'll go left into the men's department and you go right. We leisurely circle around toward the middle of the store. As we get close to crossing in the middle, you watch my six and I'll watch yours. If you see anyone following me, when we meet, just tell me what he's wearing. If not, we'll separate again and make another loop toward the door we came in where we parked the car. Okay"

"Sounds mysterious, but okay. Do I act like I know you in the middle?"

"Sure. We're shoppers, right. That's how we act. If we pick up a tail, I'll go to a register like I'm buying something and have them call security to detain them while we make our getaway."

We had reached the mall entrance to Penny's.

"See you in the middle, honey," I said, giving her a peck on the cheek. "Have fun shopping."

"Okay, see you," she said, giving me a disdainful look for my theatrics. She gave me a light jab in the ribs and I returned her look. We separated on our missions.

I walked slowly through the men's, looking at a few ties and feeling the fabrics of suits and slacks. After wandering around for few minutes, I began nearing the center counters where jewelry and perfumes were being hawked. I hadn't noticed anyone with unusual interest in me. I saw Julie coming through the women's department in the same slow manner I had used. I stopped to fondle the watchbands as she approached. She stopped beside me.

"Nothing on your ass but your trousers," she said out of the side of her mouth.

I laughed.

"Thanks, Ninety-nine. I'm off to housewares," I announced, giving her another peck on the cheek.

"Would you get smart and quit that?" she returned the pun and started her second loop.

Without seeing anyone suspicious following either of us by the time our loops brought us to the outer door, I lowered my guard a little.

"Nothing, huh?" I asked as we reunited before going to the car.

"Nope, just a tall stranger with a mustache I keep running into. Looks kind of like you, he does. Wait, it was you!" she mocked, pointing a finger in my chest.

"Ha, ha. Let's go get some cheesecake, Cheesecake. All this walking has made me a little hungry," I noted as we stepped outside.

"Wow, even after the pig-out at lunch?"

"Yeah, I'm a growing boy and need my nourishment."

"I'll say."

She wrapped her right arm around my waist. "Wouldn't want anything important to interfere with dessert."

"You being the dessert," I pointed out, fishing the Eighty-Eight's keys out of my pocket.

"Well," she started, sliding her hand down my back and grabbing a handful of my right butt cheek and squeezing it, "you could be the dessert, you know."

"Yes, I could," I confirmed, pulling her around toward me into a tight embrace.

We gave each other a slow, sensual kiss, grinding our bodies together, right there in the parking lot next to the Olds.

"Goodness, some people!" said an older woman passing by on her way into the mall.

We quickly broke our clasp and turned to look in her direction.

"Sorry, ma'am," Julie started. "We're in love and he just proposed."

I kept silent at the lie.

"In the parking lot?" the woman wondered.

"Yes, right here," confirmed Julie.

"Well congratulations on your engagement. But lovemaking should be done indoors," the woman scolded. "Privately."

"Thanks. We'll watch it next time," I assured her as she turned away from us and continued on toward the mall doors.

"I guess we'd better get going before we cause another scene," Julie managed between giggles.

I unwound from Julie and opened the driver's door. Julie slid across the seat just enough to give me room behind the wheel.

"Cozy, huh?" she said as I closed the door and fitted the key into the ignition.

"Yes, ma'am, just the way I like it," I said, bringing the engine to life.

I put the car into drive and swung my right arm around Julie to hug her closer.

"Me, too," she agreed, sliding her hand up and down my leg and finally coming to rest just millimeters from my crotch.

"Did you know it took me a couple of years to perfect my one-arm-driving-while-a-beautiful-woman-was-feeling-me-up technique?" I asked as we wound our way through the parking lot to the north side of the mall where Military Drive and the I-35 entrance were.

"I wouldn't have thought it would have taken you years. What were you when you started, sixteen?" she asked, giving my leg a squeeze.

"No, fifteen. I had Driver's Ed."

"Well, that explains why you're such an expert at it."

We had reached the parking lot exit by Military Drive and the traffic was moderate. I craned my neck left checking for an opening that would allow us into the far-left lane so we could get onto the freeway. When I saw a gap big enough, I tromped the gas and we accelerated sharply into the traffic. I must have scared Julie a little.

"You can have your arm back if you need it," she offered.

"No, I'm okay, thanks," I assured her, braking into the left turn lane as the traffic light went from yellow to red. "Missed it. But can't think of a better place to be right now, unless it was in bed with you. This is a slow light."

She turned to look at me and we kissed. Our lips stayed together long enough for us to get a honking reminder from the car behind us that the light was green.

"Whew, that was nice," she said as we made the turn under the overpass and sped up the on-ramp.

"I'll say. Now I'll have to sit in the car until I settle down a little."

"Just concentrate on the traffic, okay. That should take care of the problem."

We were on our way to the city center via I-35. When we got downtown, we took the Durango exit, then turned left on Santa Rosa to Houston. I planned on parking near the La Mansion side of the Riverwalk as close to the Kangaroo Court as possible. It was just turning five o'clock and outbound traffic was relatively heavy.

"Glad we're going in instead of out. It'll be easier to find a parking place now," I said making the right turn down Houston Street.

"You can parallel park this big boat, I hope."

"You bet. Even one handed," I bragged. "Care to make a small wager on it?"

"Sure. If you make it in, you buy. If not, you buy. How's that?" she teased.

"Sounds like I'm buying," I said as we neared an open space between the parked cars. "Let's see if I can do it in one try."

I slid past the front car on the right and stopped the Olds a fender's length in front of the rear of the other car. With my foot on the brake I shifted into reverse. Turning in the seat to look out the back window, I eased my pressure on the brake pedal and turned the wheel to the right. The rear end of the Olds was now aimed at the parking hole and we inched toward the curb. I adjusted the trajectory slightly and just as the nose cleared the car in front, I turned the wheel hard left. The front end swung around and we were in. I backed up just a bit further, careful not to touch the car in back of us and then turned the wheel hard right. I shifted into drive and pulled forward toward the curb to finish the maneuver. I turned off the motor and gave her a proud smile.

"Textbook. I'm impressed. I thought I was the only person left who could do that without bending sheet metal."

"You probably are. They still require it for a license here in Texas, you know. But it's easier to judge the distances with real cars than with the pylons they use for the test."

I pulled open the ashtray where I kept spare change and retrieved a quarter for the meter. Then I checked the left mirror before I opened the door just in case someone was in a sideswiping mood. The street was clear.

"C'mon, let's cheesecake it, Baby," I said, yanking the keys from the ignition and getting out of the car.

"I'm with you, Baby," she agreed, taking my offered hand and hopping out onto the street. "Which way?"

"This way," I said, pointing past the front of the car, hooking my finger to the right. "There's an entrance across the bridge by La Mansion. I figured we'd do a little Riverwalk before the cheesecake."

"Fine by me. I'll just work up a good appetite by the time we get there."

I locked the car, dropped the quarter in the parking meter slot and twisted the handle until the red 'Expired' flag disappeared. Two hours would be plenty of time. Then we started up the street, holding hands as we slipped between the parked cars to reach the sidewalk. At the corner, we turned right on Navarro, went a block and a half, passed over the bridge and then down a flight of metal stairs to the river.

We followed the inner bank along the river around its northeastern bend until we came to the patio of the Kangaroo Court. A twenty-something host greeted us. The place wasn't as crowded as I thought it might be.

"Hi, folks. Care to sit on the patio?" he asked.

"Sure, that's fine with us," I answered as he guided us back out the way we'd entered.

There were ten or so tables on the patio. Each had an umbrella opened over it that provided a little shade and bird-poop protection. Three other couples and a family of four were occupying the tables closest to the sidewalk by the riverbank. The waiter chose an empty one nearer the building. He pulled out a chair for Julie and left me to fend for myself.

"Just the two of you?" he wondered, looking from me to Julie as he helped adjust her seat.

"Right, just us," I said, sitting next to her. "And we already know what we want."

"Fine," he answered coming around to face us. "What'll it be?"

"Blueberry cheesecake," Julie answered enthusiastically.

"Good. One for each of you?"

"No," she said, eyeing me to make sure her choice was okay. After I nodded, she added, "We'll split it. Just bring two forks, please."

"Of course. Anything to drink?" he wondered.

"Coffee, please," I chimed in.

"Right. A slice of cheesecake and coffee for two, coming right up."

"Thanks," we said together, and he was off.

"A whole piece each would be a waste, don't you think?" she asked, making sure she had read my approval right. "As I remember, it's so rich and tasty that after about half of it, it starts tasting like cardboard."

"You're right. Last whole piece I had was too much of a good thing."

"Not like me, right?" she asked, running her foot against my lower leg and stroking my arm.

"Speaking of not enough of a good thing," I said, switching gears. "Do you have to go back to D.C. on Saturday?"

"Well, that's the plan. But since you mentioned it, I should call the general to make sure our plans haven't changed. Got some change for the phone?"

"You need to call him right now?"

"Better now, than later, honey."

"Okay, but if you're not here when the cheesecake arrives, you might miss out on your half," I warned, digging in my pocket for change for her. "No change, but here's a buck you can use."

The waiter arrived with our order.

"Here you are, folks," announced the waiter, setting our coffees and cheesecake on the table. He put the utensils, napkins and condiments in the center for us to sort out. "Anything else I can get for you right now?"

"Change for a dollar, please," requested Julie. And then, to me, "Judging from the size of that slice, there'll be plenty left for me by the time I get back."

"We'll see," I teased her.

The waiter made change and Julie followed him to the phone.

I added creamer and sugar to my coffee and stirred the stuff until it dissolved. Despite what I'd threatened, I wasn't going to start on the cheesecake without her. While she was gone, I let my eyes lazily roam over the sights of the River Walk. I had always liked this area, particularly this time of year when the weather was milder. It was also a great dating spot. There were plenty of pretty flowers for a guy's date to fawn over, some good restaurants to ply a date with food and booze and some interesting clubs for a little dancing. I was mulling over the first time I had brought Julie down to the river when she returned to the table with a smile on her face.

"Well, a little bit of good news," she started as she sat down and picked up her fork. "We're still going back Saturday, but I'm free until we get on the plane."

"That's some job you have. Are you sure you're a real secretary?"

"I'm sure. But my boss knows me and knows that I have a thing for you. So he's borrowing someone from the conference to do my job while I'm messing around with you. Pretty neat, huh."

"I'll say. But I'm not complaining," I confirmed, watching her take a bite of dessert. "Having more time for you and me is how I like it."

"Me, too. Mmm, this is good," she said between mouthfuls.

It didn't take us long to polish off our slice of heaven. We washed down the sweetness with our coffees.

"I don't know why it is, but coffee tastes so good with something sweet."

"Could be the bitterness of the coffee offsets the sweet taste," I offered.

"I suppose. It just tastes good. Want another cup?"

"No, I think it's just about time I had another type of dessert, don't you," I said after draining my cup and setting it carefully back onto the saucer.

"Why, whatever do y'all mean?" she drawled, batting her eyelashes at me.

"Well, it's time, Scarlet, to demonstrate your appreciation to the man who's been showing you a good time all over San Antonio."

"And who would that be, sir?"

"Why, me, of course," I said, waving a hand to the waiter and making bring-me-the-bill motions.

He nodded and started toward us, tearing our check from his pad on the way. I stood and peeled a twenty from the fold of bills I had taken from my pocket. I handed him the money as he arrived at the table.

"Thanks. It was really good. Keep the change."

"Thank you, sir. Come back again, anytime," he invited, stepping away from the table.

"We will," I assured him, pulling the chair back for Julie.

She took a last sip of coffee, stood up and stretching upward, turned and dropped her hands on my shoulders.

"Let's go back to my place, my fine young fellow. I have some things to show you," she said smiling up at me and pulling me closer to her.

"Like what?" I teased.

"Like smooth, soft skin, tiny tan lines and tender, moist places," she said softly into my ear.

"Can I ask you a question first?"

"Sure."

"What are we standing here for? Let's get a move on."

"Let's," she agreed, sliding her arms down until she had one wrapped around my waist.

We turned and began retracing our steps along the riverbank. When we reached the Navarro bridge, I steered us past the stairs to the street level and continued on toward the La Mansion bridge just ahead of us.

"Hey, big boy, where are you taking me?" she wondered, turning her head to look at the Navarro street sign behind us. "Wasn't that our exit?"

"It might have been if there hadn't been a change of plans."

"What change of plans? I thought the plan was you and me and a bed on the west side of town."

"It was," I began to explain as I guided her up the stairs of the arched bridge leading to La Mansion. "But then I had a bright idea and my money's burning a hole in my pocket. So I decided on a detour."

"Detour to where?"

"Have patience, my dear, and you'll see."

We had reached the top of the arch. I stopped and turned her to look back down the river the way we had come. The air was just beginning to get a little cool. The sun was casting early evening shadows over the scene in front of us.

"Beautiful sight, the river, huh?"

"Yes it is, mystery man," she nodded, then turned to face me.

"And it's all the more beautiful with you here with me."

"It's special for me, too, being here with you."

"So, I don't want to leave it just yet. I don't know when the next time will be that I'll have you in my arms in such a romantic setting."

"What are you suggesting? That we should find some secluded place and christen the riverbank?"

"Not quite, but close. Come with me," I said, leading her the rest of the way over the bridge and into the courtyard of the hotel.

We started up the steps into the lobby when the light went on inside her.

"Oh, mister, are you going to get us a hotel room?" she teased.

"Hush, young lady, I'm going to sign us in as married, okay," I told her in a tone just above a whisper as we neared the front desk.

"May I help you sir," ask the nicely dressed desk clerk.

"Yes, please. My wife and I would like a room for the night. One that over-looks the river, please. We're newlyweds and the river is just so romantic."

"It is, isn't it?" he agreed, handing me a registration card and a pen. "Would a guest room be sufficient or would you care for a suite?"

"A guest room would be fine," I answered.

While I filled out the card and signed at the bottom, the clerk picked out a room and set an ornate key on the counter between us. When I was finished with the card, he turned it around so he could read the name.

"Mr. and Mrs. Davis, welcome to La Mansion. Your room number is three fourteen. The stairs are behind you on your left and the elevator is beside them.

The restaurant is open until nine-thirty tonight. We have twenty-four hour room service available. The concierge can handle any tickets to events you might care to attend. The bellman will help you with your luggage."

"That's okay. We don't have much and I'll get it later from the car," I informed him as I reached for the key.

"Is there anything else I can do for you tonight, sir?"

"No, that should do it."

The bellman appeared at my elbow.

"Your key, sir. I'll show you to your room."

"Thank you," I said, handing him the key.

We followed him to the elevator. On the third floor he turned right out of the elevator and then left along the hallway by the river. At three fourteen, he unlocked the room and ushered us in to inspect it. There was a queen-sized bed to the right past the entrance with a dressing bench at the end of the bed. A low dresser was against the wall opposite the bed with a table and chairs just beyond. The French doors at the end of the room were closed. The door to the bath was to the right of them. The room was done up old-Spanish style, with white walls, dark wood accents and roof beams showing.

"This looks fine," reported Julie, running her hand over the bed covers as she took a tour of the accommodations.

"Thank you, madam," the bellman said, walking the length of the room and opening the doors onto the Riverwalk view. "You'll find toiletries and robes in the bathroom. Enjoy your stay."

"Thanks," I said handing him a folded five-spot as he passed back by me.

"Thank you, sir. If you need help later with your luggage, let me know," he offered, retreating to the doorway.

"Thanks, I will. Good evening," I said, closing the door behind him.

When I turned around, she was gone and the bathroom door was closed. I walked over to the French doors and stepped out onto the small balcony. Nice view, I thought, scanning the river below me. Twilight was setting in and the lights at establishments on the river were coming on. I heard the toilet flush and Julie came out to join me, wearing one of the robes the bellman had mentioned.

"Nice choice, Dave. You're full of surprises. So you just couldn't wait to get me alone in a romantic setting, huh?"

"No, I couldn't. Besides, I figure it would be a good idea to hide out from the villains while we wait for the clock to tick," I said, wrapping an arm around her and pulling her to my side for a squeeze.

"Well," she began, letting the robe gape open tantalizingly. She was nude underneath it. "Ready to unwrap your gifts?"

"My, my. I'd say they were already unwrapped," I observed, looking from her face down past her cleavage to her closely shaved pubic area. "You undressed pretty fast in there."

"Your turn," she said turning back into the room and walking slowly over to the bed. "Don't take long."

"I won't," I said, pulling off my jacket and draping it over a chair back.

I left the doors slightly open for atmosphere. I unbuttoned my shirt, laid it over my coat and kicked my shoes off. Wearing only my trousers and socks, I stepped into the bathroom. Julie's clothes were in a neat pile on the counter. I flipped the toilet seat up, unzipped my trousers and peed. My penis was already hardening, getting ready for the night ahead. I finished stripping and went back into the bedroom, my trousers in hand. Julie was lying stretched out on the bed, her arms over her head, her back arched, her nipples pointing in my direction and her left leg brushing up against her right. When she saw me, she patted the sheet beside her. I quickly hung my trousers over a chair.

"Come here, young man. I'm ready to show you my appreciation."

"I think I can see it from here," I quipped.

"Ha, ha. You need to come closer and get a better look," she invited, momentarily spreading her legs and giving me a quick peep show.

"Right you are, ma'am," I said, sliding into bed beside her.

We kissed and rubbed against each other and then she rolled me over and sat across my hips. She reached behind her and stroked my erection.

"Well, well," she said, giving me a squeeze. "It looks like we didn't take all of the fight out of him last night, did we? Guess we'll just have to do better tonight."

And we did.

I woke up about ten-thirty. We were lying on our left sides, spooned together, my right arm nestled between her breasts. Only the sheet covered us. Music and lights from the river were filtering in through the open doors. My stomach growled. I probably should be hungry, I thought.

"Julie, are you awake?" I softly asked into her hair.

"Yes, barely. Was that your stomach I heard?" she asked sleepily.

"Yeah. I'm going to get up and give room service some business. Do you want anything?" I asked, not moving from my spot beside her.

"Mm-hmm. What are you going to get?"

"I don't know. Whatever they have, I guess. Want me to make it two orders?"

"Mm-hmm. Wake me up when it gets here."

"I could wake you up now," I said, lightly grinding the beginnings of another erection against her.

"Greedy, greedy. All you want to do is have sex with me. You never want to take me out for a hamburger," she murmured, wriggling against me. "Bring me a real piece of meat and I'll think about it."

"Lady, you got a deal," I said, pulling away from her. I slid from under the sheet and sat on the edge of the bed, fumbling for the light on the nightstand on my side of the bed. The brightness blinded me temporarily. There was a hotel brochure next to the phone. I picked it up and thumbed through until I found the hotel's room service menu. With the brochure on my·lap, I picked up the phone and punched the 8 for the room service desk.

"Las Canarias restaurant. How may I help you."

"Hi, this is Harry Davis in room three fourteen," I repeated. "I'd like to order room service, please."

"Certainly, Mr. Davis. What can we serve you."

"We'd like two filet dinners, please, if they're still available at this time of night."

"Yes, sir, they are. How would you like your steaks cooked?"

"Both medium, please."

"What vegetables would you like?"

"Green beans with shallots, wild mushrooms and jasmine rice."

"Good. Would you care for salad?"

"Yes, please," I said, flipping back a page. "Do you have the spinach and goat cheese one?"

"Yes, sir. Two of those?"

"Please. With Italian dressing. And a bottle of medium priced Merlot, please."

"Certainly. Anything for dessert?"

"Sure. Just a minute," I paused, turning another page. "I'd like one of the chocolate avocado and banana tarts and a slice of Love Creek apple pie."

"Excellent. Will that be all, sir?"

"Could you add some ice water and a carafe of coffee, too, please."

"Of course. Anything else we can get for you tonight?"

"No, thanks. If that doesn't do it, probably nothing will. Thank you."

"Your welcome, sir. Your meal should arrive in about twenty-five minutes."

"Thanks. We'll be waiting."

"Good-night, sir."

"Good-night," I said, quietly hanging up the receiver.

I stood up and walked naked into the bathroom, not bothering to turn on the light. I fumbled for the other robe and slid into it. Soft, I thought. As my eyes adjusted, I found the tube of complimentary toothpaste on the counter with the other freebies. I squeezed a bit onto my right index finger and gave my teeth a scrubbing. I made a mental note to put a toothbrush in my jacket pocket for nights away from home like these last two. Julie came in behind me and unceremoniously lifted the toilet cover and plopped onto the seat. She peed, wiped, stood up, and flushed. Then, she came over and slid in between me and the robe, so that it draped loosely over both of us.

"Boy, you sure do know how to show a girl a good time. Give me some of that stuff, please," she said, reaching for the toothpaste.

She used the same technique as I had for getting out the mouth cooties.

"Did I hear you order salad and steak and wine and dessert?" she wondered, stopping her swabbing finger for a moment.

"Yes you did," I answered, spitting into the sink.

"Good. I'm hungry, too."

I fumbled for a glass to wash out the excess paste. I filled it with water and had just moved it out of the way before Julie spat into the sink. I gulped a mouthful, swirled it around and swallowed the minty mixture.

"I'll take some of that, too, please."

I handed the glass to her. She swished and again spat into the sink.

"That's better," she brightened. "Now kiss me," she demanded, turning around inside the robe to press against me. We kissed.

"So, you're not done yet, eh?" she observed when our lips finally parted, gyrating her hips against my returning stiffness.

"It'll wait until after we eat. Room service will be here shortly and I wouldn't want to start something we couldn't finish."

"Betcha I could finish it before they get here," she challenged.

"All right, you're on."

She won the bet. I was just giving her a thank-you kiss when there was a knock on the door. We were still in the bathroom.

"I told you I could finish it. I'll get the door. You rest up for the next round," she offered, padding out into the bedroom wearing nothing but a smile.

"Seriously fine ass," I said to her departing bottom.

"I heard that."

"Well it's true, it's true," I insisted, pulling on the robe that had fallen to the floor and making myself presentable.

I heard the door open and the room service cart being rolled into the room, the dishes clinking lightly. I came out of the bathroom and a robed Julie was helping the waiter set up our meal on the table. I grabbed my trousers and pulled a bill from my pocket. It was a twenty. I handed the folded money to him when he retreated with the cart.

"Thank you, Mr. Davis. Let us know if we can be of any further service."

"Thanks. Oh, there is something you can do for us, if you wouldn't mind," I added as an afterthought.

"What would that be, sir?" he wondered.

"We need two toothbrushes and a razor, please. I left ours in the car and I'm too lazy to go get them."

"Of course, sir. I'll see what I can do for you," he said at the door.

"Thanks," I began, then in a low tone, while scrubbing at my chin, "my wife doesn't like my scratchy face, if you know what I mean."

"I certainly do, Mr Davis," he said, matching my near whisper. "I should be able to fix you right up, sir. Anything else I can do."

"No, I think that will help a lot. Thanks."

"You're welcome, sir," he said, closing the door behind himself.

Julie was waiting patiently for me before diving in.

"What a meal. This will be great," she prophesized.

"Food looks good. Wine, my dear?" I asked, brandishing the Merlot.

"Why, yes, please."

The cork had already been loosened. I pulled it out the rest of the way with a pop and filled the two wine glasses, setting one by Julie's plate and one by my own. I re-corked the bottle and set it between us on the left side of the table.

"Here's to romantic settings and you, my dear," I toasted.

She picked up her glass and clinked mine lightly.

"Here's to you, love. You sure do know how to make a woman feel special."

We sipped our wine.

"Julie, it's a lot easier making a woman feel special when she's a special woman."

"Flattery, sir, will get you nearly anything you want. Now let's eat. I'm starved."

FRIDAY

A little after midnight, as we were drinking coffee with our desserts, there was a knock at the door. I answered it and traded our waiter a ten-dollar bill for toothbrushes and a razor. I put our new equipment on the sink in the bathroom before returning to the table. When we finished our meal, I called the desk and asked the clerk to wake us with coffee and a light breakfast at six-thirty. Our hunger for food satisfied, we returned to the bed and tried satisfying another type of hunger. We made love a couple of times during the night, each time better than the last. We napped between sessions. At six-thirty there was a tapping on the door. I felt Julie slip out of bed and heard her exchange trays with the waiter while I played possum. I smelled coffee and heard the shower running a few minutes later. I threw back the covers and sneaked into the bathroom. I quietly opened the shower door and startled Julie when I embraced her from behind.

"Oh, where did you come from, mister? I thought I had locked that door to keep intruders such as you away from my virginal body."

"I can fix that virgin problem for you, my dear," I leered. "But first let's clean up that body of yours really good," I said while lathering her with soap and using myself as a washcloth.

"You are insatiable," she accused.

"Around you, I am."

We were in the shower nearly thirty minutes. Our breakfast of sweet rolls, fresh fruit, juice and coffee was all about room temperature when we finally emerged from the bathroom.

"Only problem with spur-of-the-moment hotel rooms is no deodorant and no fresh clothes," I observed. "We need to make the rounds to our respective abodes before we meet with the bad guys today."

"And no makeup. Not that I need any," she gloated, striking a pose. "Besides, do you think those bad guys would notice that we're a little stinky?"

"Probably not, but I would like a fresh pair of socks. And you're right. You do look fine without makeup. Still, fresh clothes would be nice."

"Then we'd better get a move on, pal, if we're going to my motel and then to your house before ten," she remarked, tugging on her clothes in between bites.

"Relax. I think we have enough time to get freshened up before our date with destiny."

"It's nearly seven-thirty. Don't forget about rush-hour."

"You're right again. I'll get a move on," I said, slipping into my slacks.

While munching on a sweet roll, I sat at the table and pulled on my socks and shoes.

Fifteen minutes later, we were at the front desk checking out.

"How was your stay, Mr and Mrs Davis," asked the clerk as he discretely showed me the bill in exchange for the room key.

"It was wonderful," Julie answered. "The food and service were great. And I loved the atmosphere."

"We had a great night, thank you," I added, handing over the pair of one hundred-dollar notes that I had peeled from the center of my money roll.

"I'm glad you enjoyed yourselves," he said, giving me my change from his cash drawer. "Please come back whenever you're in town. It was a pleasure having you stay with us."

"Thanks, we will," I assured him, stowing the money and picking up the receipt and tucking it into my jacket pocket. "Good-bye, now."

"Good-bye, madam and sir," he said as we turned to leave out the main entrance onto College street.

We went down the steps and into the morning air with our arms around each other's waists. The city was humming with traffic and there was a slight breeze blowing between the buildings. The overcast skies of yesterday had given way to a light drizzle, just enough to be a little chilly, but not enough to make our walk to the car miserable.

"Well, Mr Davis," Julie started, pausing and looking up at me, smiling. "You are Mr Davis, aren't you?"

"Depends on who's asking. But, I'll humor you. Let's say I am Mr Davis. What can I do for you, ma'am?"

"I just wanted you to know that stopping at that last place overnight was a stroke of genius."

"I do have my moments."

"Then I suppose you're genius enough to know where you parked the car?"

"I certainly do. We make a left here on Navarro, like so," I demonstrated as we reached the corner and wheeled left. "Then we go one block north to the next intersection. That's that-a-way," I said, pointing up the street. "Then left again and voila, a large tan Oldsmobile will appear. Hopefully without a ticket on it."

"You shouldn't have one, should you. You fed the meter last night. And there's free parking from six to six, isn't there?"

"Right you are. But it's nearly eight a.m. and I'm sure the cops have been making rounds already. We'll soon know."

"Oh, well, the way you were spending money yesterday, I'd say you can afford a small parking fine. Besides, if everything goes sort of according to plan today, you should be able to buy your own private parking place."

"True. There is a big payout due today, isn't there," I confirmed as we made a left at the corner of Houston and Navarro. "Thar she blows," I announced on seeing the Eighty-Eight a half-block up the street.

"It is indeed a whale of a car. Shall I get the harpoons ready, sir?"

"Are you making fun of my large ride?" I asked, poking her lightly in the ribs.

"Kind of," she yelped, jumping away from me. "With a big payday coming, one might think one would consider an upgrade to something more gasoline friendly."

"Maybe. I'll think about it," I said as she rejoined me. "Meanwhile I like the big ride because it has room for stuff in the trunk and trysts in the front seat. Or back seat for that matter. Those Hondas and Toyotas don't have enough room in them for proper snooping tools or for proper sex."

"What would you know about proper snooping sex tools?" she kidded, making a joke of my argument as we reached the Old's front fender.

"I thought I'd made it clear last night just how much I know about a snooper's proper sex tools," I said, retrieving my keys from my pocket and fitting the right one into the passenger door lock.

"You'll have to refresh my memory. Last night was last night and you're only as good as what's going on right now," she countered as I opened the door for her.

"Is that so? Sounds too Zen-like for me. I'd rather concentrate on what's happening around me at the present time," I said, returning the joke and closing the door behind her.

She laughed as she slid across the seat and pulled up the knob for me. I waited for a car to go by, then stepped into the street and pulled open the driver's door.

"And what's happening right now is that we're off on another adventure on a brand new day," I said, closing the door behind me and bringing the big engine alive with a turn of the key.

"Yes, we are. We're going to my place first, right?"

"Right," I nodded, backing up the Olds until it just kissed the car behind me. "Oops, a little too much there. Sorry, pal," I apologized to the car's absent driver.

"Contrary to popular belief, folks, Dave isn't quite as good getting out as he is getting in."

"I just wanted to see what that car felt like," I explained as I cranked the wheels to the left and eased away from the crime scene. I flicked on the headlights and turned the wipers on low just to clear the accumulating drizzle.

We made it to the freeway without further mishaps and started south on I-35.

"Anything special you want me to wear today?" she asked as we hit the ramp for 90 west.

"You mean aside from the obviously facetious answer of 'Nothing, my dear. Absolutely nothing at all'?"

"Yes, aside from that," she confirmed, smiling at my crude attempt at humor.

"No, nothing special. Something like what you have on right now will be fine. Because after our meeting, I plan on taking you out to lunch somewhere and then back to my place where I'll keep you locked up until it's time for you to fly out of my life."

"Locked up at your house, huh? What for, to make me clean it up?"

"No, dear, as my love slave. I don't want to send you back to the Beltway unsatisfied."

"I could leave right now and be just fine, horny fellow," she informed me.

"I don't want to take any chances that I'll be forgotten any time soon. I know how it can be with all those rich and powerful men around to tempt you."

"What do you know about rich and powerful men?"

"Well, I've heard stories. How they can corrupt an innocent young woman like you."

"You spoiled my innocence last night, rogue," she pointed out. "Or was that early this morning? I get confused."

"See, are you sure it was even me who spoiled you?" I teased.

"I was sleepy, but not that sleepy."

"Was it before or after dinner?"

"Both," she answered as I turned on the right blinker to signal our leaving the freeway for Military Drive.

At the traffic light at the bottom of the ramp, I signaled a left turn. When the light went green, I wheeled the Eighty-Eight under the overpass and through the next light. A right turn put us past Denny's into the La Quinta parking lot. I pulled up in front of Julie's room and killed the engine.

"We've come full circle. It seems like a week since we were here," she observed, getting out of the car on her side. "This shouldn't take long."

She pulled her room key from her front pocket and opened the door. After locking the Olds, I followed her inside where I sat on the edge of the bed, watching her swap clothes. She stripped off her outer clothes. She was only wearing a bra.

"Went commando, did you?" I noted.

"Sure. Didn't you notice that when I was dressing this morning?"

"No, I must have been blinded by your beauty or something?"

"Probably the 'or something'," she said, turning to pose. Besides, that's the way you like me, isn't it? Easy access."

"Absolutely true."

"Then you'll really like what I'm going to wear today."

"I will, huh? What's it going to be? That slinky black dress you had on the other night?" I guessed.

"No, but close," she said, picking out a couple of things from her suitcase on the stand by the bathroom door. "I'll be back in a little bit."

After several minutes, she emerged from the bathroom wearing a black spaghetti-strap blouse and a black mid-thigh skirt. She had two-inch pumps on which helped emphasize her spectacular legs. The blouse disguised her prominently pointy nipples, at least from the front. When she did a spin for me, the disguise was lost. I let out a breath.

"Whew, where did you get that body, baby?"

"You like?"

"Lady, it's going to be hard keeping my mind on the job today knowing you're around."

"Keeping it hard will be good for you, Dave. Consider me the prize you'll get at the end of the day."

"Any chance I could unwrap my presents before we leave?"

"No way, buddy. We have places to go and people to see. So roll up your tongue, et cetera, and tuck them away. We'll use them later."

"Okay, but only if you promise."

"I'll promise you one thing," she said, sitting across from me on a chair she had spun around from the table. "This," she began, crossing her left ankle over her right knee and giving me a view up her skirt. "This will be waiting for you at day's end."

My jaw dropped. No panties, again. It was difficult taking my eyes off what she was offering, but I managed, barely. Even though we had made love all through the night, she could still turn me on at the sight of her. She stood up, terminating the mesmerizing vision I had witnessed.

"Then by all means," I drooled. "Let's get started."

She took my hand and pulled me to my feet. She handed me the key to her room.

"No pockets," she explained. "And I don't want to carry a purse."

"Okay, I'll put it right here, next to Mr Stiffy," I told her, sliding the key into my left pants pocket. "It'll be safe there."

"That's about the only thing that would be," she observed, brushing past me on her way to the door.

She opened it and stepped outside. I shook my head to clear my thoughts and followed her. It was raining a little more earnestly now and the breeze had picked up noticeably. As she slid across the car seat I received another sneak peek. Boy, I thought, you have got to keep your mind on business today. Someone is going to get hurt if you don't. I reminded myself that a couple of days ago I had warned Wilson's son about greasy kid stuff. Now, here I was with only that on my mind. Focus, pal, you must focus. I got into the Eighty-Eight beside her and cranked the engine. It was after eight-thirty when we rounded Denny's going south on Military Drive.

"Wouldn't the freeway be faster?" she wondered.

"Maybe, but it would be longer, distance-wise. If we take it easy, at about the thirty-five mile-per-hour limit, we can make nearly every light from here to Pleasanton Road. We'll pass right by the mall, too. That way we can scope it out beforehand."

We passed by the mall twenty minutes later. The parking lot had a few scattered cars in it with a heavier concentration by the grocery store near the K-Mart end. The grocery opened at six-thirty so people could buy food to take to work and school. We didn't see anyone hanging around that looked out of place. When we reached Escalon, we turned right, went down through the residential streets, and finally ended up in my driveway.

"Looks just like we left it," I noted.

"Yep. Same old scraggly lawn. Bet the maid didn't make it back either," she taunted.

"No bet," I said, shutting off the engine and opening the door.

The rain had stopped for the time being and the breeze was punching small holes in the overcast. After I climbed out, Julie followed by sliding across the seat toward me. Once again I was treated to a heavenly view. When she swung her legs out to stand up, I faked dropping my keys at her feet and then stooped down to retrieve them, giving the scenery an appreciative nod.

"Young man," she scolded. "Are you looking up my skirt?"

"Definitely, ma'am. I wanted to see again one of the most wonderful sights of the modern world."

She touched my chest with the toe of her right foot and gave me just enough of a shove to send me scrambling to regain my balance.

"That should teach you not to be so fresh, peeping Tom," she admonished, standing up beside the car and smoothing down her skirt. "There will be plenty of time for freshness, later."

"I sure hope so," I laughed, finally righting myself and following her up the front steps after closing the car door.

I stepped past her and unlocked the dead bolt and door handle locks. She grabbed a handful of my left butt cheek as I went by.

"My turn to be fresh, sonny."

"Madam, you'll kindly unhand my hiney and wait patiently in the living room while I change," I instructed, stepping over the threshold and pointing to the couch.

"If you insist, sir," she said, releasing her grip on my butt and taking a seat.

I went into the bedroom, selected a pair of charcoal slacks and a clean shirt from the closet. I put on clean socks and briefs before I got dressed. After applying deodorant and donning my shirt, I traded jackets for one that matched what I was wearing and reloaded my pockets. It only took me a few minutes to get dressed. I checked myself in the mirror and returned to the living room for a second opinion.

"You don't look nearly as good as I do, but you do look good enough to eat," she offered with a smile on her face.

"Same to you," I said with a smile and a slow nod.

After locking up, I escorted her back out to the car where I once again was presented the opportunity to marvel at the beauty of human female anatomy. I must have had a dreamy look on my face or something, because Julie kept watching my expression as we drove toward the mall.

"You love looking at my legs and other things, don't you?"

"Yes, I do," I said, glancing down at where her skirt had stopped riding up. "You are put together extremely well, you know. The only thing better than looking at you is touching what I'm looking at."

"You definitely have a one-track mind."

"I know. But I'll tell you a truth. There is nothing I can think of that's better than a fine looking woman."

"Better than Mexican food and beer?"

"Yes, better than that. When I look at you, it's like I'm a desert plant and you're a cooling rain that's finally come to give me moisture. I just can't get enough to drink."

"Gee, you're a poet, too. Stop with that or we'll have to pull over and take care of your freshness right here," she said, giving my right leg a squeeze and leaving her hand to warm my thigh.

"As much as I'd like to do just that, we're only ten minutes away from mall opening time."

"I know. Business first," she acknowledged.

Her hand was still on my leg when we parked in the lot outside the locked entrance to the mall. I turned off the car, opened the door and stepped out.

"Okay, beautiful creature, one more time for us thirsty cacti," I said, holding the door open for her.

She slid across the seat in slow motion this time. I was jealous of the fabric clutching at her rounded bottom. Her skirt slid up nearly to her hips and she took her time putting her feet on the ground outside the car, spreading her knees apart and deliberately gave me an achingly slow exposure shot of her pubic area. Finally she was up on both feet and pulling her skirt down. I looked around to see who else was watching. We were alone in that part of the lot. The show had been just for me.

"You know, I'll be an old man and never forget that. Thanks."

"It was just for you, honey," she pointed out, stepping close to me and giving me a light kiss on the lips. I encircled her waist and pulled her to me, making the kiss last longer and adding some tongue to the action.

"You're welcome," she gasped when our lips finally broke apart. "And now you're going to have to find a pole to beat him against, you know?"

"I don't have to find a pole. It's right here," I said, thrusting toward her.

"Come on, Horny Dave, time to go to work," she laughed, disentangling herself from my grasp.

Reluctantly I released her and busied myself locking the Olds. With it secure, I opened the mall door with my key and let us inside. When we reached the office, Ruth was at her spot and my two heavies were sitting in the chairs opposite her desk, talking with her, coffee cups in their hands. They watched us come in the door and had a hard time looking away from Julie.

"Waiting for us, were you?" I asked.

"Right," they said, simultaneously, their eyes flicking from me back to Julie.

"Okay, here's the drill. Swap places from yesterday. Deets is in here and Sanchez is by the hallway. The bad guys have seen you, Sanchez, so stay out of sight. Julie will occupy the restroom between Bobby's and my office, just like yesterday. Any funny business and Ruth calls the cops. But I don't expect any problems. So, unless it's a real hazard, we just let these guys do their business and walk out of here. This is bigger than a local thing, by the way. The feds are in on it and they don't know about you two," I informed them all, pointing to Sanchez and Deets. "I want you around just in case. You're my personal backup. The feds want these two guys to lead them to their superiors, so don't do anything to spook them unless there's bloodshed, understand? There will be some federal agents in the mall, so just ignore them if you can pick them out. Any questions?"

"No, sounds clear to me," answered Deets.

"None from me," echoed Sanchez.

"How about you, Ruth?"

"Yeah, am I going to get that raise?" she wondered.

"Tell you what. If this goes down without a hitch, you'll all get a raise. And a modest bonus."

"Me, too?" asked Julie.

"Oh, yeah, Julie, you'll definitely get a raise when this is over," I joked, giving her a wink. "So, if there are no other questions, then everybody take their places."

Sanchez left through the outer door and walked up the hall toward the main mall corridor. After unlocking my door, I went with Julie into my office. Deets picked up a magazine and perused it, acting like a travel agency customer.

"Julie, better make sure the bathroom doors are unlocked," I said, going over to the wet bar and setting up a pot of coffee.

Julie left through the bathroom door and returned a few minutes later. The coffee was perking merrily by then.

"All set, boss. Anything else."

"Nope. Boy, you sure did get looks from Deets and Sanchez," I noted.

"Yeah, I noticed. Those two guys could be your brothers the way they look at women."

"You think so? Do I really ogle as much as they did?"

"You're a bit more subtle than they were, but you still look."

"I'll do that until I'm dead, I guess. I just don't want to be too overt about it," I said, remembering Niki's words to me about women.

"Well, I'd like a bit more eye-contact now and then."

"Oh, sorry. I'll do better."

"I'm sure you will," she encouraged.

When the coffeepot was finished gurgling, I poured her a cup and added a spoonful of sugar. Then I poured a cup for myself. After adding sugar and creamer, I hoisted it in a toast.

"Here's to skullduggery. May it always pay well."

She laughed.

"Right. Here's to skullduggery," she returned, touching mugs with me.

We sipped. I glanced at the clock. It was ten-fifteen.

"Time for you to hide, my dear."

"See you in a bit," she said, taking her cup and retreating to the restroom and closing the door.

After she left, I turned the dial on the Mossberg until all of the tumblers but the last one were in place. I also unlocked the drawer in my desk where the Beretta was hiding just to make it more available should I need it.

Ten minutes later the phone rang. I was sitting in my desk chair with a refill of coffee in my hand. I set the mug down on the desk pad and picked up the receiver after the second ring.

"There are two gentlemen to see you, Mr Harris," came Ruth's voice.

"Are they the two guys from yesterday?"

"Yes, sir. Shall I send them in?"

"Yeah, send them in."

My office door opened and in walked the two Libyans. They were dressed pretty much the same as yesterday. Mohammet carried a large, black satchel, the kind that book salesmen tote around. The way he held it I could tell it was heavy. I motioned them into the room and indicated they should take a seat by the coffee table. I stood up, picked up my coffee mug and went over to greet them. They had that same limp handshake and sat in the same places as yesterday, one on the couch and one in the opposite chair. Mohammet set the case down on the floor beside him.

"Good morning, gentlemen. Did you bring the money I asked for?"

"Yes, we did. Do you have the package we want?"

"I do. It's in the safe," I assured them, sitting in the chair I had turned around yesterday and putting my coffee mug on the table. "Let me see the cash."

Mohammet pushed over the satchel with his foot, keeping an eye on me.

"You two don't have to worry about me," I promised. "I'll be in this same office tomorrow. You'll know where to find me if I cheat you. What I don't know is where you'll be tomorrow in case you cheat me. But frankly, I don't care as long as I get what I want."

They relaxed a little and I opened the satchel. Inside the bag were two folded shopping bags. I plucked them out of the satchel and laid them on the coffee table between the two men. Under the bags were packets of used hundred dollar bills, held together with rubber bands. I guessed there were probably a hundred bills per packet. They watched me as I pulled out the bundles and stacked them in four piles on the table beside my mug. I counted twenty-five packets when the bag was empty. I picked up one packet at random and quickly counted the number of bills, riffling the packet to make sure it was all hundreds. Satisfied on the count, I fished out a couple of bills from the center of the bundle. Returning to my desk, I pulled a white sheet of paper from the center drawer and scrubbed the green side of the bills across the white paper. A slight green tint showed up after several passes. The money felt real, it had silk strands running through the paper and the old test of the green ink rubbing off made me take the bait. I folded the bills and stuck them in my trouser pocket.

"Did you think we would give you fake money?" asked Mustafa.

"It occurred to me you might," I admitted, walking back over to where the money was stacked up. "It looks real enough, but it could still be counterfeit."

"It isn't. I told you yesterday that we have enough money to pay for what we want without cheating. Now, where is our book."

"I'll get it right now," I said, scooping the money bundles back into the briefcase and taking it with me around to the safe.

"We don't need the case, just the book," said Mustafa.

"Don't worry, you'll get it. Just as soon as I lock up the money."

I dialed in the last number and pulled the right-hand door open. I glanced down at the CZ sitting on top of the packaged book behind the left door, then hefted up the satchel and set it on the right-hand shelf. I would make a safety deposit box stop later, I thought. When I was done, I extracted the package from under the gun and tucked it under my arm. I had kept the pistol hidden from their view while I made the transfer.

"We need to inspect the merchandise, Mr Harris," stated Mustafa.

"I know. I'll be right there," I said as I closed the Mossberg and spun the combination dial. I tried the handles to make sure the safe was secured. It was.

I returned to my seat near the two men and handed the package to Mustafa.

"Check it out," I invited.

Mustafa tore off the outer paper. Inside was an exact replica of the book I had turned over to Leo on Wednesday. He handed the book to Mohammet. The Libyan thumbed the book open and looked at each drawing and schematic very carefully. He pulled a paper from his pocket and compared some writing on it to a couple of written passages in the blue-bound book. Finally he nodded his head and said something to Mustafa in Arabic.

"It is what we wanted, Mr Harris," Mustafa said, picking up one of the shopping bags from the table and rising to go.

He spoke Arabic to his accomplice who put the book into the other bag, stood up and headed toward the door.

"Good-bye, Mr Harris. Don't try to follow us, please. You have what you want and we have what we want. Our business is finished."

He retreated toward the door that his partner was holding open for him.

"I suppose it is," I said with finality.

He closed the door behind him and I let out a sigh of relief. My coffee was getting cold, so I picked up the mug, drained its contents and set the empty cup down on the corner of my desk. A couple of minutes later, the bathroom door opened quietly and Julie peeked in.

"How did it go?" she asked, coming into the room. "This time, I could barely hear a word."

"It went fine," I told her. "Better than I thought it would. It was nearly too easy."

"Did you get the money?"

"It's in the safe. Do you want to see?" I offered.

"Sure. I've never seen a quarter million dollars before."

I stood up and went over to the safe. A couple of spins on the dial and I pulled open the right door revealing the satchel. Julie came over to my side and reached past me to pluck a bundle from the case.

"Is it real?" she asked, fanning herself with the bills before replacing the bundle.

"Well, it has the right feel and there are silk threads in the paper. It also rubbed green on white paper," I said, retreating back to my desk and holding up the white sheet of paper as evidence.

"Wow!" she exclaimed, running her hand over the money. "This is a lot of dough."

"Want some of it?"

"Maybe later. I don't have any place to put it right now."

"I can see that," I said, eyeing her up and down.

She laughed at my obvious leering.

"Tell you what, I'll save it for you," I promised. "It'll be right here whenever you need it. Just let me know and I'll even send you some."

"Sounds like a good deal to me," she agreed, closing the heavy door and locking my private vault. "So now all we have to do now is wait a bit until those guys get completely clear of the building, then we're home free."

"Well, Julie, I actually think we're home free right now," I said, settling into my swivel chair. "But we'll wait a little while longer before we leave. Then in, oh, about an hour or so, I'm going to call Leo's office and see how things went."

"Do you think he'll know anything by then?"

"He'll probably know something. In the mean time, you could come over here and sit on my lap and we can discuss whatever comes up," I joked.

"Yes, I could," she agreed, taking hold of my right knee and slowly spinning me around to face my desk. Then she stepped past me and hopped up to sit squarely on my desk pad facing me. She put a foot on either armrest of my chair and said, "How's this?"

I couldn't believe my eyes. I was looking right down her skirt at the place I'd been admiring all morning. Funny thing was, it looked like she had grown more pubic hair than the last time I had had the same view. I looked up at her face. It was blurry. I rubbed my eyes and my arms suddenly felt very heavy.

"Shit," I drawled drunkenly. "I think they drugged me or something. The coffee. They must have put something in my coffee."

"Oh, damn," I heard Julie say, and she disappeared from view.

I heard running feet and muffled noises. Just before I blacked out I had the thought that I was going to die. And I kept wondering if, when I woke up on the other side of life, I'd be seeing angels or devils.

I was either dead or dreaming. I could see a bright light in the darkness. It was getting bigger in diameter. I vaguely wondered if it was the train in the tunnel coming straight at me or a preview of heaven or the bright lights of hell. I thought again about angels or devils, then had a vision of a big festival and girl angels in frilly white dresses with wings flapping, dancing with red boy devils who waved pitch forks and had pointy tails swinging in time to the music. It was the kind of dream I get when I eat too much pepperoni pizza. The pizza thought had me seeing red devils again, then angels shooing them away. Then I heard a slow, regular dinging sound. Another angel came into view. She had blonde hair and a pretty face. There was a luminous radiance around and through her whole body. She was holding a shiny metal triangle dangling from a golden string with her left hand and slowly striking a metal rod against it with her right. Just as I was getting used to the ding-dinging sound, she sped up the pace until the noisy clanging was nearly doubled. A devil appeared and grabbed the rod from her. The red apparition stuck the rod on the inside of the triangle and began making a loop of noise like an angry dinner bell. Clang, clang, clang it went, faster and faster. The devil's motion was now so fast that the individual clangs merged into a steady tone. Bells began ringing. There were angels and devils running around everywhere with their hands up to their ears in an attempt to block out the noise.

The vision disappeared as quickly as it had developed but the noisy din continued. I became aware that I was lying on a bed with something shooting air into my nose. I took a deep breath and my foggy brain began clearing. The noises were right next to me. Or, rather, in the room with me. I heard running feet coming nearer and groggily propped myself up on an elbow to see what was going on around me. I was in a hospital bed. My recovery from Leo's gunshot flashed through my mind. Same two-tone walls, white on the top half and sea-foam green on the bottom. I briefly thought that they should get a decorator with more imagination.

The door to the room was on the left just past the foot of my bed. Across the room from where I lay was a sink with a mirror hanging above it and the long door of a cabinet built into the wall. I surveyed myself and noted that the air shooting into my nose came from the plastic tubing of the nasal cannula that I was wearing like a bolo tie. I also had an IV catheter taped to my left arm that was attached to tubing running through a pump on a pole next to the bed. Satisfied that I was okay and getting better, I turned my attention to the beeping noises coming from the other side of the curtain that hung a few steps away on my right and partitioned my bed off from the rest of the room. It was the same sea green color. My tax dollars at work.

Suddenly several people, two women and three men in varying hospital attire, rushed into the room through the door and bustled around the curtain. Whoever was on the other side of the curtain was in trouble, judging by the alarms going off and everyone's hurried movements. Then a woman in a white uniform came through the door and wheeled a large rolling toolbox past the end of my bed and around the curtain.

"It's asystole. Is there a pulse?" a male voice asked.

"No pulse," came the answer from one of the females.

"Get the backboard under him and begin CPR," ordered the same male voice. "Get the bag out and give him fifteen liters. And warm up the defibrillator. Start with two hundred joules."

There was some movement beyond the curtain, then the whooshing of air and the creaking of bedsprings like someone slowly jumping up and down on the mattress.

"Give him an amp of epinephrine."

"What's going on over there?" I croaked, rather loudly.

"Who's that?" the voice asked.

"That's Mr. Harris. He's a GHB poisoning that we're holding until he comes around."

"Sounds like he's around. Nurse, get him out of here," demanded the obvious leader of the mob next door.

The white-uniformed person that had been pushing the toolbox came around the curtain and began lowering the bed rails.

"Mr. Harris, I need to move you to another room," she said over the commotion next door.

"What's going on? Is someone dying?" I wondered.

"Maybe. We're working on him," she added, helping me stand up and gently pulling the nasal cannula from its perch on my face.

I was in one of those flattering hospital gowns with the gap in the back. At this point I really didn't care who saw my butt. The nurse unplugged the IV pump and with it in one hand and my arm in the other, ushered me out of the room. Just as we cleared the door I heard the boss next door yell "Clear" and the sound of electrical discharge that was trying to restart the guy-next-door's motor. I looked over my shoulder and saw his legs stiffen with the jolt.

"Who's the guy and where am I?" I asked as the nurse escorted me down the hall to another room. This one had two empty beds. She parked me on the one by the door after she turned the covers down.

"You're in Wilford Hall, seventh floor, and the guy in the room with you is Robert Garcia."

"Robert Garcia?" I stammered, mouth gaping. "Are you sure?"

"Of course I'm sure. He had a heart attack last Sunday and heart surgery on Monday. He was recovering nicely until today."

I was still dumbfounded.

"What day is it?"

"It's Friday afternoon," she answered in a tone that indicated she thought I was probably demented. She consulted her watch anticipating my next question. "It's just a few minutes after three p.m."

"What happened to me? I heard you say GHB. What's that?" I continued the questioning.

"Someone poisoned you with GHB, a sort of knock-out drug. It caused your unconsciousness. You were brought in by ambulance, stabilized and sent up here until you came around. Since you're better, I'll tell your doctor and he can fill in the gaps. Now, I need to get back to Mr. Garcia's room."

"Wait. Did anyone, a woman, say, come to the hospital with me?"

"I don't know. You haven't had any visitors since you've been up here on this floor. Now, I really must go."

"What about this?" I asked, holding my left arm up and pointing to the IV.

"I'll take that out as soon as the doctor says it's okay for you to be discharged," she said at the doorway.

"How about my clothes?" I called to her retreating back.

"I'll bring them to you in a little bit," came her answer from the hallway.

I lay back in the bed, my mind swirling with questions. So Garcia wasn't missing after all. Had Leo known where he had been all the time? If so, then Leo had been playing me the whole time. I really wasn't surprised by that possibility, just a little miffed. Assuming I had been set up, the question was by whom? Wilson had set me onto Garcia. Or rather, his maid had started the ball rolling. What part did she play in the whole charade? It could be that she and Wilson were legit and I had just stumbled into a set-up by Leo and his spies. I wondered what would have happened had I not found that book in the freezer and the attic or had not taken it to Leo? One other thing, he seemed in control of the situation from the start, not really like someone that had been blind-sided. I was confused about who was involved with what. And I missed Julie. She had been by my side for nearly three days and I was getting used to having her there. I was thinking of her when I fell asleep.

I awoke to a hand gently shaking my shoulder. It was the same nurse in white that had moved me down the hall. With her was a man in a white lab coat.

"Mr Harris, this is Doctor Carter," she introduced me to the man beside her and then turned and left the room.

"You mean, like the little liver pills."

"That's an old joke, Mr Harris. How are you feeling?"

"Good enough to make dumb jokes, doctor. How do you think I'm doing?"

"Pretty good, considering your were probably given a dose of GHB that was potent enough to put down a small horse."

"GHB. Yeah, the nurse mentioned that someone poisoned me with it. What exactly is the stuff?"

"It's gamma-hydroxybutyrate, street name Scoop. It's an odorless, tasteless, colorless, non-lethal concoction that is used primarily as a date-rape drug. I understand you became unconscious after you drank some coffee laced with it. There were traces of it found in the residue in your cup. It could've knocked you out for a day or so, depending on the amount. You metabolized it pretty quickly. We didn't have to do anything drastic to detox you except to guard your airway and wait for you to come around. I'd say you were pretty lucky that you had someone nearby when you passed out so an ambulance could be called."

"Were they trying to kill me?"

"I don't think so. The effects of GHB usually subside completely once the general effect of unconsciousness wears off."

"Good. When do you think I can be discharged from the hospital?" I asked, anxious to get out of the place.

"Well, medically, I'd say you could leave anytime. But you'll have to stick around until you're cleared from this floor by security."

"Cleared by security? What floor am I on?"

"You're on the seventh floor. The high-security wing. You can't get out of here until you're cleared."

"Fine. How long will that take?"

"I don't know. Sometime later this afternoon I suspect. I'll go write your discharge orders pending your clearance by security. That way you'll be free to go as soon as you're cleared. Does that sound okay to you?"

"Thanks, doc, that sounds fine to me," I said as the doctor went for the door. "Say, Doctor, what happened to my roommate, Robert Garcia?"

"Was he a friend of yours?"

"No, actually. I know his fiancé," I said, establishing a sideways connection so he would tell me how Garcia was doing.

"Well, he died this afternoon."

"What of?"

"His heart stopped and we couldn't revive him."

Great, I thought, bad news for Dallas. And just wait until I get hold of Leo.

Five minutes later the nurse came back into the room holding a blood pressure cuff. She also had a stethoscope draped around her neck.

"Mr Harris, I need to take your blood pressure and then take out your IV."

"Okay," I said, holding my right arm out for the cuff.

She took the measurement and switched arms. After stopping the pump and pulling the IV out, she pressed a piece of square cotton over where the fluid had been running into me and taped it in place.

"If this bleeds, just put some pressure on it until it stops."

"Thanks, nurse. Come back anytime. Can I get dressed now?"

"Yes. I put your clothes in the cabinet over there," she informed me, pointing to a locker-sized cabinet door in the wall opposite my bed. "I'll bring you some toilet articles so you can freshen up if you want."

"Thanks, I need to. My mouth tastes like hell."

"I'm sure it does. I'll put the stuff by the sink," she said, leaving me to dress.

I sat up on the side of the bed and waited until my head stopped spinning a bit before gingerly walking over and opening the cabinet. My clothes, including my socks and shoes, were neatly placed inside. The jacket and shirt were hanging on one hanger, my slacks on another. I retrieved my belongings and took them over to the bed. I pulled the dividing curtain around the track in the ceiling and dressed. My pockets hadn't been stripped of their contents, for which I found some solace. At least I could pay for a cab if I needed to. I had just finished pulling on my shoes when I heard a voice on the other side of the curtain.

"Mr. Harris?"

"Yes."

"Mr. Harris, I'm Sergeant Brooks. I'm in charge of the security detail on this floor."

"That's nice," I said pulling the curtain back and revealing a uniformed security policeman about my height and weight standing just on the other side. "When can I go, Sergeant Brooks?"

"Right now, Mr. Harris. Major Ramirez told me to escort you out as soon as the doctor cleared you."

"Major Ramirez, eh? Any other instructions from the major?" I asked, a bit of hostility in my voice.

Brooks ignored my irritated tone.

"He only told me to escort you out, to tell you to call him tomorrow at his office, and to give you this envelope," he said, holding out a plain white envelope with lumps in it.

"What's in it?"

"I don't know. I'm just supposed to give it to you and see you out."

"Let me brush my teeth first, okay?" I said taking the envelope and shoving it into my right pants pocket. Without waiting for an answer, I walked past him to the sink. The nurse must have delivered the toilet articles she had promised while I was dressing. There was packaged soap, a plastic-wrapped toothbrush and a tube of unopened toothpaste lying just where she said they would be. I pealed the plastic wrapper from the toothbrush sitting on the counter and lubed it up with paste. After swabbing away any lurking oral critters, I rinsed, spat, dried off my mouth and moustache and turned to the sergeant.

"Now I'm ready," I announced, heading out of the room.

He followed me out the door. When I stopped in the hallway to determine which way to go, he tapped me on the shoulder.

"This way," he said, starting down the hall to the right.

I followed him to a bank of elevators. He produced a key from his trouser pocket and fitted it into the slot by the elevator door. He turned the key and pressed the down button next to the lock. In less than twenty seconds, the elevator doors opened and he ushered me into the box. The key went back into a lock on the panel inside the car. Another turn of the key and push of a button and we were descending.

On the way down, I pulled the envelope from my pocket and felt its bumpy contents more closely. It felt like keys. I ripped open the end and dumped the treasure into my right hand. Keys, all right. Mine. The whole set I had put into my pockets this morning. I stuffed the empty envelope into my jacket pocket and stared at the keys for a second or two.

"You said Major Ramirez gave you these?" I asked, dangling the ring in the air between us.

"Yes, sir," he confirmed without elaboration.

"Did he tell you where he got them?"

"No, sir."

"Was there anyone with me when I came into the emergency room today?" I asked as the elevator settled to a stop.

"I don't know, sir. I was just told to…"

"I know," I said, cutting him off. "Your job is see me out, have me call the major and give me the envelope."

"Yes, sir," he agreed, stepping from the car as the doors opened.

I followed him down a hallway into the hospital's lobby. I walked beside him as he went over to a window looking out onto the parking lot.

"The major also said I should tell you that 'your Yank tank is parked in the third row'," he quoted, pointing toward the lot.

"Thanks, sergeant," I said, fingering my keys and turning toward the glass lobby doors.

"Sure, sir," he said without emotion and retreated the way we had come.

At least the rain had stopped completely, I thought as I stepped out of the hospital. The gray skies of earlier had broken a little and there was blue sky peeking through.

It didn't take long to locate the big car's tail end. Who could miss it? The thing clearly took up the full width of the parking space it was in. I unlocked the driver's door, slid under the wheel and inserted the key without turning over the ignition.

"So, David Andrew Harris, what are you going to do now?" I wondered aloud. 'I'm not sure' was my mental answer. What did I know about this weird case? Let's see, I mused. Garcia stole a book of secrets. Fact, because I found half of it in his freezer and half of it in his attic. Had it been planted there for me to find? Maybe. Some out-of-towners who lived over the back fence had made a deal with Garcia to buy the book and had followed me when I visited Garcia's house. But Garcia had suffered a heart attack, was hospitalized and died before he could collect. I had turned the book over to the OSI, gotten it back from the OSI and sold it to the bad guys. The bad guys drugged me and took off with the book. To where? They were being tailed by OSI and other agents, according to Leo. What if they weren't? Where would they be right now, six hours after knocking me out? Time to call Leo for some answers. But first I wanted to check on Julie's whereabouts. Afterwards I could call my office and Leo's from Julie's motel room. I turned the key in the ignition and the V-8 came to life. After backing out and carefully winding my way through the parking lot, I followed Burquist out to Military Drive.

Wilford Hall is the Air Force hospital complex right next to Lackland Air Base. The La Quinta Inn was just down Military Drive from the hospital in the direction of the Fox. A few minutes later I pulled into a parking space outside Julie's room. I put the car in park, switched off the motor, and opened the door. Before exiting the car, I took a deep breath. I walked up to number 114 and knocked loudly on the door. I breathed a long sigh when the door opened. A middle-aged woman stood in the doorway.

"Can I help you?"

My how you've changed, Julie, I thought.

"When did you check in?" I finally managed to ask.

"This afternoon about three o'clock. Why?"

"Oh, just wondering," I said, recovering from my slight shock. "I had a friend staying here and I guess she checked out."

"I guess so. No one's here but Horace and me," she confirmed, nodding her head toward the interior of the room. I could just see a gray-haired man about the woman's age lounging on the bed. The television was blaring a news show.

"Sorry to bother you. I'll check at the desk. Thanks."

"You're welcome. Good luck," she offered as she closed the door softly.

I drove the Olds back to the lobby area, parking under the portico. I didn't lock it when I went inside the lobby. There was a man about my age behind the counter. He looked up as I approached.

"May I help you, sir?"

"Hi. My name is Dave Harris. I'm a friend of Julie Newton's who was staying in room 114. Did she check out?"

"Just a moment while I check," he said looking down at some paperwork.

"Oh, yes, Miss Newton. She checked out today around noon. Well, she didn't. She had a friend check her out."

"A friend?" I asked suspiciously. "What did this friend look like?"

"He was a tall Mexican gentleman. Nice looking, as I recall. Big, like a wrestler or weight-lifter."

"Was his name Leo Ramirez?" I guessed after hearing the clerk's brief description.

"It could have been. Why do you ask?"

"Well, I was supposed to take Miss Newton out to dinner tonight and now it looks like I've lost track of her."

"Sorry, sir, but she checked out," he said with finality.

"Do you know where she might have gone? Maybe there's a forwarding address."

"No, sir, no forwarding address or messages," he said while thumbing though some more papers.

"Right. Say, mind if I use your phone for a couple of local calls. It won't take me a minute."

"Sure. Here you go," he said, setting a yellow phone up on the counter beside my elbow. "Just try to limit the calls to a couple of minutes each, okay? That's our business line."

"No problem," I assured him as I picked up the receiver and dialed my office. It was just four-thirty and Ruth picked up on the second ring.

"Good Afternoon. Nelms Travel Agency, Harris Investigations," she said.

"Ruth, it's me, Dave," I told her.

"God, Dave, are you all right?" she gushed into the phone. "We were worried sick when they took you out of here. What happened? Where are you?"

"I'm okay. I just left Wilford Hall. I'm calling from the La Quinta where Julie was staying. What happened was the two Arab-looking guys poisoned me with some street drug to incapacitate me while they made their getaway. Right now I'm fine."

"Whew, I'm glad to hear it."

"Ruth, what happened when the guys left?"

"Let's see. Your girlfriend came running out of your office and had me call for an ambulance. Then she went back in to see if you were okay. She waited for the ambulance and then left after they took you to the hospital."

"Do you know where she is now?"

"No, she didn't come back. And your Olds is gone. I thought maybe she took it and followed the ambulance to the hospital. So she's not there with you now?"

"No, I haven't seen her. And she's checked out of the motel. I have the car. Leo left the keys with one of the security people at the hospital."

"So now what? Is your business with the Arabs over?"

"I don't think so. I'm not sure. No one has been back to my office, then?"

"No, I locked the door after the ambulance and your girlfriend left," she confirmed.

That meant the money was still in my safe. Good.

"Is Bobby still there?"

"Yes, do you want to talk with her?"

"Please."

"Hold on and I'll transfer you."

"Hey, big boy, how the hell are you doing and what the hell have you been up to?" Bobby asked as soon as we were connected.

"Oh, just the usual, Bob. I made a deal with some bad guys, delivered the merchandise, got paid, got poisoned, landed in Wilford Hall and then got better. Now I'm a little pissed off at them for drugging me, so I'm going to raid their lair for maybe a little payback and I need your help."

"What kind of help?"

"I need a driver. There's just a little danger involved, I believe."

"A little danger, huh? Little, like the last caper?"

"About the same, maybe less, since we're in the U.S. And the bad guys aren't likely to be missed by anyone if we need to get rough."

"Rough? Does that mean I get to carry a gun?"

"Maybe. I just need you to drive and provide backup."

"How long will this take. I have a date at eight o'clock."

"That's okay, Bobby. We should be back at the mall in time for your date. Anyone I know?"

"Maybe, but it's none of your beeswax."

"All right. So how about I pick you up in thirty minutes. That'll give us a couple of hours to play with Garcia's pals before I have to return you to romance."

"Okay. See you in thirty. Bye"

"Wait," I shouted into the receiver.

"What?" she said after a second.

"I forgot a couple of things. First is, have you seen my girlfriend, Julie? She checked out of the motel and I have no idea where she is."

"Sorry, guy. I haven't seen or heard from her since Ruth said she left following the ambulance. Sounds like you need a sitter or something."

"Very funny."

"What's the second thing?"

"I need Leo Ramirez's number from my flip file."

"Sure. Hold on a minute and I'll get it," she said and then clunked the phone down on her desk.

In a couple of minutes she was back on the line.

"Okay, Dave, here it is," she said, reading me off the number.

"Thanks, Bobby. I'll see you in thirty."

"Okay. Bye for sure this time."

"For sure. Bye, Bobby" I said, pushing down the button on the phone.

I pulled my finger up, heard the dial tone and dialed Leo's office. I just hoped it wasn't too late in the day that I'd missed them. Military hours are usually from seven-thirty to four-thirty. This time it took four rings before the receiver was lifted off its cradle.

"Major Ramirez's office, Sergeant Acres speaking," said the familiar voice.

"Hi, Sergeant Acres. This is Dave Harris. Is the major around?"

"Er, no, Mr. Harris. He's not available right now. Can I take a message for him?"

"Two things. Can you get in touch with him?"

"I can try, but not likely. What's this all about?"

"Find him, please. Tell him I think I know what he's out looking for and I may know just where to find it. If it's where I think it is, I'll bring it to him. So, he needs to hustle back from wherever he is. Tell him the villains are getting away."

"Sounds mysterious. What's the second thing?"

"Have you seen Julie Newton? She's sort of missing in action."

"No, I haven't. I thought she was hanging out with you."

"She was, but I seem to have lost her about six hours ago and don't know where she is."

"More mystery. If for some reason I see her, I'll tell her you're looking for her. Any special message for her?"

"No just for Leo. Just tell him what I said and we need to talk."

"Where can I reach you, if I can contact him?"

"I'll be on the move and calling back in a little while. Okay? It'd be better if he's there when I call back. Understand?"

"Sure. I'll get the message to him," she assured me. And then just before hanging up she added, "Somehow."

"I heard that. Do your best. Talk with you later," and the line went dead.

I placed the receiver onto the cradle, my mind racing. Weirder and weirder, I thought. It seemed strange when I woke up at the hospital and Julie wasn't there. Now she had left her motel early. I was beginning to smell a rat and the rat's name was Leo.

"Thanks for the phone," I said finally, focusing on the clerk's face.

"You're welcome, sir," he said flatly, retrieving the phone. "Good hunting," he added as I retreated toward the lobby door.

I think the young fellow had been eavesdropping. I didn't care at that point. I saddled up the Olds and drove quickly south on Military Drive in order to keep my date with Bobby. In the process, I pinked a few lights and caused more than one fellow driver to salute me in the traditional way one does to drivers without manners. I arrived at the mall after about thirty-five minutes and pulled the Olds into a parking slot that was as close to the Chevy van as I could get. The bad guys knew the Olds, so we would take the Chevy, instead. I unlocked the mall entrance by my office and found Bobby sitting in the waiting room opposite Ruth. She was examining her watch when I came in.

"Close, pal," she noted, tapping her watch face.

"Sorry, Bob. It took a little longer with afternoon traffic. You haven't heard from Julie or Leo have you?" I asked both of them together.

"No," they chimed.

Then Bobby added, "When did she check out of the motel?"

"About noon, according to the clerk. But not by her, by Leo."

"That's funny. What's she got to do with Leo? Did she know him when she was here before?"

"I don't know, but I'm beginning to think it."

"So where do we go from here?" she wondered, getting to her feet.

"Right now we go into my office, get some protection and then we're off to Garcia's neighborhood," I stated, finding my office door key on the ring in my hand. "We're going to use the van because I don't think the bad guys have made it yet."

I unlocked the door and led the way into my office. To check on the money and retrieve the CZ, I unlocked the Mossberg while Bobby looked on. I pulled back one of the satchel flaps. The money was still there, just as I had left it. I shielded it from her view with my body. I picked up the Czech pistol and holster and set them on my desk. Then I opened my top right desk drawer, pulled out my lock pick case and the Beretta and placed them next to the CZ. I had left both weapons with rounds up in the chamber ready to fire. I wanted to be as ready as possible. After I secured the safe doors, I shrugged out of my coat and pulled on the shoulder holster rig for the CZ 75. I dropped the pick case in my coat's left inside pocket and handed the Beretta to Bobby.

"Bobby, there's a round in the chamber. All you have to do is pull the trigger. So, be careful with it," I warned.

"I will," she assured me, taking the gun. "Where should I carry it?"

"Got a purse?"

"Sure. In my office."

"Well, get it. You can put it in there. Remember, backup only. Okay?"

"Right, backup only," she repeated as she went though the bathroom door to her office.

While she was gone, I called Leo's office. Still no news about Leo. Next, I got Garcia's file from the cabinet and looked up his fiancé's number. While I was in the file, I wrote down Garcia's address on a slip of paper from my desk drawer. Then I called Dallas. The phone was picked up after the third ring.

"Good afternoon, this is Mr. Fitch."

"Hi, Mr. Fitch, this is Dave Harris, from San Antonio. Is Maria Garza there? I need to talk with her, please."

"Of course, Mr. Harris. Please hold."

I waited on hold long enough for Bobby to return with her purse.

"How's this?" she asked, modeling the clutch handbag she had brought back with her. The pistol inside her bag was unnoticeable.

"Fine," I said, covering the mouthpiece. "I'm on the phone to Dallas and they put me on hold."

"Okay," she said as she made herself comfortable on the couch.

Another thirty seconds of waiting and the line came alive.

"Good afternoon, Mr. Harris, this is Daniel Wilson," came Daddy Wilson's voice on the line. "What can I do for you?"

"Well, hello, Mr. Wilson. I didn't mean to disturb you. I needed to talk with Ms. Garza about Robert Garcia."

"Ms. Garza isn't here this afternoon. I can convey a message for her if you would like me to."

"Okay, but I have some bad news that I'd rather tell her myself."

"Trust me, Mr. Harris, I'm pretty good at delivering bad news," he promised.

"All right, here goes. Robert Garcia died this afternoon of a heart attack."

There was a moment's silence on the other end while it sunk in.

"A heart attack, you say?"

"Yes sir, a heart attack. The reason he didn't call her was that he was hospitalized with a heart attack last Sunday. On Monday, I believe it was, he underwent bypass surgery and was in an ICU. The surgery apparently didn't take because he had another one today and they couldn't save him."

"That's very unfortunate. I'm sure Ms. Garza will be devastated."

"Yeah, well, sorry to be the bearer of such sad news. And sorry you'll have to be the one to tell her."

"It's okay, Mr. Harris. I'll tell her."

"Oh, and since the investigation was not really an investigation, where should I send your refund?"

"No refund necessary. You did what we asked. It just didn't turn out well."

"That's okay with me if it's okay with you, Mr. Wilson."

"It is okay with me. Thanks for calling, even if it was to report Mr. Garcia's death."

"You're welcome, Mr. Wilson. Glad to be of service, even if the outcome wasn't a happy one." Then as I watched Bobby tap her watch face, I added, "I have to go now, but please let me know if I can be of further service."

"I will, Mr. Harris. Good-bye."

"Good-bye," I said and returned the receiver to its cradle.

"Well, that went well, huh?" Bobby commented at my solemn expression.

"Yeah, just swell," I said, folding up Garcia's file and putting it into the bottom drawer of the filing cabinet.

"Dead letter file?" Bobby teased.

"Sort of," I answered, pulling on my jacket and moving toward the door. "Let's roll out of here."

She followed behind me. Ruth looked up at us as we came through my door.

"Ruth, I'll have her back before eight o'clock. If we're not back by then, call the police and have them go to this address out by Medina Base," I instructed, handing her the piece of paper with Garcia's address. "Tell them you think the house has drugs and dealers in it. Then, call Leo Ramirez's office and give them the address, too. Any questions?"

"Yeah. Will you two be in any danger?"

"Nothing we can't handle ourselves. I only want the cops involved if they need to be. Otherwise, having them around just complicates things. And I'm not sure if there will be anyone at the house, anyway. It's just a precaution. Anything else?"

"Nope," she confirmed. "I've got it. Good luck."

"Okay, see you before eight," I said, holding the door open for Bobby.

On the way out of the mall, I handed Bobby the keys to the van.

"You can drive that thing, right?"

"Of course," she said, snatching the keys from my grasp as we stepped out in the evening air. "First thing I ever drove was a tractor on my grandfather's farm south of Dallas. Besides, I've driven your TR-3 plenty of times, remember?"

"Yeah, I remember. I also remember a crunch or two in the old Triumph's trannie."

"That was just your teeth gnashing with jealousy of my driving skills."

"Right," I snorted as she split away from me on her way to the van's left front door. "We'll be using your skills tonight if we find culprits at Garcia's"

She unlocked the driver's door, hopped in, set her loaded purse on the floor between the seats and finally leaned across to pop up the lock on my side. I opened the door and got in, making sure to fasten my seat belt with a flourish she couldn't miss.

"Are you that unsure of my driving or are you just scared?" she wondered as she fit the key into the ignition and turned over the starter.

"Both," I answered. "I just wanted to make sure nothing happened to me before we get to the west side."

"Oh, I'll get you there in one piece, alright," she said as she found reverse gear and backed the van from its mooring place.

She handled the Chevy without any problems.

"Now tell me, just what is your plan when we get there?" she asked after we had gone up the I-35 on-ramp and successfully merged into the evening traffic.

"Maybe I'd better fill you in on the background a little."

"Maybe you should. First, though, tell me where we're going."

"We're taking I-35 to 410, then northwest toward Highway 90. We'll get off at the Medina Base Road exit. Got it?"

"Sure. Now tell me a story."

"I'll make it sort of short."

"Okay, short is good if this is one of your longer stories."

"Funny. Anyway, Tuesday, while dropping off Wilson in Dallas, his father asks me to do a favor for one of his employees."

"What kind of favor?"

"Find out what happened to her fiancé who happens to work at the nuke farm at Kelly. Seems he's been missing and she's worried. I go to his house on the west end, get inside, see it's been tossed, snoop around and locate a package in the fridge that the first searchers had missed."

"What's in it?"

"I'm getting to that."

"Okay."

"I bring the package back to my office, discover it's a classified tear-down manual for a nuclear weapon and take it to Leo Ramirez. He says thanks, he'll deal with it and I'm on my way. That night I run into Julie at the Fox and we spend the night at her motel. Yesterday, two guys show up at our office. They say they tailed me from Garcia's and want the book back. I make a deal with them and after they leave call Leo with the news. He tells me I retrieved only about half of the book from Garcia's; that there's another half that's missing."

"You didn't know that before then, huh?"

"Right. So Julie and I rush out to the van and follow the bad guys to Lackland and then to the west side. Turns out they're in the house just over the back fence from Garcia's."

"That's how they knew who to follow, right?"

"Right again. In the driveway of their house is a brown Chevy van. I figure they're keeping tabs on Garcia and that's where they've taken my missing man, hoping to get the book from him without using cash."

"You mean, torture."

"Exactly. But I need the rest of the book to make the deal work. Leo wants me to be the bait so he can follow the guys to their leaders, but the back half of the book is missing. Well, without Garcia to tell me where it is, I need to re-search his house. So, Julie and I play like plumbers and go back in. It takes us a couple of hours but we finally find the last twenty or so pages in a paper bag in the attic under the rock wool insulation."

"Pretty clever of Garcia. Sort of a back up plan for a possible double cross, eh? So where's Garcia?"

"At that point I don't have a clue. We take the back half of the book to Leo. He tells us to go somewhere for a while so he can get the book together for exchanging. We eat at Mamacita's and return that afternoon for the whole edition. Then we store it back in my office safe. Since I had promised Julie a slice of Kangaroo Court cheesecake, we head to the River Walk. While we're there I get a bright idea and we spend the night out of harm's way down at La Mansion. This morning we finish the transaction."

"La Mansion. Geez, you never took me there."

"Oh, sorry. We could go there tonight if you call off your date."

"Sorry, buddy, but knowing you, the room is probably still a wreck."

"We could rent another," I leered across from her.

She laughed at my ungentlemanly behavior.

"You'll never change, will you, Dave? Still horny as ever."

"It's the town, you know, Bobby. Charged up with GI's and salsa."

"So, back to the short version," she started. "Where's Garcia?"

"Well, I didn't find out anything about him until today. Which is suspicious. Leo didn't seem to know or want to know anything about him, it seems. Like he already knew. Which is what I suspect. While I was in the hospital, the guy in the room with me had a heart attack and died."

"Wait, let me guess. The guy was Garcia," she stated.

"Wow, you are good."

"Not really. For you to mention some guy in the hospital, who else could it have been?"

"Right. Then I had to call Wilson to let him know the bad news."

"Oh, no. A funeral instead of a wedding. How morbid."

"Yeah, I know. Kind of sad. Anyway, after the doctor makes sure I'm alright, a security policeman gives me an envelope with my keys in it and then shoos me out of Wilford Hall."

"Who took the keys to the hospital? Julie?"

"Julie, probably. But then I found out that Leo had checked Julie out from the motel. Makes it seem like they're in cahoots or something."

"Yeah, you'd think your true love would have stayed behind to make sure you were okay. Kind of funny, don't you think?"

"It is funny, isn't it."

"So, anyway, what's your plan once we get to Garcia's neighborhood?"

"Well," I started, refocusing on the job at hand. "Since I don't know where anyone is right now, that's why I need to go back to the houses to check for connections that I might have missed. We'll drive by the front of the bad guys' house to recon vehicles. If the house looks empty, we pull up and I check it out through the front. If there are cars there, we'll circle the block and you drop me off at Garcia's. Since they have the book they probably won't be watching his place anymore. While I'm tackling their house from Garcia's side, you continue on around the block and park at the top of the street facing the house. If you hear or see anything, come on down to the house. If any cars leave, follow them as best you can."

"That'll leave you stranded, won't it?"

"I'll probably have a blown cover by then. They'll be running because I flushed them out. If I don't meet up with you somewhere out in front of their house that means I probably can't. It would be better if you followed them than if you came to my rescue. Besides, we have Ruth as the backup plan. Anyway, nothing can happen to me, right? I'm armed and dangerous, remember?"

"I believe the last part of that statement."

My explanation had taken long enough for us to have just passed the sign that informed us the Medina Base exit was one mile ahead.

"When you get off 410, use the U-turn lane and go under the freeway heading back the way we came. Garcia's and the bad guys' streets are right over there," I explained, pointing to the large neighborhood area on the other side of the freeway to our left.

"Okay. I understand. How far from the U-turn lane is the street I turn on?"

"The distance is just a couple of blocks. It's the first street on the right after the underpass. Lake Valley is the name of the street."

"Okay," she nodded, easing the van down the exit ramp and slowing for the sharp curve under the freeway.

We paused on the other side as a car went by, then Bobby accelerated a little so the van was just rolling as we turned right down Bad Guy Lane. We crossed the intersection with Sun Valley and in a minute the house Julie and I had seen yesterday came into view. The brown van was still in the driveway, but now it was parked backwards just inside the open garage door on the right. As Bobby eased past the front of the house, I noticed the van's back doors were open inside the garage, effectively blocking our view. There was also something hanging down inside the van that kept us from seeing though it into the garage. In the driveway next to the van was a large two-axle utility trailer.

"That trailer wasn't there yesterday," I observed, looking at Bobby after we had passed by the house and neared the corner.

"What do you think they're doing?" she wondered, stopping our ride at the corner before turning right.

"I don't know, but since they're home, plan B is in effect. Drop me off at Garcia's and wait for me to signal or them to run."

"Or a gun shot or lightening or something, right?" she asked, wheeling the van around the half block to Garcia's.

"Right, but less dramatic."

"Less dramatic. I'll remember that."

We made a right onto Garcia's street and she slowed to stop where I told her to, next to Garcia's driveway.

"See you in a few," I said encouragingly as I dismounted the van and closed the door.

"See you," she said, then accelerated up the street.

I walked up the driveway to the back gate under the carport keeping my pace leisurely, like I belonged there. All my senses were on high alert. There were two people casually walking up the street the way we had just come. Their gait indicated a decided lack of interest in me. I heard the traffic on 410 and some kids playing and laughing a couple of yards away. A dog barked in a yard nearby. I flipped the latch on the gate and stepped quietly though into Garcia's back yard and eased the gate shut. I walked slowly along the fence to my right, getting a feel for the background noise of his neighbors across the fence.

The wooden privacy fencing between the yards was slightly offset because of the lots the houses sat on. The fence along the left of Garcia's yard was smooth, with the cross rails on the neighbor's side. To the right, the cross rails were on Garcia's side. The fence separating Garcia's yard from the bad guys' also had the rails on Garcia's side. The corner I wanted to use as my entryway was just what I needed. I stepped up onto the lower rail and did a periscope move with my head and shoulders, surveying the adjoining yards for occupants. Children's toys and lawn furniture littered the neighbor's side. A garden shed occupied the corner of the bad guys' yard. I hadn't noticed the shed before because the top of it was just below the fence line. There was a two-foot space around the shed. As I looked down the fence line I spotted a three-step ladder leaning against the smooth side of the fence. So that's how they gained access to Garcia's, I thought. They were living right under his nose.

Then I quickly vaulted up and over the top rail and dropped into the yard where my adversaries were holed up. I landed quietly and paused to listen for any sounds that someone had noticed my gymnastics. A dog barked in the back yard a couple of houses away and I heard the same kids-playing noises I'd noticed when I entered Garcia's back yard. No real change in any of the background sounds as far as I could tell. I waited another moment or two in the space between the shed and the fence, then pulled the CZ from its holster and carefully peeked around the corner of the shed.

The back of the house was flat, the outside of the bedrooms on the left lining up with the kitchen in the middle and the wall of the garage on the right. Curtains on the bedroom windows kept out any prying eyes and the kitchen door had a curtain covering its four panes of glass. Two folding chairs were lying on the concrete slab of patio along with a rake. They were guarded by a small once-red barbeque whose two wheels looked in need of a retread. There was a door on the right side of the garage that led out into the back yard. The concrete stoop held a couple of one-quart oilcans and a wash bucket. Two brooms leaned against the door trim. The small window in the middle of the top half of the door was covered by something, possibly newspaper.

With the CZ hidden from view in my right hand, I stepped quickly from my hiding place to the wall by the garage door. I very gently tried the door handle. It was locked. Next, I tried looking through any breaks in the window covering and found a small gap that allowed me to peer into the garage with one eye. A wooden workbench ran along the wall from the door where I was standing toward the house as far as I could see. There were various tools and other items on top of it with a large vise attached to the end by the door. A wooden crate about four feet square and maybe twelve feet long occupied a space along the wall to my right toward the garage door. Several wooden palates were stacked in front of the crate. On top of the stack was a silver container about two feet in diameter and four feet long. On the floor in front of it was another silver container about the same diameter but shorter that appeared to be standing on its end. The two pieces looked like they could fit together. The short piece had been badly damaged by something or someone. There was a terrible dent in the closed end that caused it to be deformed out of round. Several odd pieces of metal were haphazardly strewn over the garage floor.

On the side of the garage that had the van backed into it was an engine hoist with two men fiddling with it. The men were dressed in tan slacks, undershirts and brown loafers. An odd combination of clothing, I thought. Their outer shirts were hanging from the left door of the van. At first I thought they were the two guys I'd dealt with earlier today. As I watched, I decided by their profiles that these were two other bad guys. Their builds were bigger and their hair was a little longer. Neither had a mustache. They were both sweating some from their labors.

While I peeped, they began hoisting up a round container the size of the larger of the other two but apparently weighing much more, judging by their struggles. The container was nearly six feet long and attached to the hoist with a crude piece of metal stuck through the two lift lugs spaced evenly apart on the top of the container. Attached to the end nearest my view were several small boxes of different colors. The two men were taking extra care not to bang the boxes against the hoist parts. So they did have a bomb after all. The question in my mind was where the hell did they get it? And where were they going with it? As I pondered my next move, the hoist was doing its work and the bomb swayed in the air poised to be shoved in through the van's open doors. Carefully the two bombers pushed the hoist with its teetering nuke warhead into the van's waiting mouth. These guys were going to be on the road before I could stop them, if I didn't hurry.

I jammed the CZ back into its holster, pulled out my pick case, extracted two lock picks and started to work on the door's lock. Before I popped it, I looked through my peephole to see if they might hear me. By now the hoist's boom was well inside the van along with the bomb and the two men. I twisted the picks and the lock snapped open. I returned the picks to the case and the case to my pocket before I quietly twisted the handle and let myself into the garage. They were fussing with the bomb, making enough noise to cover my movements. I shut the door quietly. There was a piece of two-inch pipe propped up in the corner behind the door. I picked it up. While I really had no problem with shooting these two guys, I had something better and quieter in mind. Besides, I wasn't sure just how many of them were around.

With pipe in hand like a baseball bat and keeping out of sight of the van's interior, I stepped over to the closed garage door and made my way along it to the side of the van nearest me. I had no sooner reached my spot of attack when one of the guys hopped out of the vehicle with his back to me and gently twisted the hydraulic release on the hoist's body. As the boom arm went slowly down, so did my pipe onto the man's head, but much faster. The pipe hitting his head and the bomb coming to rest inside the van made a clunking sound nearly simultaneously. The object of my attack staggered back toward me, turning to see who had hit him. I clunked him on the head again. His knees buckled and the light in his eyes went out. As he fell, I eased him down to the concrete floor to limit the noise. I pulled him away from the other gentleman's line of sight and stepped back into my ambush position.

"Rashid," the other guy called to his comrade.

No answer, of course.

"Rashid!" he called again with a little anger in his voice.

He mumbled something I didn't catch and then, pushing the freed hoist out of the van's interior, he followed it from the van into the garage. When he turned toward his prone crony, I swung the door of the van I was standing behind hard into the fellow. The door caught him right in the face before he could get his hands up in defense. His nose gushed blood. The door rebounded and I slammed it into him again. It was his turn to stagger. The door rebounded and I pushed it toward him again. This time it missed him, slamming shut against the vehicle's doorframe like it was designed to do. I stepped toward him and gave him a bonk on the top of his head with the pipe. His knees wobbled, his eyes rolled up and he was on the ground, out cold.

I surveyed my handiwork, listening for any sound of other accomplices. The garage was quiet except for some snoring coming from Rashid. I stepped over my victims and put the pipe on the workbench. There were a couple of cabinets above the bench and some drawers built into the thing. I rummaged through the cabinets and found a roll of silver duct tape in the second one. With tape in hand, I returned to my sleeping bombers and began applying the sticky stuff to number two's ankles. I pulled his arms behind his back, taped his wrists and forearms together and after pulling his taped ankles up behind him, looped the tape through his secured ankles. I taped up his pal, Rashid, the same way. Number two's nosebleed had subsided somewhat by the time I finished trussing up Rashid. Both men were breathing raggedly though their mouths. So, I thought, no murder today. Time to call in the reinforcements.

I pulled the men's shirts off the left rear door of the van, tossed them inside by the bomb, eased the door shut and stepped outside the garage into Bobby's line of sight. I waved her to me. She put the Chevy into gear when she saw me and rolled quickly down the block, squealing the tires to a stop in front of the bad boys' house. She came up to me at a near trot, her hand in her purse, no doubt wrapped around the 380.

"Everything's okay in here," I told her quietly, guiding her past the side of the brown van into the garage. "You watch these guys while I check inside the house. I suspect it's empty, but if someone comes out the door and it's not me, I give you permission to shoot them. Okay?"

"Sure. Man, you made short work of those two. There's a lot of blood on the floor. Any of it yours?"

"No, Bobby, the number two man caught it on the nose," I explained as I moved over to the door leading to the interior of the house. "Just keep an eye on them."

"I will. Holler if you need me."

I retrieved the CZ from its holster, opened the door quietly and listened for movement. The house was silent except for the hum of a nearby refrigerator. I stepped over the threshold and into a laundry room. The kitchen was just beyond. I peeked around the corner into the kitchen. It was unoccupied. I crept through the house, my expectations of finding anyone else decreasing with each empty room I encountered. These guys were just about ready to leave the area, I thought. There was a minimum of furniture in the place, just enough to live on while spying on Garcia. In the living room by the doorway to the kitchen I found two packed suitcases, one large and one small.

I tucked the CZ back into its nest under my armpit and then opened both cases and inspected the contents. The larger of the two held an assortment of clothes, including socks and underwear. In the smaller one I found some clothes and toiletries along with four rubber-banded bundles of hundred dollar bills and a small black velvet bag. I fanned one of the bundles. About fifteen grand each, I guessed. Next, I opened the little cloth bag and nearly gasped at its contents. The stones inside looked like diamonds. I had no clue what they were worth. Easier to haul around than a bunch of cash, I thought, as I slid the bag of jewels into my left outside pocket and stuffed a cash bundle into each of the inside pockets of my jacket. I had no second thoughts about stealing from these characters; served them right for being bad boys. I left the other two wads of cash on top of the stuff in the suitcase and snapped them both shut. Then I picked up the suitcases and returned to the laundry room. The door to the garage was ajar, as I had left it.

"I'm coming out, Bobby," I called quietly.

"Come on out," she invited. "No one here but me and two sleepers."

I lugged the two suitcases out the door and set them down by the back of the van.

"Whose are those?" Bobby wondered.

"These guys', I guess. I think they were planning a getaway when I put their lights out."

I opened the van doors and tossed the larger suitcase in on the left side of the bomb. It was then that I noticed that the bombers had placed wooden blocks under the sides of the warhead to keep it from rolling from side to side. Then, I set the smaller case on the floor behind the bomb, opened it and extracted the two money bundles.

"Is that what I think it is?" Bobby said behind me.

"You mean the bomb?" I asked, not sure if she had seen the money or not.

"Well, yeah."

"It sure is. Unless I miss my guess, you're looking at the warhead of a B-28 nuclear weapon."

"So those guys had more than just a book, huh?"

"Yeah, except these two aren't the same two that I made the book deal with."

"They aren't?"

"Nope, these are two different guys," I clarified, closing the suitcase and flipping its catches.

I tossed the case on the right side of the bomb, turned and held out the two bundles of money to Bobby.

"What's this?" she asked, looking down at my offering.

"Spoils of war. It's your pay for helping me catch these two criminals."

"Well, thanks," she said, reaching out for the bundles. "It looks like a lot of money. Don't you get some?"

"How about this," I said as I passed her the cash and held open my jacket so she could see the bundles in my inside pockets.

"Now what am I going to do with these? They won't fit in my pockets or my purse."

"Wait a minute," I said, going over to the workbench and picking up one of the shop rags piled there. "Wrap your cash in this."

Something blue sticking out from under the disturbed pile of rags caught my eye. I pushed the pile out of the way and there was the teardown book I had sold earlier today. Or its double.

"Well, looky here," I said, picking up the book and holding it up like a trophy. "The book of the month."

"Great. You've got the book and the bomb. So now what are we going to do with these two?" she asked.

"Well, you and I are going to load them into the van and give the whole mess, less our pay, to Leo."

She chuckled at the thought. So did I. I tossed her one of the rags. She wrapped up her part of our haul as I placed the book on the floorboards behind the warhead.

"So give me a hand," I said, turning my attention to the unconscious duo on the floor.

She put her loaded purse and wrapped money down on the garage floor and helped me drag number two over to the van. Avoiding the blood on his face and shirt, we pulled him up against the back bumper and heaved him through the doorway where he came to rest on his side next to the bomb. Rashid was a little lighter but we treated him with no more gentleness. Then I retrieved a couple of rags from the pile on the workbench and lightly gagged the two men. I didn't want them making too much noise in case they woke up too soon, but I didn't necessarily want them to drown in their own barf, either. Next, I grabbed three of the packing blankets I had seen stacked under the workbench and unceremoniously threw one over the bomb and one over each of the bad guys. I slammed the van doors shut, opened them again and patted down number two for the van keys. They were in his left trouser pocket. I extracted them, recovered him and closed the doors again.

"Time to go, Bobby. You follow me. We'll go through the back gate of Kelly. Okay?"

"Sounds fine to me," she agreed, retrieving her purse and money from the floor and slipping outside between the van and the side of the garage door.

Following her, I got into the front of the bad guys' van, turned over its engine and pulled it forward enough to get the garage door closed. I left it running in park, hopped out of the van and went back to the house and pulled the door down. Bobby had started up the Chevy and was sitting there idling while I secured the villains' lair. Back in the driver's seat, I put the Ford into gear and eased the heavy load out of the driveway, turning right down the street so Bobby could follow me without turning around.

The van drove like an overloaded whaler. I guessed it was a three-quarter ton truck but it felt maxed-out because of the way it bounced whenever we hit even a slight bump in the uneven road. It took several seconds for the chassis to settle when we stopped at the corner. The fastest, straightest way to Kelly was left on Roy Ellis Drive to Pearsall. I put on the left blinker, waited for two cars to go by and eased into the eastbound lane. Bobby followed. Ten minutes and much bouncing later we reached the southeast gate at Kelly. The guard saluted me through the checkpoint. I hadn't noticed, but this rig must have had an officer's base sticker on the bumper. I saluted the SP and eased on past him. I smiled to myself thinking what he might have done if he had known what my cargo was. Bobby was waved through behind me.

We continued down Berman Road until we came to Tinker. I put on the left blinker and our convoy turned left toward Leo's building. When we got there, the parking lot was nearly deserted. Only a Mustang and a Nova occupied stalls in it. It was seven-thirty. I pulled into a parking place and Bobby wheeled into the one next to my door. Before getting out, I checked the status of my captives.

Still out, snoring a little. They would be coming around soon, I figured, so I had better hustle with the hand-over.

I locked up the Ford, dropped the keys into my pocket and opened the side doors of the Chevy. Bobby stayed behind the wheel, watching me. I put my stolen money bundles into the footlocker in the back of the van and covered them with my jumpsuit.

"Dave," she started. "There's something about finding the book at that house that bothers me."

"What's that?" I asked.

"Well, if Leo had a bunch of people following the book guys, how come we didn't see any of the good guys at the house?"

"Good question. I'll bet they pulled a switch somewhere. When I gave them the book, they put it into one of two identical shopping bags they had with them. They probably handed off the book to those two somewhere in the mall," I guessed, using my thumb to indicate the sleepers in the Ford.

"That would mean Leo is on a wild goose chase," she observed.

"You're right. Pretty clever of our bad guys. This bomb was right under Leo's nose and now he's off somewhere chasing shadows. This just gets better and better."

"So what do we do now?"

"Well, it's close to eight, so you need to go on your date. You take the van back to the mall. Hide the pistol in your desk. I'll get it later. Meanwhile, I'll go inside and present the goods to Acres or Leo if he's around."

"How are you going to get back to your car?"

"I'll have Leo or someone, maybe Acres, drop me off. Oh, yeah, I'll need my car keys," I said, stretching my hand out toward her.

She pulled the keys from the ignition and passed them over. I unwound the van key from the ring and gave it back to her. I stowed the rest of the keys in my pocket.

"Sure you're going to be okay?" she asked, sticking the key back into the ignition.

"Sure, I'm here on a base surrounded by military. I'm still armed. What could happen?"

"Okay, if you're sure."

"I'm sure. See you later," I said, closing the doors and slapping the side of the van.

"See you," came her muffled reply.

I moved up onto the grass at the front of the vehicles. She waved and I waved back before she started the Chevy, put it into reverse and backed out. I watched her motor toward General Hudnell before I turned toward Leo's building.

There were still lights on in the hallway on the second floor. Good, I thought, seeing light shining under Leo's outer office door. Acres had taken me seriously and stayed put. I opened the outer door and stepped across the threshold. Acres was at her desk and looked up when I came in.

"So, I have you alone at last," I joked with a smile.

"So you have," she said, smiling back at me. "But not for long. The Major is on his way back and should be here by eight o'clock. Have a seat."

"Good," I said. "Because my gifts for him are outside getting ripe."

"What gifts are those?"

"I'm returning some of the stuff Leo gave me yesterday, with interest."

"I see," she said with a tone that meant she didn't.

"Got any coffee for a thirsty guy?" I asked, changing subjects.

"Sure. Same as before?" she asked as she got up from her desk.

"Yes, please."

I watched her as she came around the desk. Today she had on blue slacks instead of a skirt. I preferred the skirt, but kept my opinion to myself. She watched me watching her as she circled my chair and walked down the hall to the coffee room. A few minutes later she returned with a cup of tan liquid and set it on the edge of the desk beside me. I resisted the urge to pat her bottom. She must have sensed my thought because she looked at me sideways before turning and retreating behind her desk.

"Where is your friend, Julie?" she asked at last.

"I have no idea. I was hoping you would know," I said over the rim of the cup as I took a tentative sip of the hot coffee.

"I've heard nothing about her since you called earlier. Only thing I know is your message for the Major caused quite a stir. Did you find what you were looking for?"

"Yes, I did. And speaking of which, I had better go check on it. You said the Major would be here around eight? Where is he coming from?"

"Yes, he said eight o'clock. I believe he is coming back from Washington."

"I thought you didn't know or wouldn't tell me."

"It was easier not to tell you where he was on the phone. It's harder to lie when you're sitting here in front of me drinking coffee."

"You been in the OSI business for long?" I wondered, changing gears.

"Do you mean I need to learn to be a better liar?"

"Sort of. But how long have you done this?"

"I've been with the Major for about eighteen months. I was in the SP's before that. I worked a couple of cases with the OSI and the Major recruited me."

"How come I've never seen you here before Wednesday?"

"I don't know. Maybe you haven't been around much."

"You weren't at the Halloween party last year, were you?"

"Nope, I wasn't invited."

"That's too bad. They didn't know what they were missing."

"Thanks," she said, blushing just a little at my compliment.

"Well," I began, finishing my coffee and setting the cup down on her desk. "I need to go check on my gifts."

"Want me to come along with you?"

"Sure," I said as I stood up and went over to the door.

She came around her desk, retrieved her hat from the rack by the door and followed me out into the hall. We were halfway down the stairs when we saw Leo coming up. He apparently hadn't seen us yet.

"Hey, Leo, where the hell have you been?" I asked loudly.

It startled him just a bit and he looked up at us.

"Never mind that. Where have you been?"

"I've been doing your dirty work. Catching bad guys and saving the nation."

"Yeah, I'll bet," he said as we met on the landing.

We shook hands as we met.

"Where were you two going?" he wondered.

"Outside, to check on your gifts."

"What gifts?"

"C'mon, I'll show you," I beckoned with a wave and led the way out of the building.

Acres and Leo followed in my wake. I fished the Ford's keys from my pocket and walked around to the back of the van. When they were beside me, I opened the door and pulled back the blankets I had covered my cargo with. The two gentlemen trussed up in the back were awake now, making muffled noises through their gags. They were struggling a little against their tape, but it was holding well.

"Well, I'll be damned," said Leo with amazement in his voice.

"I guess you will. Not only did I bring you two would-be terrorists and their bomb, but also the book they were using to make it go boom," I said as I picked up the manual from the van's floor and presented it to Leo.

"Where did you find them?" Leo asked, taking the book.

"In a house on Lake Valley, over the back fence from Garcia's. Speaking of Garcia. I guess you know he's dead."

"Yeah, I heard about it on my way to D.C.," he confirmed. "That was too bad. He was a good man. Had a bad ticker, though."

"Nice touch Leo, putting me in the same room with the guy."

"I thought you'd like that," he said with a grin.

"Yeah, I woke up right when he was dying."

"Yeah, the doc told me you would be out for awhile. I figured it was the best place for you until you came around."

The men in the van struggled a bit, drawing our attention back to them.

"So, what are you going to do with your presents?"

"Well, shit. I've got to get them jailed until I can interrogate them."

"Sergeant Acres, go call Miller and Tandy. Have them get here ASAP. Meanwhile, we'll just sit on these two."

"Yes sir," said Acres, leaving us at a trot.

"Are you sure that tape will hold?" Leo wondered.

"So far, so good. How long will it be before your men get here?"

"I don't know. Twenty minutes, maybe."

"Good. While we're waiting, you can fill me in on just what the hell is going on."

"What do you mean?"

"Hah," I snorted. "As if you don't know."

"What do you mean?" he repeated.

"Tell me what's going on, from the beginning," I demanded.

"I'll tell you what. As soon as we get back in my office, I'll give you the low-down. But I won't discuss it now in front of these two."

"Okay. Have it your way," I said, handing him the keys to the Ford. "This is your party now."

"Yes, it is," he said with finality.

As we waited for reinforcements, Leo hoisted his bulk into the back of the van and tested the tape restraints on his prisoners while I looked on. When he was satisfied the trusses would hold, he hopped back out and closed the van doors. Just over twenty minutes of us looking at each other and his men arrived. He took them aside and gave them their marching orders. He also gave them the Ford's keys. I didn't hear what he intended to do with the prisoners, but I knew I was glad I wasn't one of them. When he had things under control, he turned back to me.

"Okay, now we can talk. Back in my office," he said, turning and walking briskly toward the building's entrance without waiting for my approval.

I followed him to his lair.

As soon as we entered his outer office I could smell fresh coffee cooking. He asked Acres to bring us both a cup before retreating into his office. I was on his heels and left the door open for Acres. He parked his big frame in his desk chair and I sat opposite him in what was now my usual seat. Before he could start talking, Acres brought the two cups in and set one of them on the edge of the desk near me and the other by Leo's elbow on his blotter. Mine was the way I like it. If Acres ever left the service, I thought, maybe I'd hire her. She left the office, closing the door behind her.

"Where do you want me to start?" he asked at last.

"From the beginning. And don't give me any crap about classified information. I think you owe me the whole story."

"All right, here goes," he began. "Have you ever heard of Chrome Dome?"

"No, but it sounds familiar."

"Well, Chrome Dome is the Air Force code name for the flying of alert B-52s carrying nuclear weapons out to their fail-safe areas. Once they're out there flying around, KC-135s refuel them as long as it takes for them to pull their rotation. Each base with B-52s and nukes rotates the Chrome Dome alert duty so not all the birds are in the air at the same time."

"Alright, I've got it."

"In late 1973, during a Chrome Dome flight taking place over the Mediterranean, a KC-135 refueling a loaded B-52 collided with the bomber and crashed. Before the 52 went down, the four nuclear weapons on board the plane were jettisoned by the plane's pilots. They were dropped in the safe mode and deployed their parachutes before pranging in. Two hit some farmland in southern Sicily and two landed in the Med. We paid those Italian farmers some big bucks to keep it quiet while we recovered the pieces. We pulled one of the bombs out of the ocean, but never located the other one."

"Good grief, a lost nuke," I interjected. "How long did they look for it?"

"The Air Force and Navy quietly hunted for it nearly six months before they gave up. Then last year our intel folks learned that a large bomb had been recovered by some Libyan fishermen and that it had fallen into the hands of Qaddafi. Ever since then, we've been trying to pinpoint its location and get it back. Our breakthrough came when some Libyans posing as Saudi student pilots looked up our man at SAAMA and wanted a book on how to take it apart."

"Your man at SAAMA was Garcia, right?"

Leo nodded.

"How did they know who to contact?"

"It appears they knew some sympathetic foreign military students at one of the exchange schools on Lackland. They got together and made some initial inquiries that were reported back to us. We snuck Garcia into the game as a tech writer. We had to go with them wanting a disposal book in order to track them back to the bomb."

"So, let me guess. Before Garcia could do the deal he had a heart attack and that's where I came in?"

"Sort of. Garcia was supposed to make the trade on Monday, but had heart trouble, which landed him in Wilford Hall. He underwent heart surgery, so that took him out of the game altogether. We couldn't wait for him to heal up. So, I needed someone not attached to the military to finish the deal. I figured you'd be the guy but you weren't in town. That's when I found out that you were down on the border on some fool jail break mission."

"How did you find that out."

"Now that part I won't tell you," he said flatly. "Just be satisfied that I have resources everywhere, my friend."

"Okay, you can have that one. You set up my contact through Wilson though, didn't you?" I accused.

"Right. Easiest way to involve you was have you come into the case sideways, first getting the bad guys used to you being around and then having you be the person to finish the deal."

"So Maria Garza isn't Garcia's fiancé?"

"Right, she isn't. We just used her to get you into action."

"Geez. No wonder Wilson took the news a little casually."

"You called Wilson?"

"Of course. Well, actually I called Maria Garza to break the bad news. But Wilson took the call. He said she wasn't there and that he would take a message. When I told him, he seemed a little nonplussed by Garcia's death."

"Now you know why."

"Yeah, I guess I do," I agreed, thinking that I needed to call Wilson back and ask him a couple of questions. "So, Leo, what would you have done if I hadn't found the book at Garcia's?"

"Then I'd have contacted you directly to get you to play along."

"How did you know that I would?"

"Ever hear of the Internal Revenue Service? I'll bet what Wilson paid you would make some mighty interesting audit material."

I think I actually heard my testicles shrink when he said that.

"And judging by the look on your face, I'd say I was right. But not to worry, old pal. You just be the nice, cooperative person that I know you can be and nothing will ever happen."

"So you were going to blackmail me into doing your dirty work, but I took the bait out of greed and here we are," I guessed.

"Not quite," he stopped me. "When you brought me half of the book before the Libyans contacted you, I nearly shit. But things worked out. Your greed helped things work out. Besides, there was the backup plan of blackmail."

"Did you have any idea they were going to poison me?"

"Nope. It was a good thing I had agents all over the place, though. We had to let the bad guys leave unhindered before we could rescue you."

"Yeah, but they pulled a fast one on you, didn't they? They passed the book on to the bomb guys right under your nose."

"Yeah, you're right. We chased the wrong pair. We'd still be chasing them if you hadn't had Aeres call to let us know."

"You're welcome, Leo."

"Anyway, we chased the phony couriers all the way to D.C."

"And while you were chasing, I was flat on my back at Wilford Hall. It was a good thing Julie was with me when I blacked out."

"It, um, certainly was fortunate."

"Wait a minute. Was she in on this, too?" I asked, my eyes widening.

"I'm going to tell you something now that I'll deny telling you all the way to my death. It's something that you can never repeat, no matter what, okay? Under threat of national security and the FBI and IRS crawling up your ass. Okay?"

"Okay, okay, I get it. What?"

"Julie is an Air Force Captain in the O.S.I. and has been working undercover on this case for months."

"You have got to be shitting me!" I stammered in disbelief. "My girl friend is an agent?"

"Yep, one of the best ones we have. When we got you on the hook, she flew down from Washington to keep you from getting killed while you were nosing around with our bad guys."

"Man, that's hard to believe," I said, thinking back to the phone calls she'd made checking in with the General. But she was also pretty cool during our bad guy chase and the ransacking of Garcia's. "Boy, I feel like such an idiot."

"Don't take it so hard. You did a great service for your country. You got to spend some quality time with a foxy spy and you got paid for your trouble. Fifty grand ain't hay."

Fifty grand, I thought. Julie knew the number was two-fifty but hadn't told them what I'd negotiated. I suppose I owed her for that one. My suddenly plummeting opinion of her began to take wings again.

"Say, speaking of Julie, where is she?"

"When the bad guys took off and she saved your ass by getting you to the hospital, she was told to join the team following the Libyans. Right now," he said, looking at his watch, "she should still be tracking those couriers somewhere inside the Beltway."

"She's back in D.C.?" I said, surprised again. Damn it, I hadn't finished playing with her yet. "Why is she still on their trail. Don't we have all the players cornered now that the bomb and book have been recovered?"

"Well, yes, we have most of what we need. She's still on the trail because we need the rest of the group. And they're most likely in D.C."

"Is that where they were going to take the bomb?"

"Best we can figure."

"So it was in the U.S. all the time," I said, thinking back onto how those two had conned me into believing there was no bomb.

"Yeah. We initially thought that they were going to try blowing up Tel Aviv once they figured out how to set it off. You know, Arabs against the Jews and all that. Then we got word they had snuck the bomb into the U.S. through New York and were going to nuke the Big Apple. But we couldn't locate the device there."

"How in the hell could you find the thing in a place as big as New York?" I wondered. "It'd be like looking for a needle in a haystack."

"Well, that's true. And to add to that we were looking in the wrong haystack. They must have brought the thing through Houston and then moved it to San Antonio."

"There was a big trailer parked in the driveway at the house today. They most likely hauled it on that. There was also a big packing crate. Looks like they snuck the thing in right under everyone's noses. Good thing I wanted a little payback for knocking me out. Otherwise you would still be going in circles."

"We would have probably found the bomb once it was moved to its target."

"Again, how in hell would you be able to find the damn thing?"

"Okay, are you ready for another piece of information that isn't to leave this room?"

"Yeah, I'm ready. And I suppose the same rules of disclosure apply?"

"Yes, they certainly do," he nodded. "The other piece of info is something that's been in the works since 1969. The loss of this bomb finally forced the government to get off its tight ass and create an outfit that hunts for lost nukes or improvised nuke weapons, either the dirty kind or the ones that actually can give nuclear yields. The official version was that this new agency was created because of a nuke threat in Boston, but the real reason was to find the very bomb you brought to me in the back of that van. Ever since that bomb was lost, the government has been working furiously on a project called NEST, the Nuclear Emergency Search Team."

My questioning look caused him to explain.

"NEST is a group of scientists and spies along with the military who have special equipment that could locate a luminous watch from a helicopter flying overhead at five thousand feet. Until your call, they were scouring the East Coast looking for the bomb's radioactive signature. We didn't realize they had brought the bomb to the book."

"They probably wanted to fix it up before delivering it to their target," I guessed.

"Yeah, makes sense. And since D.C. was where our Libyan couriers went after they did the book-drop thing on us, that's where we were concentrating our efforts. That's also why Julie Newton went there and is still there."

"Any idea why they didn't kill me instead of poisoning me?"

"My guess is that they wanted you out of action while they made their break. If they had murdered you, they'd have had the cops on them pretty quickly. By paying you and just knocking you out, they probably figured they could escape with the book and stay away from the law. Besides, they paid you, right? They probably thought they had bought your silence. Anything else?"

"Maybe. You didn't seem too excited about that big-ass bomb in that van in the middle of your Air Force base. How come?"

"Well, I was assured that even if the terrorists had figured out how to set it off, it wouldn't have gone nuclear. In fact, it might not have gone off at all."

"How do you know that?" I wondered.

"Because, as I was told, the thing had been underwater for several months, just like the one they recovered. When they took the recovered bomb to Los Alamos to test the components' reactions to submersion, none of them worked. The high explosives in the thing wouldn't even go off."

"Do you mean that during this whole exercise we were after a dummy bomb?" I asked incredulously.

"Not really a dummy. The best the terrorists could hope for was a bunch of scattered plutonium and enriched uranium. And they would've probably had to pack the thing in their own explosives to get that to happen. We were concerned more with the components and technology reaching the wrong hands."

"So they would have done better to dismantle the bomb and see how it worked?"

"Right. That's why we figured they wanted a teardown book in addition to the bomb, so they could tear it apart without ruining it. But it looks like the two bombers in the van just wanted a big explosion."

"Well, too bad I spoiled it for them."

"Yeah, too bad. Anything else you want to know?" he wondered.

"No, I think you answered all my questions. So far."

"Well, then," he began, rolling back his chair and standing up. "Since we have all the goods, you're free to go."

"Swell, Leo. Let me know if you ever need a patsy again," I said, taking a big swig of coffee, setting the cup down a little hard and getting to my feet.

"I will. No hard feelings, okay?" he asked, standing and sticking out his hand for a shake.

I grasped the big paw and gave it a squeeze.

"No, Leo, no hard feelings. Only that I already miss Julie," I lamented, dropping his mitt.

"Oh, I dunno, she may find her way back into your life sometime. You can never tell," he said, seeing me out the door.

"You're right. You can never tell. Right now, though, I think I need a stiff drink," I admitted, thinking of how far away the Fox was from Kelly.

"You still hang out at the Black Fox," he wondered.

"Yes, I do. And I was just thinking of going over there as soon as I can find a ride."

"That was their van, right?"

"Yeah," I admitted.

"How did you get to their place?"

"I had an accomplice," I admitted.

"Some good looking blonde who works as a travel agent?"

"Could be. I had to have someone help me since you stole away my other partner."

"That's too bad. Still, you could do a lot worse than have Bobby as a side kick."

"Yeah, you're right. Now how about that ride?" I asked, guiding Leo back on track.

"Give me a minute. I'll see what I can do."

While I had hoped it would be the delectable Sergeant Acres behind the wheel, what Leo arranged was an SP vehicle with a decidedly unhandsome male driver. In twenty-five minutes I was standing next to the Olds fishing around in my pocket for the keys to the big beast while the SP waited for me to unlock the door. I still had a sack full of diamonds in my pocket and the CZ under my jacket. I had to disarm and dis-treasure myself before going drinking. I separated the key to my private entrance from the ones on the ring and held it up to the SP.

"I've got to go to my office," I explained. "I forgot something. Thanks for the lift."

"You're welcome," he said, and drove away toward Military Drive.

Then I walked over to my private door and let myself into the mall. The light was on in Ruth's area when I walked in and she was typing something on her electric machine.

"Hey, Ruth. How are you?"

"I'm fine. Question is, how are you?" she asked, looking up from her typing.

"I'm doing really good, now that this little adventure is over except for a couple of loose ends."

"What kind of loose ends?" she wondered.

"Well, I need to call Dallas and ask an ex-client a couple of questions."

"Okay, but that's only one end. You said 'ends', plural."

"Well, there's the matter of your raise. What do you think is fair?"

"I don't know," she said, her interest rising. "How about eight-fifty an hour?"

"Oh, I dunno," I said, frowning and watching the disappointment flash across her face. "How about ten?"

"Ten? Really?"

"Yep, really. I'll talk with Bobby. I'm sure, between the two of us, we can come up with ten. Is that okay."

"Dave, you just made my day," she said with a wide smile. "Thanks."

"You're welcome," I said, turning my office doorknob.

"It's locked. Just like you left it. Bobby came back just before eight, said to tell you your van key was on your desk, locked up and went on her date."

"Thanks, Ruth," I said, finding the right key on my ring and fitting it into the lock.

I let myself into my office, turning on the light as I went. On my desk was the lone car key. I picked it up and added it to its brothers on the ring. When I was done, I put the keys in my pocket and facing the Mossberg, opened it up. I took the bag from my jacket and without looking at the contents, placed it into the top right drawer. Then I pulled off my jacket and draped it over my desk chair. I unhooked the CZ rig and put the safety on the pistol before storing it in its place in the safe. Next, I pulled out the small roll of bills from my pocket and counted how much cash I had on me. Four hundred eighty dollars. I opened the black satchel and extracted ten or twelve more hundreds that I folded into the center of my pocket roll. That should be way more than enough for tonight, I thought. I pulled out two more hundreds and put them in my shirt pocket before closing the safe doors and spinning the dial. I retrieved my jacket, shrugged it on and retraced my steps out of my office. I locked the door on my way out. Ruth was still attacking the typewriter. She looked up as I came out.

"Here," I said, fishing the two hundreds from my shirt pocket and extending my hand toward her. "Here's a little bonus for your help."

"Hey, thanks, Dave," she said. And then added with wide eyes when she saw the denomination, "Wow. Thanks a bunch, Dave."

"You're very welcome. It's just a small token of my thanks."

"You can keep those small tokens coming," she said enthusiastically as I reached the outer door.

"I'll see what I can do. Good night, Ruth."

"Good night, Dave."

When I reached the parking lot I thought about the money hiding in the footlocker in the van. It could wait until tomorrow. So could calling Dallas. Right now I wanted a drink or two. I unlocked and climbed into the Olds. Julie's perfume was still lingering inside the big car. I couldn't decide if I wanted to air it out or not. I started the engine and left the windows up.

It was a little after nine-thirty when I pulled into the Fox's parking lot. The place was jumping. It's Friday, I reminded myself. I also reminded myself to go easy on the booze tonight. There may be some residual effects from my Scoop ingestion. But to be frank, even though I had scored a huge consolation prize with the diamonds and cash, Julie's being gone kind of put me in the dumps and I didn't really care if I got trashed. Well, I thought, nothing like taking on some depressants when you're feeling depressed. I found a parking place at the far edge of the lot, squeezed the Olds into the spot and slithered out the door. I made sure all four doors were locked before heading to the Fox's entrance. A blast of music and laughter greeted me when I pulled the door open. Maybe I'd feel more festive with a little alcohol on board. My mood lightened immediately when I saw Niki behind the bar. I considered seeing her again so soon after the other night to be a minor miracle.

I slid into the one empty seat at the far corner of the bar by the hall to the restrooms. Niki came over and set a coaster down before me.

"How are you doing tonight, Dave?" she asked over the din.

"Fine, Niki, now that I'm looking at your face," I said, gauging her reaction.

She smiled. I watched her eyes and decided I might be just fine right here and right now. She seemed to light up right before me.

"It's good to see you, too. Where's your girlfriend?"

"She went back to Washington this afternoon."

"That's too bad," she said, brightening a bit more. "What can I get you that'll cheer you up?"

"I'll start with a Glenlivet over ice followed by you with me for breakfast."

"You don't waste any time, do you?" she accused.

"I can't afford to," I admitted. "Smart, good-looking women are hard to find."

"Yes, we are," she said without bragging. "I'll bring you your drink."

While I waited for the alcohol, I scoped the action in the bar. It was a usual Friday night. Girls looking for guys. Guys looking for girls. And probably every other looking-for combination imaginable. There were a few couples gyrating on the tiny dance floor. I watched them, remembering how Julie and I had meshed together at the Back Way Inn.

"Here's your drink, sailor," Niki announced.

"Thanks, Niki," I said, pulling a twenty out of my pocket and sliding it toward her.

"Don't get too tipsy," she advised.

"Why not?"

"Because I quickly thought about it and decided to take you up on your breakfast offer. It's my rain check from Wednesday, you know. And since your friend is gone, I'm going to cash it in tonight. But first, I want to go to the Back Way and dance a little."

"That suits me fine. What time do you get off work?"

"Ten-thirty."

"Sounds great. We can stay out late, too. I don't have anything to do tomorrow except make a phone call and check a wire tap."

"A wire tap. Are you a spy? Or just a private eye?" she joked.

"Just an eye," I answered, winking each eye at her. "An eye for beauty."

"A flatterer, too, I see. Do you think that will help?"

"It doesn't hurt, does it?"

"No, I suppose it doesn't."

"Good. I have a lot more where that came from."

"I'll bet you do. See you in a bit."

"I'll just be sitting here and contemplating you and my next compliment until then."

"Not much longer to go," she observed, tapping her watch.

"That's good."

A couple of more drinks and I was feeling much better. Ten-thirty came and I noticed that Niki had disappeared. I called over one of the other bartenders. Rick was his name, I thought.

"Rick, have you seen Niki?"

"No, she got off work at ten-thirty."

"I know. I was supposed to take her to breakfast. I owe her a meal."

"I don't know where she went. Sorry," he said, turning back to his other customers.

A minute later I felt a tap on my right shoulder. I turned around. It was Niki.

"Hey, you changed clothes," I observed, looking up at her wearing a near copy of the black dress Julie had worn Wednesday night. "You look fabulous," I added, standing up and taking her hand, giving her a spin.

"Why, thank you, Dave. I borrowed it from a friend."

"Anyone I know?"

"Maybe."

"Uh, huh. The shoes, too?" I asked, noting the similarity between this and another pair of pumps I had seen on another set of good-looking legs.

"Yes, the shoes, too. Pretty nice of my friend, huh?"

"Boy, I'll say. Are you ready to go dancing?"

"Why, yes, I am. And I'm ready for some breakfast later, too."

"Before we go," I began, steering her toward the door, "I have a personal question to ask you that may be a bit forward so early in the course of our first date."

"So, this is a date?" she wondered.

"Well, yeah. Sort of. We're going dancing and then have breakfast, right? So, yeah, this is a date."

"Okay, it's a date," she finally agreed. "Now what is your personal question?"

"Well, I was just wondering if you were, uh, wearing anything under that dress?"

"Wow, that is a personal question," she said, watching me for a moment like she was trying to make up her mind. Then finally, "Okay, I'll give you an answer. It's for me to know and for you to find out."

I did.

About the Author

Steve Frye was born in 1947 in Fort Worth, Texas, where he spent most of his childhood. At nineteen, he joined the Air Force at the height of the Vietnam War. In the military, he was a bomb disposal technician for eighteen years after spending his first two years working on nuclear weapons. He spent four years stationed in Turkey, six years in Germany, four in San Antonio and six at other bases throughout the United States. Retiring from the Air Force in 1986, he returned to college and eventually became a registered nurse specializing in emergency care. Mr. Frye now resides in Montana with his wife Bobby.

978-0-595-34188-7
0-595-34188-8